HER Steadfast Protector

ALESSA KELLY

"On the left side of a strong woman, stands a strong man; he is strengthened by her character." ~ Ellen J. Barrier

1

MORGAN BLACKWELL

Los Angeles, California

'You're Morgan Blackwell? I didn't know you were a girl.'

A line I sometimes got from researchers or scientists when we met for the first time. I guess a wolf biologist called 'Morgan' had to be a guy in their heads.

I didn't mind surprising people like that, though. Especially when they learned about my age. *Nineteen?* Sometimes their eyes would flicker as if computing whether that was possible.

Even so, impossibility is there to be challenged.

I'm a self-confessed girly girl who loves makeup and making cupcakes. Yet, they could throw me among the beasts in the middle of Yellowstone, and I'd feel at home.

But three days ago, I discovered an impossibility I never saw coming.

My parents were murdered, my little sister is missing, and I've been on the run since.

So far, those men haven't found me. Sheltering in place has

helped, but today is the day. Or I'll never make it to the rendezvous point.

Hauling a backpack that hardly leaves my shoulders, I blaze my way to my old campus library. I've got one thing to collect before leaving this city.

The woody scent of vintage hardcovers, mixed with the smell of modern toner, swirls around me like nostalgia. I used to spend hours here, not to mention the late nights.

Before she told me to run, Mom had packed an escape bag for me. Apart from a few clothes and essential items, she had included cash, a new ID, and a pile of books, which I know had nothing to do with my love of reading.

Once I get to the Biology section, it only takes me a few seconds to locate the publication, which used to be my bible. *Wolves: Behavior, Ecology, and Conservation.*

There's a piece of paper wedged in the middle of the book. Written on it are sets of numbers I'm sure will correspond with the books Mom had packed for me. In time, I will decipher the hidden messages. For now, I've got to go.

A librarian walks past me. The 'returns' trolley in front of her creaks as she navigates the aisle. My peripheral catches sight of two men wandering along an adjacent shelf.

That's the thing about a library. You know when people don't belong. My only hope to get away is my knowledge of this campus.

"Stop!" one calls out when I slip past them.

My back takes a pounding from my wobbly pack as I gallop, working through shortcuts to get to my car. I don't even care to glance back to see where they are.

I hit the road as fast as I can, gripping the steering wheel as if my car would fly without me if I let go. My gaze hops briskly between mirrors.

Normal L.A. traffic.

I think they've lost me. "Take that, fuckers!"

But my unhinged escape is short-lived. That car driving erratically behind me must be my pursuers'. They're still far away, but I can't lead them to my real destination.

Think! Morgan, think!

When hiding or running won't work, I have to blend in. It's Saturday, and it's summer. There'll be nowhere else in L.A. like Venice Beach.

I chance cutting across lanes. Horns blare, tires screech, but I make it to the right side of the road in time to skid into an alley.

"Hey, you can't park there!" a woman yells, but I abandon my car on the spot. I'm going to sprint the rest of the way.

Sweat drips off my face.

The crowd at the pier is what I've expected. I slow down, weaving through rows of sunbathers, smiling at a few kids who seem to be competing to build the largest castle.

I keep strolling across the sand, glimpsing at the street every now and then.

Shit!

Those men haven't even bothered to be discreet. They want me. Bad.

My plan to blend in might fail if they're vigilant or desperate enough. It won't be hard for them to spot a girl hauling a hiking pack running around Venice.

Passing an unattended umbrella, I set my bag next to whoever's beach gear scattered in the shade. I take off my clothes, then, tagging onto a family group, I hit the water.

I swim further from the shore, occasionally diving to stay out of view. This is the closest I get to feeling peace in days, but I'll enjoy this reprieve, however small or short it may be— letting myself float, surrendering to the waves.

Then, something hits me.

In fact, whatever it is, it's obliterating me. I'm dragged under, pinned between the sand floor and...a beast.

I knew my peace would be temporary, but I didn't think it would be destroyed like this. After trying to be a ghost in the City of Angels, my life might end in the mouth of Jaws.

Amid the bubbles, I'm pulled to the surface.

A sturdy arm hooks under my armpit, stopping me from being towed back to the bottom. I don't know who has found me, but his hold is steady. It's not a tight grip, yet it's secure. Like the hand of a teacher, a guardian of some sort.

A gentle swipe clears water off my face.

My lids bat open, and a pair of eyes stares back at me. Their blue-green hues almost match the shade of the ocean.

It may be the days of isolation taking a toll on me, but this man is frighteningly handsome and curiously un-Californian. A local surfer would've given me an earful for intruding his space like this.

"You okay? You hurt?" His wet scruff glistens in the sun as he speaks.

"I'm fine." How the hell did I get here? It wasn't a shark attack, but I can consider myself lucky. He seems to be a skillful enough surfer that he managed to kick his board away despite his speed. Because my limbs are still intact.

"I'm so sorry." His voice is deep. The kind I'd expect from a man with chiseled jaws like his. But there's tenderness in his tone. More curiously, his expression is tight, as if he was at a graveyard and I was already dead.

"It was my fault," I admit.

The well-tanned man squints. His thick brows almost swallow his eyes. He's probably in his mid-twenties. That he didn't blame me for the incident tells me he's not an asshole.

"You should go back to the safe area," he advises.

But an object flying overhead reminds me that the only safe place right now is with him.

There's only one way to blend in this time.

While those ravishing eyes are still fixed on me, I pull him forward.

And I plunder his lips.

It's a kiss of survival, so I shouldn't feel a thing. The man himself doesn't seem to object despite being stunned. His mouth pouts a tiny bit as if wanting to gauge his own reaction. The longer it goes on—or the longer he lets me go on—the more I feel it. Like I was seventeen and safe, and it wasn't that long ago that I was seventeen and safe.

Still shadowed by his massive torso, I glance at his eyes and break the kiss.

What the hell have I just done?

It's more than just the heat of day melting my body. A flash of amusement crosses his face, erasing that graveyard expression.

"Don't look up! Don't look up!" I warn as the drone is still circling above us. By now, my DIY perm would've been ruined, and the saltwater might've messed up the dye, exposing my natural blonde. But I'm hoping I still appear so ordinary that my pursuers give it a pass. And I also hope that this man doesn't know the difference between bikinis and undies.

"You're a celebrity or something?" he smirks.

"Maybe. Just hide me."

"It's probably a lifeguard drone. Nothing to worry about."

He's probably right, and I feel stupid.

But he cautions, "Though you may want to worry about those suited men on shore. They're combing the beach with their binocs. Geez, they have no shame!"

"Shit. Hide me, please!"

He rotates our position so his back is to the shore, shielding me. "You've gotta swim back toward the tower. We can't hang here." He scans the surfers around us. "The two of us look a little odd. You'll soon catch their attention."

What's wrong with me that 'we look a little odd'?

I shouldn't waste time nursing my self-pride. And although I don't want to leave my newfound safety, he's right. So I step backward, leaving him. "Thanks, I—"

Out of nowhere, a wave swallows me. North and south flip. The only reference I have is that muscular shape behind the swirling water. I reach out to grab whatever I can of him. But even his slim waist is too taut for me to grip. In a panic, I resort to tugging his shorts, getting a handful of the fabric.

After a struggle, we pop to the surface. Whatever has happened, I find myself fastened to him. My cheek rests on his gleaming chest, my boobs against his abs. Sea frolicking with a stranger should feel creepy, but being skin-to-skin with this hunk doesn't give me the slightest sense of repulsion.

It must be the way he's holding me. Firm, but it doesn't insinuate that he needs to feel me like a man needs a woman. It's a safe-guarding kind of firmness. And with that, I feel like I've known this man enough to trust him and that it's my right to be protected by him.

He soon lets me loose, only to adjust his shorts that are barely clinging to his hips. But the dreaded moment comes. "All right, now go!"

I swim away despite my heavy legs, feeling like I'm flushing the only drug that will save my life. When I turn my head, I see him leaving the beach.

By the time I arrive at the family-friendly area of the water, I'm spent. I don't know what the hell I'm going to do, but I can't even garner enough awareness to feel a shred of panic. Instead, I let myself float, trying to reclaim my temporary peace and—

"There you are!"

My arms flail, trying to scramble away from the wall of flesh behind me.

"Hey, it's me, it's me."

I stop moving like a dying crab. "Shit. Why are you here?"

He can't be a part of all this mayhem, can he?

My gut had saved me a few times when I was in the wild. It has also saved me from boys trying to fool me. But I've never tested it on a grown man.

"I thought you were done with me," I grumble.

"There's a third man. He's not suited up like those two fools, but he still looks like a fool. With sunglasses and a scarf across his face."

A scarf across his face. I haven't seen that man since he emerged from my burning home. But he's here, and my companion seems able to read the situation. "Are you a cop?"

"Me? No," he denies. "Look, I don't know what predicament you're in, but I sure hope you're not running from the authorities. I'm willing to help a stranger in need, but I don't want to harbor a criminal."

A criminal?

I live too close to the law to be one. Or I did, anyway.

"Seriously? I'm a criminal to you?" I follow his line of sight. "Is it my tattoo?"

He keeps studying the black wolf art covering half of my upper arm, forming a rueful smile as if he's about to make a bad mistake. "No. Come on, let's go." He whips his head, gesturing to the shore.

"Are you crazy? They'll see us!"

"I'll help you. But you've gotta trust me."

I let out a growl, but I follow him anyway.

"And allow me to hold you," he adds, his arm lifts a little.

I slant my face, giving him a cue to wait. I don't know why I need time to think—as if this would've been the first time he held me. It must be because we're out of the water, exposed. And I'm starting to doubt that I deserve his help.

His arm is out now, giving me no choice but to lean closer. He then rounds my shoulders. His long legs wade through the water like he was in a kids' pool. Meanwhile, I'm paying the price for not wearing the right gear. My bra is dripping like a wet sponge, and my panties feel thick, sticking everywhere.

After repositioning his arm, he rests his hand on my shoulder, his giant palm eclipsing my tattoo. I don't know if my pursuers know about my ink, but it's certainly a good idea to keep it out of sight. He passes me a pair of sunglasses. "Put them on. Don't look around. Smile and talk to me like I'm your—"

Boyfriend?

"You get the idea," he completes his sentence another way.

"Where is he? The third man?" In my head, I've been calling him *Scarf-face.*

"It's better that you don't know. Come on, let's get out of here."

"I've got to get my bag."

"Okay, if you must. Lead the way, then." He waits for me to get my bearings, his chunky feet sink in the sand. "And you can put your arm around me too. More convincing, don't you think?"

Having no reason to say no, I hook my arm around his waist. What does he do to keep it so tight? God knows when I last had a romantic stroll along the beach, and it makes me question why no part of my body screams 'Awkward!'

"Thank you. My name is Morgan."

"You're welcome, Morgan. I'm Tyler."

I nip my lips. I shouldn't have told him. But this running-away business is getting to me. I'm desperate for someone to know who I am.

"That's my bag," I point out in relief, then quickly snatch it.

We soon make our way to the parking lot.

"Jump in." Tyler opens the door of his SUV. Before he takes the wheel, he slips into a T-shirt. His jaws are wrapped in more than a five-o-clock shadow—I swear that beard has grown since he was in the water. "So, where to?"

I wish I could say 'home.'

But I keep silent.

He mutters as if trying to jog my memory, "A friend's place? Family?"

I draw a deep breath. "Do you think I can hang out at your place? Borrow your shower and towel?"

"Um... sure." Hesitance rides his voice this time. "It's not much, but you're welcome to."

His place turns out to be a motel north of Venice.

"If you need to get something, don't wander out alone, okay? It's a shady neighborhood." His warning comes with a concerned stare, but *holy wolf*, that's a fiercely captivating pair of eyes.

"You're not from here. How do you know?"

"I'm not from here, but I know this part of L.A.," he gushes, then pauses. "Hey... how did you know I'm not from here?"

"You're staying at a motel. And you sound like my Montanan ex."

He lets out a laugh. "Montanans don't have accents."

"Well, I'm right, aren't I?"

Dismissing my conclusion, he fusses with his hair. Half-dry, the glossy black strands lighten to a dark brown, and a handful of his fringe starts to curl. "I'm from Bozeman. Is it so strange that a Montanan goes to Cali?"

"No. But you're the first Montanan surfer I've met."

He gives me a look as if hinting *don't read me*. Despite that, he seems curious about my story. "Did you meet your ex here?"

"No. I met him in Gardiner. I spent a couple of years there, studying the Yellowstone wolves."

"Oh, so that tattoo wasn't just for show."

I scoff at him. "You like it?"

"I do. Although it wasn't a good thing to have if you want to be anonymous in your bathing suit walking around Venice."

Bathing suit. Thank God he doesn't know I'm in my underwear. It shouldn't matter, but I can't help dreading the indecorum I've been taught since the day I was born.

He smiles, unlocks his room door, then lets me in. "Bathroom's all yours."

How life could change in a blink of an eye. Something as simple as a shower can turn into a matter of life or death. For the first time in three days, I'm cleaning myself while someone is looking out for me on the other side.

I close my eyes, feeling the warm water on my face.

After dropping my guard, contemplation fills the absence of danger.

How close was I to being captured? What would they have done to me? How long can I keep this up?

What had my parents done? That I didn't even have a chance to say I loved them before they perished?

I swallow back sobs.

Get it together now, Morgan.

Three days is nothing. Getting to the rendezvous point will only be the beginning. I have no time for self-pity. I can't let Lilly down. I have to find my little sister. She's only twelve, for goodness' sake!

I flick the shower off.

Stepping out wearing a fresh T-shirt and a pair of shorts, expecting my host to ask how my shower was, I'm taken aback when a cold face greets me. No sign of his earlier concern or kindness, he has turned downright suspicious.

"Well, I never thought you were a celebrity. But... let's cut to the chase. Who are you?" Tyler holds up a driver's license, the new ID that Mom gave me.

"You went through my things?" I glare at him and snatch it off his hand. "My name is Emma. So what? You don't just say your name willy-nilly to a stranger."

"What's a young woman on the run doing with twenty grand in her bag?"

"It's none of your goddamn business!"

"What's going on, Emma Schiffer?"

My heart is screaming *that's not my name*. If we're going to be together for a while, I'm going to ask him to call me 'M.' At least it resembles my real name, and he might think it's 'Em.'

"I just need a place to hide for the night. If you intend to let anyone know about me, you might as well kill me."

He takes a step forward, eyes ready to interrogate me.

He's in my space, and just by standing there, I can feel a force rising inside him. It's a protective force. Steady and ready. But apparently, to get through it, I will need to answer some questions.

I can't do that. So I don't give him the chance to press me further. "If you're not gonna help me, thanks for the towel!" I throw the damp rag at him and grab my backpack.

With one wide step, he gets to the door, blocking me. "All right. I won't tell anyone. Now, I'm gonna have a quick shower. When I'm done, I will see you here."

The sun is setting. I could run away now, but I know this man is my only ticket out of California.

2

TYLER SEBASTIAN HUNT

I let her get some rest while I grab some chow.

I shouldn't care if she decides to disappear. Just like what she said about the wad of cash I discovered in her bag, ultimately, she's none of my goddamn business.

She seems to be the type who likes to do things her way. But I couldn't help going into protective mode even before she pleaded, 'Hide me.' Not because she was a girl in distress, nor was it the kiss. She has stunning features, but she did well to hide the fact. Yet, her beauty wasn't the reason either.

She was simply there.

I don't even know if I keep returning to Venice to honor the life that slipped through my hands or relive the pain. But her presence broke the pattern. I've never seen a young woman so scared, and it spurred me to swear that I'd never let the curse of Venice wrap its tentacles over her.

Emma jolts when the door clicks open.

"Hey, it's me."

Her spooked face relaxes, then lifts. Whether it's because she's happy to see my return or the smell of Chinese food I'm carrying, this is the first time I see a spark in her big brown eyes.

Jesus, she looks so beautiful like that.

She's still sitting as if she hadn't moved since I left her. Her back is straight, hands clasping together as if clinging to something. Despite the spark in her eyes, her fear lingers.

My heart splits a little, feeling the urge to comfort her, take her into my arms, caress her cheek, and whisper in her ear that everything will be okay.

Perhaps she will let me give her a small kiss. Not through desperation like she did out in the water, but like—

Like she was my girl.

And I would never let my girl stay in that state of fear. No girl should!

"Thank you." Her voice is sweet, her sincerity at the forefront.

I dismiss my wayward thoughts, unpacking the food onto the coffee table.

She attacks the box of fried rice and steals a couple of dumplings before I even sit down.

"When was the last time you ate?" I pass her a glass of water. With the rate she's eating, she could well choke herself. But before she manages to gulp the water, a knock on the door chokes her.

She cringes, almost cries. "Tyler...you didn't...who did you tell?"

"Shh!" I pull her away from the table. "I haven't told anybody. Hide behind the bathroom door! But don't close it."

I reach for my gun, then pull the room door slightly. My foot is firmly planted behind it, stopping it from slamming wide, while I use my body to barricade the opening.

"The extra towels you asked for, sir."

I've forgotten about them. "Thanks." I grab the towels, immediately close the door, and latch the chain.

I watch the housekeeping boy from behind the curtain. Then I motion for Emma to come out.

"You have a gun?" she confronts me. "You're a cop! You're *so* a cop!"

"I'm not!"

"That is a cop gun! Glock 47. I know!"

How the hell?

Perhaps the more appropriate question is, *who the hell is she that she knows?*

But with her silence and eyes flaring as big as marbles, it's her who's asking the question, and she tells me she doesn't like to wait.

I stow my Glock. "Look. Why don't we trust each other? I have a gun, okay? I just do, but law enforcement isn't my business. I'm on my way to Coronado."

It's as if a spotlight had hit her face.

Is that awe? Is that disbelief?

Look at her pink cheeks!

I make the most of it, adding, "You should know what that means. I saw your books. *A SEAL for Princess Paloma*? Really?" The girl has eclectic tastes in reading—from romance and investment to self-help—but that book takes the cake out of the pile in the ridiculousness score.

She laughs at herself this time, turning a few degrees to hide her face. She then cocks her head back to me. "You're a SEAL? For real?"

"No one pretends to be a SEAL."

"And you're afraid of me being a criminal?"

"Well, I love my job, and I'd like to keep my life uncomplicated."

"Yet you let me share a room with you." Her eyes roam the four walls. Her lips subtly pucker as she skims the bed.

"My trust doesn't stretch far. So, tell me. Who's after you?" I ask before she gets carried away with this life-imitating-fiction moment.

"I don't know. And that's the truth. All I know is those men killed my parents."

The split in my heart rips wider. No wonder she's so scared. "Jesus... I'm sorry."

"And I'm supposed to be somewhere."

"Where?"

"Washington State, somewhere in North Cascades. I abandoned my car this afternoon. So I have to think of something."

"Well, we should leave early in the morning then."

Her brows cock. "You're... you're gonna drive me there?"

"You've got a problem with that?"

Her tired eyes brighten. "I don't know what to say."

"Just enjoy the ride. Not every day you're driven by a SEAL."

Her full lips curve up, revealing the kind of gladness that pulls me in as if I'm already part of her life.

As soon as dinner ends, almost simultaneously, our attention lands on the only bed in the room.

I'm the adult here. She may be smitten by who I am, but the danger she's in is anything but fictional. And I still want to keep my life uncomplicated, so I pack up any thought that touches on any form of romance.

I stride forward to tidy up the comforter—I don't know why. The bed is already tidy.

My brain has gone on autopilot, overriding my will to keep my mind clear. God, I'm seeing the sheets all messed up, with the two of us tangled in them.

For fuck's sake! Where did that thought come from?

I grab a pillow and toss it onto the couch. "You take the bed."

Wearing a T-shirt and shorts, she climbs under the covers. There's a tinge of guilt in her stare as she tries to measure my height against the sofa's width.

I leave her be, and she starts writing something on the motel notepad. I make a call to my friend. "Yeah, sorry, man, I can't make it tomorrow. Something came up."

Her head is still down, contemplating her writing, but I know she's watching me. When I hang up, she asks, "You canceled something—for me?"

"It's okay. It was a boxing match, which I would've lost anyway. Save me from having a black eye or a bruised jaw."

"What do you mean?"

"Trying to earn extra cash, I guess. My brother is going to college this year."

"Shit. I'm sorry."

"Hey, it's no big deal. I'll help you."

She tears the page off the notepad. "Tyler, could you please send this for me?"

"A physical letter?" I muse over the address she wrote on the other side of the paper.

"It's the safest option," she argues. "She's my best friend."

When your family isn't with you, you fall on a friend. It bothers me that she can't even do that. "I'll get an envelope and send it as soon as I get you to Washington. Actually, I'll send it from San Diego. Less conspicuous."

"Thank you." She slants her face away from me.

I touch her shoulder. "Hey, you okay?"

"I miss her." Sorrows coat her smile. "I call her my Chief Life Officer. She's smart, funny, generous, and she always had an answer to everything." She fails to contain her sobs. "I guess I miss everyone. I've never felt so alone."

"Hey, I'm sure you'll see her again," I murmur straight from the heart. I almost cry with her. I know how it feels to miss someone so bad. It can feel like an earthquake, where everything around you is crumbling. And I give her the only thing that may keep her standing.

I pull her into an embrace, stroking her back, letting her know I can sense the tremors inside her. She breathes into me through the fabric of my T-shirt, perching her cheek on my chest for a while.

Then, she withdraws.

I wish she had stayed a little longer. I want to be her comfort until she's entirely at ease. But I know it's not my role. Her road is way longer than the time I have.

"Let's get some z's, eh?" I smile at her. The quake hasn't passed, but I've got to let her temper it on her own. I switch off the lights, remove my T-shirt, and sink onto the couch.

An hour has passed, and I'm still fighting with my pillow. In fact, I'm fighting against the whole fucking couch.

"Tyler..." She whispers. "Tyler!"

"What?" I mumble, rustling and grunting mixed into one.

"Come to bed. Or you're gonna be dead by morning." She turns the lights back on, then shifts herself to give me room.

"You sure?" I croak, my ass bouncing against the edge of the mattress as I sit.

"Of course I'm sure. Come on."

I lie down, leaving a strip of no-man's land between us.

She slowly pulls the covers over me.

"Thanks." I rest on my side, my back to her.

I'm still fighting, not against the bed or the pillow. Despite my honor, a small part of me imagines what would happen if I rounded my arm around her, felt her curves, and pressed her soft body against mine.

Would that comfort her? Would she ask for more?

God forbid!

I feel a brush on my back. A respectful touch.

"How long have you been a SEAL?" Her fingers are on my eagle-and-trident tattoo.

I turn to face her, and my heartbeat eases a notch. "Five years."

The fight within me fades as I remind myself the only comfort she needs is me guarding her until she has found a safe place.

"It's a tough career."

"Wouldn't change it for the world."

"I suppose fiction gets it right sometimes. Most of my heroes were proud servicemen. And I imagined their pride would've looked like that." She points gently at my eyes. "Why did you trust me, Tyler?"

"I don't see any reason you would've made it all up. I've never seen a young woman so scared."

Her mouth purses as if disagreeing with my assessment. "I hate being scared, but if it has helped me earn your trust, so be it."

A different kind of honor shrouds me. "And why did you trust me, Emma?"

She cringes. "Call me Em, please."

"Right. Em. Why did you trust me?"

Her warmth travels fast to me. The brown in her irises seems to melt like caramel. "I've kissed a few liars, and you're not one of them."

"You trust a kiss?"

"I know what honesty tastes like."

"You sound like a thinker," I comment. "Maybe one day you'll figure out why the ocean chose us." With that, I reach behind me and turn off the bedside light.

I lift my elbow, covering half of my face with my biceps.

"So, where to for you after Coronado?"

"Afghanistan."

The sheets rustle as she reaches over to the bedside table. I think she's taking something out of her wallet. "Keep safe." She passes it to me.

I remove my arm from my face, inspecting her surprise gift. It's a coin. "I don't do good luck charms."

"It's not a charm. It's a Yellowstone coin, something to remember me by."

I let out a throaty cackle. "How will I ever forget you, Wolf Girl?"

She responds with a giggly hum, apparently amused by my choice of nickname.

I put the coin next to the bedside lamp.

"Do whatever you want with it. Just stay safe, okay?" she insists.

"It's me who's supposed to say that, but thanks anyway."

"Afghanistan versus Washington? There's no comparison, Tyler."

"I'm highly trained. And as a sniper, I'm usually away from the hot spots."

"You're a sniper?" The mattress jolts as she shifts her body to face me. "Aren't snipers high-value targets?"

"Look at you talking! First the Glock, now the war?"

"I just know, okay?"

The revelation seems to bring out uneasiness in her as if she was about to lose me already. "When I'm out there, I'm part of the weapon," I convince her. "So I'm damn hard to destroy."

'I'm damn hard' echoes in my head. I wish I could say it in another context, but it's no time to restart the fight inside my chest. And I don't want to go to hell because of my stupid cock. So I say, "It's late. Let's sleep."

She pulls herself up, pecking me on the forehead. "Stay safe."

I tap her cheek playfully. "I will, Wolf Girl."

"Good night, Tyler."

I angle my face to her, watching her forcing herself to sleep. "So, this place you're supposed to go to, and whoever you're joining, they'll keep you safe?"

"I hope so."

"You hope so?" I prop myself up, resting my head on my elbow. 'Hope' is never part of my repertoire. I wish I could plan out how I'm going to keep her safe. But at least I need to know what she's getting herself into. "Do you know who's gonna be there?"

"Yes. And they will keep me safe. Don't worry." She places a hand over my shoulder, then drops it to my elbow as if drawing a line—a line that I shouldn't cross.

Two Years *Later*

3

TYLER

Helena, Montana

I ROLL the Yellowstone coin across my knuckles.

I meant it when I said I didn't do good luck charms. But Wolf Girl's souvenir has become a token of change.

A lot has happened since I dropped her off in North Cascades two years ago. My following deployment to Afghanistan was my last, and after some soul searching, I quit the Navy and came home to Montana.

Thanks to a recruitment ad I found by chance, I started a new career and became a children's rescue specialist.

'You'll never forget the first child you rescued,' my Red Mark brothers told me.

Yes, it's true, but in my mind, Wolf Girl was my first rescue case. She wasn't a child, but she was too young to be alone—facing her parents' deaths, fending off grown men who seemed hell-bent on capturing her.

I kept my promise and delivered her to her destination.

Although curiously, she insisted that she hike the remaining few miles on her own.

'I don't want to drag you further, Tyler. It could be a trap.'

It's strange to say, but that was the first time someone had tried to protect *me*. She was a nineteen-year-old, and I was in my fifth year as a SEAL.

But she wasn't an ordinary girl. Her wolf tattoo wasn't for show—that girl had teeth.

Yes, she was scared. Who wouldn't, being pursued without knowing why? But she was constantly thinking, always aware, and determined to prevail. I'd never seen it on someone so young. She certainly never acted like the princess in that ridiculous romance book of hers.

I set the coin on my desk, reminiscing the moment she put it in my hand that night. Just like most U.S. coins, the reverse bears the motto *E Pluribus Unum*—'Out of many. One.'

She was definitely one of a kind. Although she and I were never real—while women have come and gone in my life—thinking about her takes me to a pleasant place. A place where I can claim that I'd saved someone, and she was special.

What if someday our paths crossed, and I told her I didn't leave her when she ordered me to? That I'd waited until she'd arrived safely in her new home before I turned back to San Diego? Truly, I could never have let her fend for herself, especially when the word 'trap' was mentioned.

It was almost sunset in North Cascades. As I observed from afar, she ended her hike at a mountain house—a well-guarded property built to blend into its environment. A man welcomed her at the door. The strapping young fellow appeared to be a little older than she was. I could even say he was every girl's dream. The two hugged as if they'd been separated for a long time.

Whoever he might've been, I was glad she wasn't alone anymore.

"Ty, they're here." My boss, Mark Connor.

I check the time, wondering how long I've been reminiscing my past that I've forgotten about a meeting.

Mark tosses me a side smirk. "Relax. They're early."

People in the office say the man has loosened up since he got married. Still, like any good commanding officer, he has a way to keep his men in check. A decorated Green Beret, together with my other boss, fellow ex-SEAL Sam Kelleher, they founded Red Mark—the company I've worked for since I left the Navy. The men lead by example, and they've saved so many families from heartbreaks. There's nothing that I won't do for them. That's how much those two leaders mean to me.

"I'm ready, boss, don't worry." I slot the coin into my wallet and then rise from my chair, grabbing a case folder.

"I know. You were born ready, Ty." He pats my shoulder.

We make our way down to the main conference room.

I wonder if people were born with qualities that drive them to be who they are. But as the oldest of five siblings, perhaps my life has been shaped so when it comes to helping someone in need, I'll answer the call without hesitation.

When I saw the opportunity to join Red Mark, I couldn't let it pass. Serving my country was an honor. The SEAL blood will always flow in my veins. But after the fall of Kabul, the endless cycle of training and waiting without any real direction almost broke me. At the same time, there's a real war happening on my home turf—families torn apart by kidnappings. So I answered the call.

"Mr. and Mrs. Grant," Mark greets our guests.

"Sorry we're way early. Carl's chemo at the hospital has been moved ahead," the woman says, guilt apparent on her face as if she and her husband had messed up our schedules.

"Not a problem at all, Mrs. Grant," Mark assures.

"Thanks for the tea, it's really nice. Not very often someone would offer hibiscus."

"I remember you liked it the last time you were here," Mark mentions, then extends his arm to introduce me. "This is Tyler Hunt, our Head of Operations. You didn't get to meet him the other day."

I shake their hands, confidently greeting them to ease those tense, desperate faces.

"Any update on Tia?" the father asks.

Tia Grant—their fifteen-year-old daughter, last seen a week ago at their home in Butte.

"Yes," I reply. "Based on the description you gave us, I believe the man you saw talking to Tia before she disappeared is Alex Cobbs. Does that name ring a bell?"

"No," both parents say almost at the same time.

I lay Cobbs' photos on the table. Immediately, they observe the suspect's face.

"That's him. One hundred percent. This was the man I saw talking to Tia," Mrs. Grant affirms.

"He's been arrested before for acting as a pimp, but there was not enough evidence, so the case was thrown out," Mark explains. "Unfortunately, we found out he's been recruiting again, and the victims seem to be getting younger."

"Why isn't he in jail then?" Mr. Grant reddens.

"Cobbs is sly, and he's very selective in choosing his victims," I inform. "He doesn't appear to have kidnapped or forced those girls. Instead, he lures them with attention and praises, even gestures that may appear like love. He is this perfect, charming boyfriend in those girls' eyes. He'll shower them with gifts and jewelry, promising better lives if they agree to run away with him."

"Tia...what have you done?" Mrs. Grant mutters to herself.

"That explains her new earrings and necklace. She was never into jewelry. But what does a mother know!" She tries to catch her breath after that venting. "I knew there was something wrong with that man. I wish I'd said something. But I was sick of fighting with her."

She shakes her head, her teeth grit.

I'm dying to tell her I understand exactly how she feels. If I had said or done something, the tragedy in Venice eleven years ago would never have happened. But mentioning that to her will only serve my ego. You will never fully understand what a mother goes through, having her daughter missing without a trace.

"You can't blame yourself, Mrs. Grant," I emphasize. "Don't let Alex Cobbs plant doubts and self-blame in you."

I pause for a moment, letting the couple take the time to absorb the revelation. The husband, although palpably frail, holds his wife steadily as if trying to stop her from exploding while at the same time comforting her.

"He's right, Betsy. We're in this together." He obviously knows how to get through to his wife because she calms. "How often do you see family ends up hating each other? Blaming each other while we should really be blaming that criminal. What's his name? Alex?"

I nod. "The police in Great Falls have advised us about the possibility of a similar case. It's still early stages. We don't know if it's related to Tia's case. But we'll keep an eye on it."

"He won't go far. We'll get him." Mark taps at the photo of Alex Cobbs.

A thought springs up in my mind. "Mrs. Grant, do you remember what Tia's earrings and necklace looked like?"

"Um, yeah." She closes her eyes as if visualizing them. "The earrings were like an S-shape, maybe an-inch long, with small diamonds set from top to bottom. They looked expensive, but I guess the diamonds could be fake. And the necklace had a similar design, although thicker. And the chain was silver. Or white gold."

"Thank you. I'll check pawn shops which Cobbs might have connections with. He couldn't have bought them from Tiffany."

Mrs. Grant's face lights up a little.

"We'll do whatever we can to save Tia," I add.

"Thank you, Mr. Connor and Mr. Hunt," the father says. "And thank you for taking our case. As you know, the police didn't take us seriously. I mean, Tia is no angel. She's been in trouble many times, and she had run away before. With all signs pointing to her simply wanting to leave home, we had no chance of convincing them she's been taken."

"This is all we have." Mrs. Grant slides an envelope across the table toward Mark. "I've talked to some of your previous clients. I know it's nowhere near enough—"

"No, Mrs. Grant, we can't accept this." Mark hands over the envelope back to her.

"We hired you, so it's only fair that we pay you," Mr. Grant argues.

"We're a business, and we need to make money. But it's also our job to make sure we're not taking what's not ours. Tia's case is ours to take, but your money isn't."

Mr. Grant, who's been composed throughout the meeting, breaks down in tears. Mark and I both know they're struggling to make ends meet with the mounting costs of his cancer treatment.

Once again, the couple comforts each other.

This is why I do what I do—for parents like them. And the way the couple stays united makes me even more determined to save Tia from that manipulative monster.

4

MORGAN

North Cascades outer rim, Washington State

Our rendezvous point is long gone. The guards were killed, but the three of us managed to get out of there alive.

We've been moving from place to place since, but our pursuers always seem to know our moves.

Now, it's only the two of us.

"Still no news from Aunt Diana?" My voice is barely audible, as if I don't want to ask the question.

"She's dead, Morgan. Let's face it," Hudson gripes, refusing even to take out his phone to check.

Aunt Diana, my father's sister, wasn't my favorite Blackwell. She'd stay in our house when my parents had to work out of town or interstate. Maybe as a young girl, my idea of 'aunties are a perfect blend of mother and friend' was distorted. She wasn't cruel in any way. She gave me everything I needed. But my memory of being under her care was almost emotionless.

Nevertheless, realizing that she may be dead rattles me. She decided to part with us to distract our pursuers, but after almost a month of no contact, I know Hudson is right. We have to move on without her.

Hudson navigates a hairpin turn with speed that I almost drop my phone. He huffs like a whale, eyes nearly as red as the sunset.

"We can't keep running, Hudson." I touch his hand, begging him to stop and take a break.

He pulls over.

"Then what are you suggesting?"

"We've got a lead on Lilly."

"And we're going to follow it through."

"We can't do it alone. I found this." I show him a website.

He studies it. "Red Mark? Who the hell are they?"

"This company has saved numerous missing children. If anyone can help us find Lilly, it'll be them. At least him." I show Hudson a profile.

"Him?"

"Yes, this man." I point at my phone screen, heart loping. I knew what safety was like, and I'm dying to be in that space again.

"Tyler Hunt?"

"He saved me in L.A. And he drove me to North Cascades."

Hudson's lips flatten. "You said you came by yourself!"

I didn't tell him. I didn't want to complicate things and worry him needlessly.

"I asked him to drop me off at Stehekin. Then I hiked by myself."

To this day, I still wish Tyler could've stayed on. But he had his own mission. The safety of our country rested on his shoulders. I couldn't drag him further into my mess, and I didn't want anybody to know about Tyler.

"You're crazy, Morgan!"

"I couldn't have made it without him, Hudson. And we won't find Lilly without his help."

"And why would I trust him?"

"He was a SEAL when we met. Clearly, he's quit the Navy, and now he uses his skills to save missing children."

"Morgan, this isn't fiction. Okay? Just because he's a SEAL doesn't mean we can trust him!"

"I know! But I wouldn't have been here if it wasn't for him. He will help us. I have no doubt in my mind."

Hudson leans back. His face droops. I don't know how many creases he has collected since we were flushed out of our rendezvous point. The man needs rest so badly.

"Let me drive," I offer.

"No, it's okay. We'll stop at a motel and plan our route to Helena."

"We fly, Hudson. We can't waste time while the lead is still hot," I beg. "We drive to Tacoma now."

Seemingly having run out of energy to argue, Hudson agrees, and we make our way to the airport.

"I can't believe we're flying to fucking Montana," he mumbles.

I give him a side smirk. "You may end up joining them. You'll be in your element."

"I study military as a hobby. It doesn't make me a soldier."

"Nothing is stopping you from becoming a civilian protector."

"And would that make you love me more?"

"I always love you, Hudson." I kiss his cheek.

Suddenly, a shot rings out from behind the trees lining the road. It must've hit a tire that we zigzag out of control. Hudson slams on the brake, but the car keeps tobogganing downhill.

The next thing I see is white as the airbag deploys.

I can barely move, it's as if a thousand needles have been

embedded inside my neck. But I turn my head to check on Hudson. He's firing back, only to incite a ferocious response from our enemy.

"Hudson, duck!" I desperately shout, trying to push my door open so we can climb out of this wreck. The shots are coming from one direction, so we should be able to escape from the passenger side.

But right when the jammed door clicks free, Hudson's body falls over me. The gunfire has become a chorus of sickening thuds—thuds of metal hitting flesh as if he was a sack for target practice.

"Hudson…" I tremble.

"Run!"

Tears burn my eyes. "I won't leave you!"

"Find Lilly." His fingers tremble against my face. No doubt his blood is all over me now. But he still has a smile as if wanting me to remember his last moments fondly—that free-spirited boy who hasn't always done things our family expects but will do whatever it takes to preserve us. "You can do it."

Upon that call, I hurl myself out of the car, taking off with my pack.

I shouldn't turn around, but deep down, I'm wishing for some kind of miracle that he manages to escape, too.

It's as if a giant hand is mangling my lungs.

No, it can't be him.

It can't be my Hudson.

He can't die!

I don't know how long I have been breathless, but I'm still alive.

I wish someone could fucking explain what Mom and Dad had gotten us into!

But it's only me. I'm the last one standing.

Finally, I'm able to take in air as I put back whatever pieces of me I can salvage. I will never be the same. The pieces won't fit. But I've got to keep standing, keep fighting, and keep running. My little sister needs me. I'm her only hope.

Shots start cracking behind me, and they're getting closer. Low, as if they're aiming at my legs.

I'm now running uphill. It's good to be on higher ground, but it is slowing me down.

Among the hisses of bullets, I feel a flick on my side. There's a tear on my jacket, and a stinging pain radiates across my waist. Those bastards have got me.

I plaster myself behind a large tree, catching my breath and gaining a sense of where my enemies are.

Facing absurdity and danger has taught me to operate on my head alone, shoving my feelings into a locked room even I don't know where. It's the only way to carry on.

Gritting my teeth, I gather whatever strength I have. I'm giving my body a crash course in ignoring, then forgetting pain. I run with speed.

As I gain more distance, the attack grows wayward.

The forest closes in on me, but my vision has never been clearer.

However long, whatever it takes. I've got to get to Helena.

5
———

TYLER

After two weeks of investigating leads pertaining Tia Grant's jewelry, we finally had a breakthrough. A burglary at a house in Deer Lodge, a town southwest of Helena, led us to believe that the earrings and necklace Cobbs gave to Tia belonged to the house owner. So the prick didn't even spend a penny on them!

Following that, we narrowed our search and received a tip from a fisherman who spotted a man acting suspiciously, with a girl seemingly locked inside a van—matching the description of Tia.

"Do you believe love is blind?" Ben Winter throws me a conundrum as we chew up the last few miles of our journey.

I've assigned him as my partner today. The Taekwondo master is the only Red Mark ground crewman with no military training. But he's the man I'd rather have by my side when it comes to cases involving teenagers. He and his sister had to grow up without their father since they were in their early teens. Their mother did her best, but Ben and his sister thrived because they had each other—they understood each other.

He continues, "I mean, being a teenage girl who doesn't get along with her parents is like hiding dynamite inside your own home. But what has Cobbs done that Tia is so loyal to him? He's not even attractive. Cobbs looks like Justin Bieber had a baby with Tori Spelling."

That was the simplest description of Alex Cobbs. However, if you tell that to a sketch artist, they probably won't get it.

"It's blindness, but it's not love," I reply. "Cobbs just wheedled his way to the weakest part of her, and she willingly became his slave."

"Well, it ends today," Ben concludes.

I sit up, adjusting my ballistic vest. I really hope I won't need it today.

My partner gives me a sneaky glance. "You lost weight or something? No one's cookin' at home?"

"Shut up!"

"Have you called her back yet?"

I puff out air, regretting the day I told him about Daisy Klein. She and I broke up almost six months ago, and out of the blue, I had a missed call from her.

"No," I hesitate.

"Tyler, I care about you, so I'm gonna say this. Don't be a stag who can't keep his harem. You've got the antlers, you've got the muscle. What's missing, my friend, is your will to claim what's yours. That desperation. When did she call? Three weeks ago?"

"I don't wanna restart anything."

"Have you forgotten the smell of pheromone?"

I really shouldn't have told him. "Cut it, Winter!"

An incoming call buzzes on the dashboard.

"Saved by the bell!" Ben quips as I tap the screen to answer the call.

"Tyler Hunt?"

"Speaking."

"Sheriff Larson. Beaverhead County." Deer Lodge is his jurisdiction, and he's aware of Red Mark's plans.

"Sheriff."

"My men just reported a shootout about five miles from my office. There were two men and two girls."

Ben and I eyeball each other. So Alex Cobbs has an accomplice, and the other girl will likely be the missing girl from Great Falls.

The sheriff adds, "They seem to be traveling back north, still on that dark blue Chevy van. Skip Deer Lodge, and you may cross paths with them."

"Copy that, sheriff. Thanks for the heads-up."

We speed up, zooming past our original destination.

"Come on! Where's that son of a bitch!" Ben leans forward over the steering wheel, eyes peeled. He's six-foot-six—in that posture, it looks like he's about to eat someone.

"There!" I point. This part of the I-15 gives us a clear view ahead for miles, and with the way the van is driven, you don't have to be an expert to spot it. "They're making a turn into Wise River."

We make the same turn, but only after traveling the narrow road for three miles, we find the van—overturned and abandoned.

"Cobbs! Give it up, it's over!" I yell, gun in my hand, carefully inspecting the front of the vehicle while Ben goes to the back.

"Clear!" Ben announces.

"Clear!" I echo him. "They must be running into the forest."

Alex Cobbs and his accomplice may be seasoned manipulators, but they're no pros. In addition to their sloppy driving, they've left tracks and clues all over the place.

Only ten minutes in, and we see movement.

Apprehension latches on me.

These guys are amateurs, but amateurs can sometimes pose more danger because they get desperate quickly.

Someone heads for a clearing. I don't recognize the man, so it must be Cobbs' accomplice. He's almost as big as Ben that it appears as though he was hauling a toddler.

To our horror, he rushes into the clearing to execute his captive. The girl is not Tia, but she's about the same age. Her hands are bound, her mouth gagged, her clothes in tatters. There's blood spattered across her face, and she's clearly in shock. She doesn't even beg or cry.

With Ben closer to the two, I signal him to strike while I press on to catch Cobbs. His head bobs down, telling me he's got this.

Leaving a partner is always a fifty-fifty call, but I know I've got to, or I'll lose Tia.

Behind me, I hear a few thuds and verbal exchanges. Ben is clearly confronting the man. So far, there's not a single gunshot fired. When you work with the best, you know you can count on them. After a few minutes of no gunshots, I'm sure he's gotten things under control. Perhaps Ben's Taekwondo moves have proven to be the winner in the close-quarter combat.

I charge on. Another presence starts becoming clear, and soon, I see two figures ahead of me.

In a given mission, you always prepare for any eventuality. Including this.

"Stay where you are!" Tia turns and points a gun at me, blocking my way to get to Cobbs.

"Tia, easy! I'm not the police. I just want you safe. I don't care about him. You don't have to protect him like this." I take one step forward.

"I said, stay where you are!"

"Tia, drop the gun."

"Don't step any closer, or I'll shoot you!" she yells.

I put my gun away. "Tia, listen to me. A man who convinces you to cut ties with your family is never a good man. He's going to sell you, like the other girls he managed to snare. This isn't his first rodeo."

Tia takes half a glance over her shoulder, obviously checking if her boyfriend has managed to get away. "He loves me! Look at that Great Falls bitch! Bound and gagged. Alex never treats me like that. I'm special. He loves me."

"Look, once this is over, you'll see what real love is. That man is certainly not."

She scoffs cynically, and the gun shakes in her hands. "Real love. You mean my family? You don't know how much I hate them!"

"No, I don't. Suppose you do hate your parents. This is how much I can tell you. Real love is when someone makes you feel special because of who you are—not because they treat others appallingly."

Tia gulps, this time unable to hide her jitters. "Who are you?"

"My name is Tyler Hunt. I'm not the police, but I must come clean. Your parents sent me. They want you safe. That's all. You don't even have to return home if you're not ready. They only want you out of danger."

She softens.

"Put the gun down, Tia."

Noises spread around us, prompting her to grip the weapon tighter, finger on the trigger.

One sharp dash out of the bush changes everything. The man coming from my right is aiming at Tia.

"No!" I lunge at the girl, knocking her to the ground and shielding her. I twist, pointing my gun at the uniformed man.

It's a deputy sheriff, rage marring his face. "What the fuck are you doing!" his voice booms. "Where's Cobbs?"

"I don't know. But she's with me," I yell back, keeping Tia behind me.

Right then, the figure of Ben Winter arrives. Seeing the deputy aiming at me and Tia, he tackles him.

"Ben, no! Let him go!" I try to persuade my partner to drop the arm wrestling while still shielding Tia.

"You're gonna shoot dead a fifteen-year-old girl?" Ben grits, pulling the deputy's collar, fist about to swing at his face.

"Winter, no!" I order.

Ben unfurls his fingers. Anger shakes him, but he's withdrawing. His eyes scorn at the deputy. "You don't even deserve to wear pants, let alone that badge!"

The deputy gripes, "My partner got killed because that bitch did exactly that! Protecting her lover! She was about to do the same to yours, and you're just gonna let her?"

Ben releases the man and then gets up. "My partner knew what he was doing! *You* almost got him killed!"

The sheriff soon arrives with backup and paramedics.

"You okay?" I ask Tia. I think she might've hurt her wrist.

"Sir, we've got this," an officer says. "Please step away. The girl needs medical help."

I let Tia sit up. "I'll stay with you."

She shakes her head. "Just go! Just go before I hate you."

I reluctantly move away, letting paramedics tend to her but still keeping an eye on the proceedings.

Ben approaches me. "Fuck that deputy!" he mumbles, flicking loose grass off my ballistic vest. I'm glad the Kevlar didn't meet with any bullets today.

I glance at the uniformed man who seems to be receiving an earful from his superior. That was a close call. I know that man just lost a partner, but when you're on duty, you switch off your emotions. Ben was right. He could've gotten me killed.

"Let it go, partner." I haul Ben away from the scene. "How was the other girl?"

"She's all right. Another deputy got her, along with a very nice lady from child services."

"You didn't need your gun?"

"I thought the girl had seen enough blood for a day. She's pretty messed up. I just couldn't shoot another man in front of her."

"She witnessed the first shootout?"

"Yeah. Cobbs blew a deputy's head off. That was why the girl had blood all over her face."

That is messed up.

The sheriff motions to paramedics to start moving. It's going to be dark soon. He walks with us until we're back on the side of the road. "No sign of Cobbs. We'll keep chasing, but your job is done here."

"No. I'm staying with the girl," I insist.

Before I get close to Tia, she screeches, "Get her out of my face!"

"Is that Mrs. Grant?" Ben's eyes follow the movement of a woman who has just arrived.

"Yeah. Wait here."

Noticing me coming, Tia soon shifts her anger at me. "Tyler! Tyler! You lying bastard!"

"Tia, calm down. I'll talk to your mother. I promise. You won't have to face her tonight." I turn around to stop Mrs. Grant in her tracks. With Ben's help, we manage to keep distance between the daughter and mother.

"Let me see her!" the woman persists. "Tia!"

"I understand, Mrs. Grant," I proceed. "Tia is okay. But she's in shock. She's angry, and she's confused. Please wait a little longer. Please, trust me."

"You may have just saved her, but you don't know her. I'm her mother. She needs me!"

"On any other day, I would say yes. But just for tonight, she needs you to keep your distance."

"No! Let me see her!" Both mother and daughter seem to be charged up.

Ben keeps restraining the distraught woman while behind me, Tia throws shouts of abuse.

"Mrs. Grant." A calm voice among the piercing chaos.

Just the man I want to see.

"Mrs. Grant, walk with me," Mark Connor persuades, and just like that, the woman relents.

My boss passes me an 'I've got this' motion, and I take the opportunity to return to Tia, who's still cursing and swearing.

"She's leaving," I tell her adamantly.

The girl observes her mother for a few moments and finally settles.

"Thank you. It's nice not to be lied to," she says. "You said you weren't the police. Are you a private investigator?"

"I'm with Red Mark Rescue & Protect. We specialize in rescuing missing children."

"God! I'm a missing child. How fucked up is that?" she rages. "So now you're gonna protect me from my parents?"

"They're not the danger, Tia. You're safe now. When or where you want to talk to them, or even never, it's not my call. You decide."

Once again, Tia follows the movement of her mother, along with Mark, who, like the seasoned pro he is, calmly ushers her to her car.

"What will happen to Alex?"

"The police will keep looking for him. And once they find him, he'll go to jail."

"And me?"

"You haven't done anything wrong, Tia. Have you?"

"I'd protected him." Then she glances at the girl whom Ben had saved. Her glance turns into a bitter stare as the girl is hugged and comforted by her parents. "But I swear, I haven't hurt anybody. I was just with him, doing what he told me to."

"He manipulated you. That's on him, not you."

Tia shrugs.

"For now, these people are gonna take care of you. Please let them," I plead with her as a paramedic gestures for me to step aside. She's with another woman who introduces herself as a representative from child services.

Tia releases a deep breath, leaning on the stretcher chair. I think she has finally run out of steam. "I'll talk to my dad," she murmurs. "Just my dad."

"Okay. I'll get your dad to meet you at the hospital."

She shuts her eyes as paramedics load her into the ambulance.

I turn around to join Ben. His attention is on our boss, who's still talking to Mrs. Grant. The giant is not aware of me watching him wince every time he moves his torso.

Ben Winter never winces.

I tap him on the back. "Hey, let's get that injury checked."

"Injury? What injury!"

"It's not a request, Winter."

6

MORGAN

I feel myself rolling down a short slope, disturbing the pile of dried leaves I have used to pad the ground.

Hudson...

My throat burns, still feeling his name surging out of my chest.

When I open my eyes, I'm lying on my belly, still in my sleeping bag. The rolling has moved me a few yards off my original spot.

I puff out air, turning over so I'm facing up. Water drips from the tree above me, landing on my cheeks and mouth.

I'm more than five hundred miles from that fatal incident outside Tacoma, and I've seen more wildlife than people since then, but this nightmare keeps finding me. And it keeps reminding me of the people I loved—people who said the same thing moments before they died, protecting me.

Run.

I'm sick of running, but I can't quit until I find Lilly. *One more day*—I tell myself every morning. Time is not on my side, but I hope my decision to choose safety over speed will pay off. When roads expose you, all you can do is stay off them. Fortunately, it's summer, or this journey would've looked a lot different.

Five a.m.

Puffing air, I shake the sleep off me and start thinking about having breakfast before moving on. But I can't stomach anything right now.

Hudson would've given me an earful. 'Never hit the trail in a fasting state.' I can hear his voice, loud and clear. He had taught me a lot, my big brother.

Dad used to take us on short hikes when we were kids—before his work got hectic. I'll never forget my first outing, the wonder when I stood at Yosemite's Glacier Point on my seventh birthday. Dad gave me a taste of what it was like to be one with nature, but it was Hudson who trained me how to survive in it. He joined a military-style boot camp as a young teenager, trying to lose weight and take back control of his life. He came out a man—buff, focused, and addicted to adventures. His addiction rubbed off on me and I begged him to give me a go. So we trekked almost every weekend until he decided to leave home and did his own thing.

If only he were here now.

Bushes a distance away rustle. I don't think it's the wind. Something is watching me.

I reach out for my bear spray.

I haven't had a bear encounter on this trip—which is a bit unusual but lucky, nonetheless. It was a common occurrence in my past explorations, although I always hiked with fellow researchers.

The rustling continues.

There's a reason why this is called the wilderness. It's *wild*. Any animals—or even plants—can kill you. If the creature coming at me is a bear, and it's determined to get me, there's no spray or move that can save me. Despite my knowledge of guns,

I don't have one myself, and I'm too chicken to learn how to shoot. But I'd rather die in the paws of a bear than in the hands of Scarf-face.

Suddenly, silence.

The creature has shown itself—tawny coat, pointy ears, bushy ruff around its neck. A lynx.

"Good kitty-kitty," I whisper, more to myself than to the cat as we observe each other. Lynxes don't usually approach humans, and I hope that's the case for me this morning. Yet, I keep the communication line open. "People around me die, Mr. Cheeto. It's probably wise for you to walk away."

The cat studies me for a few more seconds, then it about-faces and disappears.

I crawl out of my sleeping bag like a clumsy caterpillar. Stretching only brings up the pain points in my body, which seem to be everywhere.

I press my left side. Blood.

My fall last night must've reopened my wound. It fucking stings. I guess, like all wounds, it gets worse with time when you fail to tend to it. But I have no time to think about my injury. I've got to trust the good doctor in Spokane that his stitches will hold. At least until I reach Helena.

I review the map, planning my last hike. Thanks to my satellite phone, I can get a reliable connection. However, getting this phone almost cost me. Scarf-face's men were close to tracking me down when I ventured to civilization to get to a hardware store.

The forecast indicates it will be mostly cloudy with afternoon showers. I could make a detour to the next town and hitchhike. But I'd rather get wet than risk being captured.

I catch a glimpse of the lake behind me.

Weight gathers on my shoulders as I take my first steps over the rocky slope. My pack had ballooned since the last time I traveled by car. Knowing I'd be away from any lifeline for a while, I'd piled up more tools, camping gear, and warm clothes.

My feet throb, bearing the pressure like they're about to explode in my boots. But I keep going.

Now, there's only one reason I will leave the wilderness.

To hunt down a man.

Tyler Hunt.

7

TYLER

"You've fractured a few ribs, Mr. Winter," the doctor at the Helena Hospital emergency room tells Ben. "The morphine will kick in soon. Wait a little bit, then you can go home." She then leaves us be.

"A rock got me. A fucking rock got me!" Ben complains. Apparently, after kicking Cobbs' accomplice to get rid of his gun, the two engaged in fierce hand-to-hand combat. One time, Ben fell on a large rock.

"He got you good," I tease him.

"It was the rock!" he insists. Then his brows cock. "Well, I must admit I didn't expect that prick to retaliate so hard, but that fucking rock hidden under layers of leaves!"

The big man rises.

I give him a disapproving look. "Hey, where do you think you're going?"

"Dinner. I can't stay here a minute longer."

"All right."

"I'm gonna get dressed."

I bend down to get his bag, unzipping it. "What do you need?"

"Tyler, much as I long for someone to dress me up and comfort me right now, you're not my type. So, wait in the car, will you?"

I cared for my four brothers when they were still young. I guess I forgot that Ben isn't one of them.

"Fine. Be quick about it." Now that he's mentioned dinner, I don't want to miss my meal at the Thirsty Fox either!

I saunter away from the E.R.

It's moments like this when you start pondering about what's next. Gathering at the table with my Red Mark brothers is one way to cope. But it can only fill you for so long. After having been pumped to the height of distress, at the end of the day, going home to an empty bed isn't the way to bring yourself gently down. It's a brutal awakening.

Women have come and gone in my life. My relationships have been pretty much drama-free, even when we parted. But breakups always hurt.

I fish out my phone from my pants pocket. The missed call from Daisy Klein is the only one that I haven't erased from the notification list.

I almost had it all with her. But she did the right thing to call it quits. I couldn't keep short-changing her, breaking one promise after another. I should've learned before I committed —you can never have it all.

But what if a call back could lead to another try?

I shake my head. It's been weeks. I'm sure she has forgotten all about it. Finally, I decide to delete the notification.

As my heart shrinks lazily, my phone beeps.

"God damn!" I murmur, reading that Alex Cobbs has been captured.

My heart may not be at its best, but this kind of news keeps my head high and puts sense in my decision to keep my single life.

As I start wondering what the hell is taking Ben so long, a bag slaps my arm from the side as the owner darts past me.

"Hey," I call out.

She doesn't even bother to stop.

A sorry would be nice!

Montana is a hikers' paradise so it's not uncommon to see people out and about in their gear. But wearing an oversized hoodie, carrying a dirt-covered pack that towers like a punching bag, the woman appears like she just came out of the Alps and perhaps thought a bear was after her. She only slows because the doors in front of her aren't sliding fast enough.

I feel another slap on my arm. This time it's Ben. "Ready?"

"Yeah," I mumble as I turn my attention back to the doors.

She's gone.

8

MORGAN

My heart is pounding double-time. One, for leaving the hospital to escape further scrutiny from the medical staff, and two, for escaping Tyler Hunt.

I'm in Montana for him. But that 'brush with destiny' had caught me off guard, and panic got the better of me. Whatever he was doing there?

I don't think he realized it was me. My jacket hood was pulled down to cover half of my face. My pack which he was familiar with has almost doubled in size and I'd only bought the yellow rain cover after Tacoma. So I'm sure I looked different to him and was too fast for him to scrutinize. Besides, *I* didn't recognize myself. I'd seen my reflection in water during my hike. But tonight, passing a mirror at the hospital, for the first time I witnessed my sunken eyes, swollen lips, and gaunt body.

Perhaps the hospital was a bad idea to re-introduce myself to human contact. The harsh white lights, the smell, the ominous equipment—they all remind me how fragile humanity can be.

But there's no way I would fail Lilly just because I dread

going back into civilization and letting infection take over my body.

I arrive at a small motel downtown. "I need a room."

I could've picked a more upmarket accommodation, but with how I look at the moment, this is passable.

One of the books Mom had packed was an investment guide. It took me a while to figure out, but the secret words and numbers contained in that book had led me to a locker. There, I found a bank card and a new ID that proves I own a bank account with a balance big enough to buy this motel.

The woman at reception studies me as she forces a smile. I bet I look and smell funny, but there's nothing I can do until I have access to a shower.

"How many nights?"

"Just one."

"A hundred and fifty dollars."

I give her cash. "Do you have room service?"

She raises her eyes to me as she counts the money. "Not at this hour. But there's a bar called the Thirsty Fox only a couple of blocks from here. They open late." She scans me from head to toe as if hinting I may need a change of clothes to go there.

The room is cleaner and tidier than I expected.

Running water. Such a simple thing. But turning on the vanity tap feels like I'm living in luxury. And feeling the warm towel on my face is like being pampered at a day spa.

I would've stripped naked and jumped into that bath, but assessing how I am now, there's no way I would survive without food tonight. That means I'll still need my legs to get somewhere, and I need my shoes on. If I take them off now, I might not be able to put them back in.

After ditching my hoodie and flannel shirt, I put on a black turtleneck and hide my greasy hair under a beanie. My top feels damp on my skin, but at least I don't look like a tramp.

THE THIRSTY FOX is a good-looking bar. Still, I decide to pass it by, not wanting to test my sociability tonight.

I drop by a convenience store and grab a frozen pot pie, which the woman behind the counter happily heats up for me. It's almost ten o'clock at night when I stop at a small park to eat. The sky is clear, and the stars are out. The only sound I hear is the rustling leaves of elm trees around me. The night turns out all right.

A shadow moves along the path in front of me—close to the ground, its four legs swinging, tail wagging hard.

"Hello there!" I greet the short-haired canine. A village dog, perhaps with some Labrador or cattle dog blood. It breaks my heart to see his visible ribs and jutting hip bones. "When did you last eat?"

The mutt grins and keeps wagging its tail.

"Makes two of us." I toss him a chunk of meat from my pie.

Dinner with a dog. I certainly hadn't anticipated it would be part of my itinerary tonight. But somehow, it restores the balance within my psyche. The furry presence reminds me that civilization isn't as scary as my mind made it out to be.

The dog licks the gravy off the ground and keeps licking even when there's nothing left.

I give him another piece, and he does the same. "All right, Gravy. It's just you and me now."

But as soon as the pie is gone, Gravy disappears.

Once more, I glance at the Thirsty Fox. Perhaps it keeps glancing at me because the neon sign is impossible to ignore.

I imagine sitting in there a while, enjoying some music, sipping whiskey to numb my aching shoulders and stinging feet.

Maybe I simply want to delay my date with a bath—I am

not ready to test my pain threshold just yet. So, if I need to be around people again, probably the best bet would be at a bar with a fox logo.

The door is so heavy I have to ram my way in. My strength has truly dwindled. A waitress has to help me.

"Welcome to the Thirsty Fox," the twenty-something woman greets me. "Take a seat, anywhere. I'll be right with you."

Oh my God—her smile. I haven't seen such a warm, friendly, welcoming human being in... I don't know how long. And, oh my God, again. Look at those burgers coming out of the kitchen!

It's a modern country bar—clean cut, natural wood, lots of plants, and warm lights. The place is less than half-filled. I guess it's late. There's a stage for live music, but it doesn't look like there's a show tonight.

Still, it doesn't mean this place is dead. The music turns to an up-tempo beat as if it has switched playlists. It sends my foot tapping under my seat.

"Sorry to keep you waiting. What can I get you?" says the woman who greeted me at the door.

I still can't believe how lovely she is. With the lack of clean clothes, not to mention my muddy boots, I wouldn't have blamed her if she'd looked down on me. "Um, Whistling Andy Whiskey, please. Neat."

"Good choice," she utters. "My name is Cassidy. I'm the manager here. Call me Cass."

"Thanks, Cass."

She glances at my backpack as she grabs the whiskey bottle and a glass. "You're traveling?"

Pack and run. Pack and run. That's been my life for the past two years. "Yeah. Kind of."

"Why am I sensing this isn't your first time in Montana?"

Was it my choice of local whiskey? Maybe. But this woman is good at reading people. I guess you have to be, working at a downtown bar.

"You're right. But it's my first time in Helena. I used to spend a lot of time around Yellowstone."

A waiter with another tray of burgers whooshes past me while Cass serves my whiskey. She seems to notice where my eyes are wandering despite my oversized fake glasses. "Fox has the best cheeseburger in town. I'll give your money back if you don't rate it ten out of ten," she tempts me.

I should've given that whole pot pie to Gravy. My stomach is urging me to tell Cass, 'Give me that cheeseburger. With extra fries.'

But after surviving only with raw nuts and wild mushrooms in the past few days, giving my digestive system a shock won't be a good idea. Even that pie wasn't a good idea. Neither is the whiskey in my hand. But what I never failed to do during my hike was to keep myself hydrated, and I think my inner system is thanking me for it. My stomach is still in pretty good shape, I'd say.

"I've eaten, thanks."

Cass glances at my backpack again. "Have you got a place to stay?"

"Umm...yeah."

"Good. I do not mean to be nosy. But it's late, and I'd hate for a young woman like you to wander around alone looking for somewhere to stay for the night," her motherly voice strikes me deeply.

Before I decide whether it'll be wise to befriend her and ask questions, her attention shifts to a man at the door.

I recognize him. Maybe this is why my subconscious had told me to check this place out. I should've known. This bar is not far from the Red Mark office, where Tyler works, and the man who's just entering the bar is Mark Connor—one of his bosses. I've seen him in photos, but Jesus! That man is so handsome I'd imagine every single woman in Helena would flip backward to get a date with him.

Cass waves at him. Perhaps seeing my reaction, she quips, "Sorry, he's taken."

I chuckle. I know. That man is married to the previous attorney general of Montana. When she was kidnapped by a crime lord, Red Mark's involvement in her rescue made headlines. That was how I found out my only hope to find Lilly is here, in Helena.

"Another one?" Cass offers, seeing my empty glass.

"Ah, yes, please."

Soon, another man enters, and right after she refills my drink, she raves, "He's taken, too."

That's Sam Kelleher, Tyler's other boss.

"And he's my husband," Cass smirks, winking at me, amused.

That I did not know.

She giggles. "Sorry to tease you like this. I thought you needed some lightening up. But I suppose you're not in Helena to find a date."

I might be blushing, and I hope she thinks it's because of the whiskey. "I'm just passing."

She nods, then says, "Excuse me."

Cass approaches Sam and hugs him, kissing him like they were newlyweds. What a couple. Sam is so lucky to have her. Although if I were in her shoes, I would feel friggin' lucky to be married to that ex-SEAL.

Soon, more men arrive, and Cass helps the group combine some tables. From their chatters, I think they've just completed a mission. I hear the words 'she's safe,' 'forest' and 'sheriff' a few times.

I have spent a lot of time in Montana, and I have researched Red Mark during my run, but I never thought I'd feel this giddy being in their company. And that doesn't count Tyler—who's nowhere to be seen. He may still be in that hospital. Perhaps someone he knew was ill or got injured because, to my eyes, he appeared as healthy as an ox.

I drink on, observing the men.

The front door swings open, and the group simultaneously cheers.

"There he is!" Sam calls merrily. "Fresh and fortified."

He is fresh and—fortified, whatever Sam meant. Most importantly, as I'd observed, the man is healthy as an ox.

He struts his way in, wearing a simple white T-shirt and dark jeans. His thick, wavy hair is neatly combed back. With a smile worthy of a toothpaste commercial, he shakes hands and pats shoulders with everyone at the Red Mark table.

While I know who he is, I don't know if he's taken.

Whatever his relationship status, he's only a few yards away from me, within a few strides. To hug, to tell my story.

But as if a sudden snowstorm is encircling me, my body freezes. The reunion scenarios I'd pictured wash out like mud disappearing into a sinkhole. Once again the Tyler-induced panic crawls all over me. Picking up where we left off, explaining why I'm here, or even saying hello, is now a giant leap which I'm too frightened to take.

What have the years done to me? Have I forgotten what safety feels like?

Tyler takes a seat, keeping the conversation going at the table. Occasionally, he surveys the premises.

Anticipating he might see me, I turn to the bar, showing him my back. I then tuck my pack between the stool and the counter, my legs cramming it so it's out of view.

But soon, I realize he has no interest in studying the night's remaining patrons.

He laughs with his Red Mark friends, toasting their success. But the way he keeps stealing glances at the woman sitting at the table across the room is rousing my suspicion. She's wearing a purple cocktail dress, and her wavy hair falls to her bare shoulders. She's perhaps two or three years older than me. She could be waiting for someone, or she could just be spending the night alone—like me.

Tyler's gaze is not that of a wandering-eyed man. The woman's back is to him, so he can't have seen how pretty she is. He knows her. And it's none of my business, but damn! He wants her.

9

TYLER

Food starts arriving, breaking my train of thought—and my train of glances at Daisy Klein. After ignoring her missed call for weeks, she's the last person I expected to see tonight.

I'm surrounded by my Red Mark brothers, but seeing her alone at that table sends my mind back to the days when she was in my life. When she was in my bed when I came home.

A woman's touch. A dangerous thing to crave when you're trying to stay off relationships.

Yet, I'm still trying to concoct the what-ifs.

Maybe now that I'm the head of ops at Red Mark, I'll have more flexibility, which means I'll be able to spend more quality time with her and keep my promise—not to let her sleep and wake up by herself all the time, and perhaps take her on a romantic getaway.

Hell, why do I keep entertaining my silly mind?

I swipe away the thought and join the team to raise our Fallen Angel bottles once again. The mission was touch and go, but we accomplished it nonetheless and it deserved the celebration.

"I'm surprised you had enough self-control not to punch

the son of a bitch," Sam reminds Ben of his altercation with the deputy.

Sam Kelleher, my other boss, is the more laid-back of the two Red Mark leaders. I respect Mark because of his knowledge and experience, but I must admit I have a special bond with Sam—he's my SEAL big brother.

"Aren't you glad?" Ben grunts, reaching for a bowl of peanuts with his long arm. While the men call our bosses 'sir,' being Sam's brother-in-law, Ben doesn't address him that way. But it doesn't mean he doesn't respect Sam. He owes his sister's life to him. He'll do anything for Sam, I know.

Sam shakes his head. "You're on notice!"

"You worry about those deputies falling out of love with us?" Ben returns a stare. "That man almost shot Tia. He could've even gotten Ty killed! Someone had got to do something."

This is why I'm sitting next to Ben. He wouldn't let it go, not in less than twenty-four hours, anyway. He's a great fighter, a loyal man, and a capable protector. He's effective and sweet with kids, but he still has a lot of ego to iron out when he's around adult men.

Red Mark isn't in a love business, but collaboration with government agencies is critical to our success. We can't operate alone. That means we have to suck ass sometimes and rein in our emotions—staying away from the blame game, maintaining our professionalism, and letting things go when they're not worth it.

I put my arm around Ben. "You've done good. You should be proud of yourself."

Perhaps not expecting some bro-love from me at this time of night, he stops, seemingly reminiscing what he's proud of me for.

"How are the Grants?" I ask Mark, who's sitting on my other side.

"Tia talked to her father while I spent time with her mother. Well, actually, I enlisted my wife's help. I couldn't have done it alone."

I know Ivy Connor. Before she and Mark were together, I was hired to guard her son from her previous marriage. So, I knew what it was like to work for her. She's a politician, a lawyer, but she never lost touch with her human spirit. She and Mark are made for each other.

Mark carries on. "Ivy did the best she could to comfort the woman. Not easy to convince a mother that time apart may just be what both she and her daughter needed—especially after they'd already been torn apart."

"Your wife is a gem, sir."

"She is. I guess that's one of the reasons I married her," Mark gushes. "Well, thanks to her, Mom and Dad are going to try again tomorrow with Tia. If the sheriff manages to keep the girl in the hospital."

I take the next bite of my burger, once again stealing a glance at Daisy. She might've seen me and decided not to interrupt. Although now I'm wondering why she had called. It's curious that she's staying this late alone. I might just say hello. Perhaps it'll be a nice icebreaker after all these months.

"Extra Cajun fries, gents," Cass announces, setting a couple of bowls on the table.

"Thanks, sweetheart," Sam tells his wife.

"Is my brother behaving himself?" she asks. Cass is Ben's sister and she's well aware of the regular banter between him and her husband.

"The burger shut him up," Sam quips. "Are you packing up soon?"

"Come on, hubby. This place will be open for as long as

you're here. Don't worry about us," she says. "As long as you tip well."

Sam laughs, taking time to get off his seat and peck her on the cheek. That's another couple that I can consider role models.

The bar staff replenishes our drinks. Meanwhile, in the background, a man arrives, making a beeline to—

"Don't look, Ty buddy," Mark warns.

Too late. The guys have already noticed, and they start teasing me. "Fuck, Ty. My condolences."

That well-suited newcomer is kissing my ex.

"She's just one fish in a small pond, brother."

"Hey, don't embarrass her!" I warn as all eyes are starting to converge on Daisy.

Right now, her companion is apologizing to her for being late. Something she should be familiar with. But one thing I didn't do right, which that man does—he's coming late bearing gifts.

Daisy gets up, giving him a big hug. For the first time, I see her face tonight. And that smile—I think all is forgiven. The necklace has done its job for him.

Was this what she wanted to tell me in her call? That she had found a new love?

She's not my woman anymore, but never mind the brotherly teasing from my comrades. Why do I feel that I've been stabbed in the gut? Maybe it's just exhaustion, but I have no intention to let the guys make me the heart of the party. I've got to get out of here before I put a damp blanket on the celebration.

I tap my glass with a knife. "Thank you for making my first mission as head of ops a bearable one. And I expect you to do the same on this table."

Some last laughter, then quiet.

I raise my Fallen Angel bottle.

"To Red Mark, and all the people we serve."

"Cheers!" the guys echo.

"I need to jet, but don't mind me. Enjoy the rest of the night —or morning."

"Come on, Tyler boy!" Sam yells. "You forgotten how to decompress?"

"Hey, let the man be," Mark says.

I saunter from the bar, breathing in the fresh air. But somehow, I can't bring myself to leave the place. I keep observing Daisy and her new man through the window. Like a stalker. Like a proper heartbroken ex.

With how preoccupied I am, it surprises me that my peripheral is still functioning. The corner of my eye snags someone behind the glass door, trying to exit the bar. She seems to struggle to pull the door open. It is heavy, but that girl looks like she's about to collapse.

"I've got it." I rush to her aid.

She quickly bows her head down. But it's not quick enough for me to miss her painful grimace despite her large glasses.

Perhaps knowing I'm scrutinizing her, she tries to speed up her strides. But she ends up slogging like a penguin as if there's a twenty-pound ankle bracelet fastened on her legs.

That backpack!

"Hey, wait!" I call out.

She tentatively stops.

I'm not trying to be friendly. Something I'm seeing in her warrants me checking her out—as in if she's okay or not. "Didn't I see you at the hospital?" I query.

"Don't think so," she replies, still hiding her face.

"Yes, I did." I step closer, my gaze following the angle of her face. But with her beanie pulled down so low, it's impossible to see her features. "Are you all right? I'm not here to harass you, okay? You look like you're in pain."

"I'm fine!" She walks off.

She clearly doesn't want me to come closer.

Someone then approaches me from behind.

It's my boss, Mark Connor. "You okay, man? Who's that?"

"Ah, yeah, yeah. It was nothing. I thought she was someone else."

Mark stands by me. "I'm sorry about what you saw in there, man." He points his thumb back at the Fox. "That sucks. But, hey, in time, you'll find someone who's really meant for you."

"I know."

"Don't lose hope. I'm proof," my boss reasons, perhaps sensing I only gave him the answer he wanted to hear. "Years of being single, broken, and bitter, and suddenly—she was there. Ivy was there."

"Maybe I haven't done enough to deserve someone."

"It's got nothing to do with what you've done or haven't done, Ty. Because you'll have never done enough until the day you die. That's life for us soldiers—or sailors. When it comes to love, my friend, if it's your time, it's your time."

"Aye-aye, sir."

"Take tomorrow off."

"No, I'm fine—"

"Take tomorrow off. That's an order."

"If you say so."

"In saying that... could I possibly bother you on your day off?"

"Certainly, sir."

"Ivy and I are due for our next scan at the clinic. And I want to take her for a long lunch. Would you pick up Noah from school? And babysit him just a bit?"

"Of course. Gladly."

He fist-bumps my biceps. "Thanks, my man. Are you sure you don't want to rejoin us? Those Cajun fries won't eat themselves."

Perhaps I will, but something stirs in me. That girl with a backpack.

When I'm in battle mode, if I feel something isn't right, I'll call it out without delay. But when I'm Ty the man, I have let things slide, and it has cost me a life. I'm not about to do that again.

"I don't think so." I watch the Red Mark men joking around, decimating the fries. "You might want to get back in there, sir. I think you're about to miss out."

Mark laughs. "Good night, Ty." And he returns to the bar.

I run in the direction the girl disappeared to. As I thought, she hasn't gotten far, but my blood boils seeing what's unfolding.

"Oi! Let her go!" I yell. I could've chosen stealth mode and grabbed the asshole by the scruff of his neck, then punched him in the face. Screw control. No one does that to a woman!

But I can't let his force-kissing continue even for a second longer.

The man takes his arm off her neck, pushing her forward. Before I can get close to him, as I anticipated, he sprints away. I would've pursued him and given him the lesson of his life, but she needs me more than I need to catch an asshole.

"Hey... hey..." Under the dim streetlight I stoop to check on her as she's lying on the path, clutching her side. "You hurt? Did he hurt you?"

She gyrates to escape my touch but then stops as everywhere on her seems to be hurting.

"Hey. Talk to me." I touch her slightly, but she looks as if she doesn't remember how to move. Holy hell, this woman is on the brink of fatal exhaustion.

I snatch my phone out of my pocket.

This time, she lifts her hand feebly. "No! Please. No hospital, no police."

Her plea, albeit soft, is devastating. I may send her into a coma if I act against it.

"Okay. Just calm down. I'm not gonna hurt you." I reach out my hand, giving the choice to her if she wants to take it and let me handle her. Although, if I find that she's really hurt, I will take her to the hospital, and she won't have a say in it.

She takes my hand, and unexpectedly, she still has the energy to use it to help herself sit up. "I was just there, at the hospital," she grumbles after gathering herself. "Why would I want to go back?"

"Huh... finally you admit! You have been following me. It's no coincidence. I know. You were at the hospital, then you were at the Thirsty Fox."

"Oh, come on, hotshot. Don't flatter yourself. *You* have been following me!"

I can smell secrets from miles away, and I bet she has plenty.

"Whatever. Did that man hurt you?"

"No. Thanks to you," she sighs.

Now, why do I feel the need to root out those secrets? I don't even know her!

But somehow, my heart says her business is my business. "You ran away from care, didn't you?"

She grimaces—so painfully I give up my questioning.

"What's hurting? Tell me," I stop her body from rolling on the ground, offering my lap for her to rest instead.

"Tyler... it's me."

Did she just call my name?

I sort of recognize her, but then I don't.

Her hand moves, barely able to take off her glasses.

This is not how she was when we said goodbye. The faint illumination in this corner makes me doubt myself, but without those thick frames covering half of her face, I know it's her. Those unmistakable eyes.

"Wolf Girl?" I whisper. Something scrapes under my skin.

She finally removes her beanie, letting out an abundance of hair. Her curls are gone, and so is her unruly fringe. She's no longer a brunette. Her hair is so much lighter, almost blonde. Now that I can see her whole face, I notice her prominent cheekbones. She has lost so much weight.

"Emma? Em?" I can feel my eyes flare. It must appear like I've been gawking at her.

"Let's stick with Wolf Girl."

"Jesus...what the hell happened?" I observe her hand. It's still clutching her side. I feel a throb in my own side as if the pain is mine. It happens just like that—instantly, naturally. "You're hurt there?"

She nods, repeating, "No police, no hospital. I'm in pain, but I'm okay. What I'm begging you to do now is please take me back to my motel room."

"Okay. But on one condition."

"Tyler, you can call my lawyer for your terms and conditions. Right now, I just need a bed to lie in."

Hell, she needs a bed, but not in a fucking motel! "I'll drive you there. We get your things, then I'm taking you home."

A glaze of elation sweeps through her when she hears the word 'home,' and that hurts me. When was the last time she was home?

"I mean, my place," I clarify.

"Okay." She agrees. "Although I left nothing in the room. Everything's in my backpack."

"Easy, then." I haul her pack. There's at least thirty pounds of stuff in there, however she's managed to carry it. I wonder if those books are still among the loads.

With her arms around my neck, I carry her.

"You swear that guy didn't hurt you?" If he had, I'd make time to hunt him down and make him regret what he'd done to her.

"No, he didn't. But I was stupid enough to just stand there and do nothing. I couldn't even put up a fight."

She can't even stand on her own. No one would expect her to escape, let alone swing a fist against a grown man.

The thought creates a quake inside me. A familiar sensation fills my chest, but this time, it's stronger than the protectiveness she invoked in me when I first saw her in Venice. From now on, all the fighting is on me. I swear I'm not going to let her defend herself alone.

"You've done enough, Wolf Girl. You're safe now."

"Imagine if it was..." She then mumbles something that sounds like 'Scarface.'

"Is that the guy who's been chasing you?"

She shakes her head as if canceling her thoughts. Then she shifts herself up. Out of nowhere, she tightens her grip around my neck, pressing herself against me as if someone was about to separate us.

"Tyler..." She rests her face on the side of my neck.

Her hold is relentless, but I feel her fragility. She wasn't like this when I held her at Venice Beach. Now, carrying her hurts me. Something must've gone very wrong in Washington—or wherever else she has been.

She loosens her grip. "I'm sorry. I shouldn't... It's just that I haven't been..." She sighs deeply, letting herself sag as if she wants to get off me. "I shouldn't have done that."

"Hey, whatever you need to do to me, it's okay. Stay there." I prop her up, widening my chest so she can rest again.

She takes my offer. "I was scared, still am," she laments.

So, California was just the beginning for us. She and I have a long road ahead. I know for sure because I won't let her go until she's free from whatever or whoever is making her scared.

"When you said I was following you," she carries on. "Well, I had been looking for you. But I didn't plan to show myself tonight. So it's true—*you*'ve been following me."

"All right." I grant her victory. I didn't have any sister to gain experience with, but my father always said not to argue with a woman who has made her point twice.

I KEEP GLANCING at her while I drive, not wanting to miss any sign of her going into shock.

"So what happened in Washington?"

She huffs, staring down at her lap. "It was a mess."

I want her to explain, but I stop short of asking her to. If her stress level goes up even a notch, I'll make her faint. "Look, you don't have to say anything now. Once we get home, you clean up, and if you're still hungry, I have food. Or I can fix some hot drinks too, if you want. Tea, hot cocoa."

Her mouth hooks a smile—her first tonight. "Hot cocoa sounds good."

"Done."

Wolf Girl leans back, closing her eyes. I leave her in peace for now. But I will reassess the situation as soon as she has cleaned up. If she needs the hospital, I'll take her there whether she likes it or not.

The rattle of the rolling garage door rouses her.

"We're here," I tell.

She sighs in relief but quickly grows alert. "Do you live with anyone?"

"No. Just me."

"Do I need to worry about a girl knocking at your door tomorrow morning?"

I chortle. "No. It's just you and me. So come on." I offer my arms and my chest, then carry her inside.

"Nice place," she compliments as I set her down on my living room couch.

"Thanks. I just moved here a couple of months ago," I explain. My pay raise from Red Mark has allowed me to afford this three-bedroom country house on the city border. I only have two acres of land to play with, but enough to have a small garden and a veggie patch. "Wait here. I'll get the bathroom ready, and then I'll make that hot cocoa for you."

"Tyler, I'm here because I want you to find my sister."

"Your sister?"

"Look... look at this sketch." She takes out a folded piece of paper from her wallet. "My best friend sketched this. This is Lilly, and the man who took her."

I marvel at the lifelike sketch, but I'm frightened by the urgency she's showing. "Sweetheart, I'll help you find your sister. But right now, you need to go clean up, and I need to look at your wound—or wounds."

"But time is running out. You know how it is with missing persons!"

"I know. But right now, you're in no state to handle it. We need to take care of you first, or you won't be going anywhere." I stop to assess her reaction. She doesn't show any intention of arguing this time. "I'll be back."

I put a fresh towel close to the bath, arranging all the toiletries to be within her reach when she's in. When I turn around, she's already at the door.

"I really appreciate this, Tyler."

"My pleasure. Take your time, okay? And keep the towel close to you."

I leave her.

It's quiet for a few minutes. Then I hear the water running. As I take a few steps away from the door, despite the background noise, I hear whimpers.

"You okay there?"

"Yeah." She's clearly crying.

"Are you sure?"

This time, I get no answer.

10

MORGAN

"I'm fine," I finally reply to Tyler, watching my hands trembling in front of me. In fact, my whole body is shaking, trying to counter the pain that's eating my flesh.

"Can you reach the towel?" he insists on talking with me.

Now I know why he has asked me to keep the towel close. He wants me to be able to cover myself in case he needs to come in.

And I do need him to come in.

It turns out, I haven't forgotten what safety feels like. The human body has a funny way of responding to stress. Looking back, the rollercoaster of reactions I experienced earlier was likely a sign that my brain had been hijacked by stress. The panic, the urge to run away from him. I simply needed the man's touch to reclaim my normal self.

However, right now I'm terrified at the prospect of him seeing me like this. Not because I'm naked—I haven't even undressed myself—and not because I'm embarrassed for leaving mud trail all over his shiny floor.

I'm completely hopeless. And disgusting.

I've run out of adrenaline, and the whiskey has left my

system. I'm sitting on the edge of the bath with my feet still on the bathroom floor. I'm slumping forward, my arms dangling over my legs. It feels like there's a belt of thorns around my waist. I'm unable to even do the most basic things an adult is supposed to be able to.

"You're not fine. I know that." His voice sounds so close it's like he was in the room with me.

I take a couple of short breaths, gulping. Like a helpless child, I cry, "I can't take off my shoes."

"Please let me come in."

I don't answer right away, but I will pass out if I stay like this a minute longer.

"Yeah."

"I'm coming in." Soon, the door is pushed ajar, and his knuckles wrap around the edge. Even from here, I can see how big his hands are. Tyler slides himself in. "Oh... Wolf Girl. Here, here, let me help you."

He carefully lifts my upper body, supporting it with his shoulder so I stay upright.

"I'm sorry..." I whimper.

"Don't be sorry. You shouldn't be doing this yourself," he says. "Let me see your side, then I'll help you take your shoes off."

As soon as I roll up my shirt, he feels the bandage covering my side wound. "May I?" he asks.

I let him peel one of the adhesive corners and have a peek.

"It's bleeding, but I think the stitches are holding up," he asserts.

"The doctor at the hospital had given me antibiotics. And a tetanus shot as well."

"Good," he says, resealing the bandage. "Skip the bath, okay? Take a shower instead. I'll get a chair so you can sit down while doing it. The bandage is waterproof, so it should be all right. I'll clean it up and give you fresh dressing afterward."

"Okay."

"Now, let's do this," he warns, squatting in front of me, removing the laces of my boots altogether—making the openings as wide as possible.

I bite out my scream as he starts pulling my left boot out. "Shit…"

He gives me a moment to settle, then he takes off the other one. Well, he tries to.

"Tyler!" I wail, scrunching the sleeve of his T-shirt. Fuck, it hurts!

"Sorry, I'm sorry. I think your right foot has swollen a lot more."

"Gnnnawww…" I grit out when he starts pulling again, my arms wrapped tight around my chest as if I'm going to suffocate myself.

The boot is finally off.

"Goodie." He cradles my feet, feeling the socks that are almost glued to my skin. "This is gonna hurt even more. Ready?"

He peels my sock off my ankle carefully. Even so, no doubt some of my skin is going with it. It's so excruciating I could've lost control of my bladder. "Tyler…" I cry, biting my lip and digging my fingers into his shoulder.

"One more, sweetheart."

"Fuuucck!"

"It's done. It's done."

I pant, my face wet like I was already in the shower.

Tyler pulls me close, letting his shoulder get the brunt of my snot and tears.

After a moment, he says, "Sorry, I lied. It's not done, but I swear this thing won't hurt as much. Let me clean your blisters."

Agony, embarrassment, and helplessness roll up in my throat. I wouldn't let him, even if he was my boyfriend.

"No, Tyler. They're gross!" I grimace, staring at my ballooning feet. And they stink like a skunk. It's hard to see where healthy skin starts and where blisters end. Not to mention the dirt and mud attached to them like it's tattooed on.

"No part of you is gross. Just let me help you."

No doubt he's seen wounds and injuries more atrocious than those blisters. But it's not his experience that makes him willing to handle my disgusting feet. It's just in him. Never have I seen such genuine kindness in a man—like my father or Hudson.

"Tyler, please... no..." I helplessly give one last chance for him to bail out.

"I'll get my kit." He unwraps my arm off him and lets me sit on my own as he leaves the bathroom. He then returns with a plastic chair and a medical kit bag.

"Come, sit here, you'll be more comfortable."

I sit down, taking advantage of the back and armrests. "You don't have to do this, really."

"I don't. I *need* to," he says and starts dabbing water on my feet, which he pours out of a bottle labeled 'distilled.' Then he applies some ointment. "It'll wash off after your shower, but I'll take care of them after I sort out your side. At least the ointment will keep the blisters reasonably protected and you reasonably comfortable. So you can enjoy the quiet time with yourself."

"Thank you. I don't know what to say."

"Go on, have that shower. I know you can't wait."

Tyler helps me settle on the chair under the shower.

"By the way, my name is Morgan."

Lines form on his forehead. "You told me that was your name at the beach before I saw your ID."

I cock an eyebrow, telling me I'm impressed that he remembers. "Every teenager has got to have a fake ID," I quip.

He lets out a chuckle. "Okay, Morgan. When you're done, put this on and call me." He hangs a bathrobe on the shower door, within my reach. "Don't try to walk by yourself. You might slip, and I can guarantee you'll spend the next few days in a hospital bed if that happens."

If there was a time to listen to him, it would be now.

WARM WATER, fruit-scented soap, a soft towel, and a robe. And a gorgeous man carrying me with such care like I'm his baby. This is no homecoming. I've already gone to heaven.

Soon, the fruity smell is taken over by a whiff of fresh chocolate as we pass the kitchen. I'm definitely in heaven!

"You comfy there?" he checks after he lets me sit on his wide couch.

"Yes."

He hands me a cup. "Your hot cocoa."

"Thanks, Tyler." A strange kind of guilt crawls on me. He's too good. After living nightmare to nightmare, it should be hard for me to trust anyone. Yet, two years on, nothing has changed about this man. And the way he's been treating me simply reinforces that my feeling is right.

I've got nothing else to hold on to. No one else. Tyler is the last rock I hang onto, the only one that'll stop me from plunging into the bottom of the cliff.

"You can call me Ty if you like."

I sip the frothy cup of cocoa sprinkled generously with cinnamon powder. They say whiskey is the best drink to numb pain, but Tyler's hot cocoa is a beverage that calms your heart and reminds you of the taste of home.

He thumbs some chocolate stain off the corner of my lips. "You're definitely a Morgan. Emma is kind of...generic."

"A good name for someone who needed to disappear," I reason. And I haven't told him about 'Audrey' and 'Meredith.'

He peeks into my empty cup. "You want more?"

"No, thanks. That was good, though. Very good."

Tyler then hands me a tablet and a glass of water. "It'll help with your pain."

I take it. "Thanks."

He gives me a look. I know it's time for round two of my pedicure. So, I let him handle my feet once again. This time, he pops some of the biggest blisters using a sterilized needle and then reapplies the ointment.

"You've lost a few toenails too. What have you been doing, Morgan?"

"I had to avoid people for the most part. So I took the wilderness routes where I knew how to survive."

"I've got to ask. Who the hell are you?"

I feel he already knows me, and I don't even realize I haven't told him who I really am. "My family name is Blackwell."

His face blanches, almost matching the color of the bandage in his hand. "You're... you're one of the missing Blackwell girls?"

"Yes."

"God! I'd never—" He inhales as if needing to collect his thoughts. "It was big news, I guess. I heard about it even from Afghanistan. But I never actually saw your photo or followed the case. So what happened in Washington?"

"After about a year of hiding, we got flushed out."

"Who's we?"

"Me and the remainder of my family. My aunt—my dad's sister—and my older brother."

"Oh." He sighs as if reminiscing about something he shouldn't have done. But then he smiles a relieved smile. "So it was your brother?"

"What do you mean?"

He clears his throat. "I saw him at the door—I mean when you got to that house."

"Ty? Did you follow me?"

He drops his guilt. "I did, Morgan. I couldn't just leave you in the middle of North Cascades."

I bow my head, not believing how far he'd gone to protect me. We were strangers—he didn't even know my real name. I stopped him from getting too close because I didn't want anything to happen to him. Yet he stayed. "You were with me the whole time?"

"Yes. Until I was sure you were safe."

My head bobs up and down, still digesting the revelation. A part of me wished he would've stayed on and protected the three of us. But with the brutality that followed, I'm glad he didn't.

"I was hoping Lilly would've come to the house with my aunt. My brother and I weren't terribly close to her. But my aunt absolutely adored Lilly."

"I didn't see your aunt there."

"She arrived months later."

"There were guards at that house. What happened to them?"

"All dead. It was a calculated attack. We managed to escape because of Hudson's quick thinking."

"Hudson, your brother?"

"Yeah. He was never in the military, but he had an interest in warfare and weaponry. Our attackers used night-vision goggles. So my brother created a fire, messing up those men's vision while we slipped past them. Once we were out, there was no resistance. We even managed to steal their car and drove off."

"So, where are your brother and aunt?"

"At some point, my aunt separated from us. She said she had to secure some information left by my parents. She didn't tell us what. She said once that was done, she'd try to distract our pursuers, so they let me and Hudson go." I shake my head, remembering her last smile. "We never saw her again."

"I'm sorry," Ty murmurs. "And your brother?"

My heart is pounding so hard it reminds me of the sickening sound of bullets hitting flesh. My breathing quickens as I try to close the curtains, refusing to relive the moment.

I can't. Not now. Not tonight. I'm already in pieces. Even a glimpse of the scene would obliterate me.

"Hudson and I carried on without my aunt, hiding in one place to another. Until—until—" I gulp saliva and air. "We were ambushed outside Tacoma. We were on the way to Helena to find you."

"To find me?"

My eyes fall shut for a few seconds, hinting a yes to him and at the same time regretting what happened next. "But our car was hijacked, and he didn't make it," I rush through my explanation, stopping sobs from coming out.

"I'm so sorry." Tyler abandons the bandages, wrapping his palms around my hand and pulling it away from my face.

My lips quiver as tears flow down my cheeks.

"We'll make sure your family's sacrifices aren't in vain," he determines. "You're one tough girl. But you're here now, and your running days are over. You know that I will help you—all the way."

"Exactly what I told my brother." If only he made it, he would've adored Ty, maybe even idolized him.

Tyler settles my hands on my lap, then wipes my face gently. He then continues with his medic work, bundling up my feet with gauze bandages. "How did you find me?"

"I first read about Red Mark when your attorney general was kidnapped. And I learned that you were part of the rescue and that your company specializes in finding missing children. I convinced my brother to come here."

"I'm really sorry about your brother, Morgan. But I'm glad you decided to see me."

"I had no other choice."

"You always have a choice," he contemplates, his hands still wrapping my feet. "Anyway, that's enough rough for tonight," he decides. He then checks the bandages and gives his seal of approval. "Now, Bigfoot, I need to check your side wound."

I sigh on a smile. "So, more rough?"

"I'll be gentle, I promise." He hints at me that he may need my help. He's got to know I'm naked under the robe.

I nudge him. "Can I ask you a favor?"

"Of course."

"My clothes are all wet."

"You can wear one of mine," he offers.

My acceptance earns a smile sweeter than the cocoa he made.

He dashes to the back of the house and returns with a bundled T-shirt. He then leaves me in peace to get changed.

It's a Red Mark top, and coming out of the bundle is a pair of boxer shorts.

"I'm ready," I announce, observing myself inside the oversized T-shirt and hoping the shorts will stay on.

"Let me see the stitches again."

I roll up the T-shirt just enough to show him the wound. He then removes the bandage completely.

"How is it looking?" I ask, not wanting to see it up close myself.

"Not bad. I'm just gonna clean it now." He examines it carefully, and he almost kisses my waist. "Don't tell me you got shot."

"I got clipped."

"You got shot, Morgan," he asserts while examining the wound. "Lucky the stitches have held up. You just have to rest and not move so much."

"Really, I got clipped." It was only one bullet. Nothing compared to however many my brother took.

Ty replaces the bandage gently, then rolls the bunched hemline down. If I pull it all the way, it will drop to almost to my knees.

He reaches out to me. "Come, I'll take you to bed."

"Aren't you sick of carrying me around?" I comment as he offers his arms for the... I don't know... maybe the sixth or seventh time tonight.

"It's part of the service," he casually answers.

In the corner of my heart, I'm hoping I'll be sharing a bed with him tonight. Just like Venice. But he takes me to what appears to be a guest room.

"Do you have something that'll help me sleep?" I request softly as he pulls the covers over me.

He cocks a brow. "Well, I got rid of those pills a long time ago. I sleep with the sound of the ocean these days. Would you like to borrow the machine?"

"Ah... that's all right. It might make me want to pee."

He laughs. "Well, there's an option to play forest sounds too. Although they don't include a wolf howl."

I smirk, realizing how lucky I am to have found him. When

was the last time I was pampered like this? By a man whose caring nature almost outshines his hotness?

Whether I can manage to sleep without him in the room remains to be seen. But I want to make the most of my newfound comfort. "Maybe you've got an extra blanket? Something that I can... um... hug?"

His face creases, and his light scruff wraps the smile on his face. Then he turns to open the closet. "Will this do?" He shows me a brown, wooly blanket.

"Thanks, Ty." I roll it into the shape of a bolster as soon as he gives it to me.

"We'll talk tomorrow, okay?" His eyes apparently try to make out what this extra blanket really means to me.

"Goodnight, Ty."

"If you need anything else, just yell. I'll be next door. Goodnight, Wolf Girl."

I'm surprised at how much my body has relaxed. Not having him in the same bed doesn't seem to matter. My body knows he's close.

No rain will drench and freeze me, no bullets will fly my way, and I don't have to wonder where my next meal will come from. I think I can actually give in to my sleepiness. And I hope this peace will keep my nightmare at bay tonight.

11

———

TYLER

I decide to sleep without the sound machine. I don't want to miss Morgan's call if she needs me.

Two hours later, I haven't had a wink of sleep. I might've formed some kind of dependency on the sound of the ocean, but I don't think that's the issue. My protective instincts are in overdrive. I feel like I'm on duty—guarding that incredible woman sleeping next door.

Whatever path my life was on before tonight, it has changed. I'm on her path now, and I won't look back. My earlier longing for Daisy Klein suddenly feels insignificant—if it's still there. That's how much power Morgan Blackwell has over me. And I'm honored to be part of her life. Not just because of her beauty but because of who she is—her strength, her determination, and her trust in me.

And I shouldn't think about it, but I'm glad the young man was her brother. Not her lover.

Suddenly, a moan.

This is why I can't bring myself to sleep.

I slip into my T-shirt and jump off my bed.

She has let me leave her door open so I can see in. I know

she won't always say it when she needs help. I whisper, "Morgan?"

But Wolf Girl seems fast asleep, still hugging the extra blanket like it was her pet. Perhaps she's dreaming about hugging one of those Yellowstone wolves she used to study.

I plod back to bed, ditching my T-shirt. I wonder what can help me sleep. If it were me before Red Mark, I would've popped a pill or two or three.

Suddenly, I hear Morgan scream. I would've heard it even with the ocean sound playing at full volume. And then there's a thud.

I rush to her room, wearing only my boxer shorts. I don't want to show up topless, but my priority is to get to her in time, not keeping my chest covered.

"Morgan!" I call out. She's on the floor, coiling next to the bedside table. I hug her, lifting her up so she's lying on my lap. "Morgan, Morgan, sweetheart. Wake up."

She almost sits up while her scream is relentless. Her fingers claw at my arms.

"Hey, it's me. Tyler. Come on, wake up. Wake up, sweetie."

Her scream stops. Then she mumbles something while her eyes remain shut. Bit by bit, her face drops to my shoulder, and it keeps dropping, trailing along my bare chest.

Clearly asleep still, she nuzzles her way to my pec, rubbing her cheek against the coat of hair I haven't got around to shaving. Seemingly satisfied with what she's resting on, she rounds her arms behind me, holding herself steady.

Have I become her wolf? Maybe. The way she hugs me looks exactly like how she hugged that bundled blanket.

Soon, she purrs.

And then snores.

"Snore away, Wolf Girl," I whisper happily, letting her cling to the peace she manages to find. After losing all of her family, being able to hug someone like this must mean a lot to her—although I don't know who she thinks I am, unconsciously.

I find myself drifting to sleep following the rhythm of her breathing (well, snoring, but it's not *that* loud, compared to one that I was used to during deployments). Her peace is contagious, it seems.

Moments later, I find Morgan resting on my belly, but her body is stretching awkwardly on the floor. She shivers a couple of times.

I lift her gently, settling her back on the bed. Then I pick up the extra blanket off the floor, rolling it up as she did to the shape of a bolster.

Trying to balance myself so I can place the bundle without waking her, Morgan's hand reaches up to me. As if guided by another dream, with one move, she glues her palm on my pec, feeling the hairy surface.

Then her eyes bat open.

Never mind my body looming over her and the close proximity between our faces. The first thing she sets her eyes on is my chest. I guess she hasn't seen me with hair before. But the awkwardness of my presence and position soon catches her attention.

"Fuck! Ty! What the hell are you doing?"

"Morgan, I'm not doing anything. It's not how it looks."

Then she stares at her own hand, which is still firmly on my pec. She quickly withdraws. "I'm sorry. I'm sorry. It was me, wasn't it? What did I do to you?"

"Nothing, Morgan. You had a nightmare."

"Oh... oh...." She sits up, clutching her side.

"You okay?"

"Yeah. Thanks for waking me up."

"Can you get back to sleep?"

"I don't know."

"Do you want me to stay?"

Her eyes shine with hope for the first time since I saw her, ever. But she blinks, and her somberness returns.

"No. It's okay. I'll be fine."

If I had my way, I would stay with her till morning, hold her tight so she doesn't fall again. Perhaps I would kiss her, whispering to her that I will never leave her side. But she's not here for the love of a man. She wants me to find her sister.

I step away. "You sure you're not gonna fall off the bed again?"

"You've just gotta be faster so you can catch me in time."

I chuckle. "I'm fast. But I'm not *that* fast. Good night, Morgan."

After I take a few steps away from the room, she says, "Ty, wait."

"What is it?"

"Suppose I asked you to sleep here. Would you do it?"

"Of course I would."

"I would ask you. But I'm afraid."

"Afraid of what?"

"Of what I'll do to you."

I smile. "And what is that?"

"Come here," she whispers.

I round the bed, getting to her side. "Yeah?"

"Closer."

I kneel, my arm reaching out over her, supporting myself so I can lean toward her without crushing her. "Close enough?"

We're almost nose to nose. Her breath is battering my face. After a short silent moment, she answers me with her lips.

God, woman...

I grow weaker as if I'd never been kissed. Just like her ocean kiss, I can taste her trust, her need, her fear. And this time, I can even feel my own will in the contact—that I will fulfill whatever she's asking of me.

"That was what I was afraid of," she confides, breaking the kiss.

"I can live with that," I grin, hiding the fact that perhaps what she's afraid of is what I'm feeling between my legs at the moment.

"Hop in, then," she invites.

I lie next to her, calming myself the hell down. She wastes no time to come to my side and rest her cheek on my chest. What is it with her and furry things?

Her fingers twitch over the side of my neck, her breath caressing my skin. Who needs sleeping pills or a sound machine when you've got this amazing woman sleeping next to you? On you?

A woman's touch.

Not any woman's, but hers.

I crave it. But what I need even more is to erase that haunted look in her brown eyes.

"Don't let me fall, Tyler."

"No. I won't, I promise."

The only thing I *will* do is to let her fall asleep.

THE SUNLIGHT HURTS MY EYES. I've never slept here. I didn't know it got this bright so quickly.

Fortunately, it doesn't seem to bother Morgan.

She's lying across the bed diagonally, using my torso as a pillow. Her breathing steady and quiet, no sign of snoring. It looks like she has found a spot on my abs where her neck is perfectly supported. Her left arm stretches out, following the length of my leg, while the other is hugging mine, locking my hand in position—right on top of her side wound. I think she's liking the pressure. Perhaps the warmth, too.

I haven't seen anyone sleep like this before. But she's welcome to do whatever she wants here and use me however she wishes.

Besides, it's a gorgeous sight.

Her long hair drapes over my side like a waterfall bathed in the morning sun. It's a darker shade of blonde—which I think they call honey blonde. Her face tilts to me. It's sunburned, but it hasn't erased her pretty features. All in all, I think nature has taken good care of her.

Last night at dinner, my boss told me we'll never do enough until the day we die, and the coming and going of love doesn't depend on what we'd done. But I still wonder. What have I done that she's here with me? In my home that used to be a place for me to sleep and eat—because my work is my life. My home is just a house. Why is my heart feeling such content-ment as if I'm not wanting anything else?

That kiss she granted me last night might've simply been an expression of her gratitude. Functional, not emotional. Just like her first kiss was in helping her disguise herself. But the connection that I felt was real. Hell, I still feel her lips on mine. I hope she felt it, too.

God, what am I thinking?

She's here so I can help her find her sister—I remind myself.

Then I hear my phone. It's my day off, but there was some-thing else that Mark said last night before I left.

"Shit!"

Now I know why it's so bright. Because it's almost fucking midday!

"Sorry, sweetheart," I murmur, shifting myself sideways. Luckily, she's really out, so I manage to escape without waking her up. She mumbles when I reposition her, but she soon carries on with her serene breathing like the slumbering angel that she is.

"Mr. Connor," I answer the call.

"Ty, my man. You okay?" It must be my sleepy voice that prompts my boss to ask that.

"Yes. Yes."

"You haven't forgotten about Noah, have you?"

"No, of course not. Twelve thirty?"

"Yeah."

"I'll pick him up, Sir. Then, can I take him to my place? I've got a friend visiting."

Mark pauses for a couple of seconds. "Of course. Although, if you're planning to spend time away from my house, the boy comes with the Dane."

"Understood, sir. I'll pick up Jasper after I get Noah." That dog is trouble. He only listens to Mark and no one else, but you don't back down on your boss.

"Sounds good, Ty. I'll see you later this afternoon."

"Good luck with the scan, and enjoy lunch, sir."

"Thanks, Ty."

I shuffle my jeans up my legs, then rush back to Morgan's room while buttoning my shirt.

"Morning." She yawns. But apparently noticing me rushing, she asks, "Hey, everything okay?"

"Yeah. I've got to go, but I'll be back soon. I'll put the alarm on the door. The code is 3517, but don't let anyone in, and don't go out. Okay?"

"Okay..." she mumbles.

"You're safe here. I've got all the food and entertainment in this house. If you need something that's not here, please wait for me."

Morgan sits up, readying herself to leave the bed.

"Wait, wait!" I stop her, dashing to the storeroom and back in less than a minute. "Do you know how to use these?"

"Seriously? Crutches?"

"Unglamorous, I know, but you'll have to take pressure off your feet. At least for today. We can reassess things tomorrow." I adjust the height of the crutches, three holes down. They used to be my third and fourth leg when I was recovering from my knee injury—one of the four bullets that got me when I was facing eight men on my own. Although, in the end, they brought me down and sent me to the ICU. At least Noah managed to get away. "You're pretty tall, so I think this will work."

Morgan studies the walking aid with bewilderment. "I haven't used crutches before. But how hard can it be?"

I don't think she likes the idea. Imagining her losing her balance on them, I suggest, "Stay in bed then. I won't blame you if you want to sleep for the next few months."

"Where are you going?"

"School. To pick up my boss's son. I promised to babysit him today. You've got nothing against kids in the house, I hope?"

Her lips curve up. "How old is he?"

"Almost nine."

"He can be my little brother."

I send a smile her way. She'll be a perfect big sister.

"Try not to hurt yourself. Feel free to raid my library or kitchen. Bake a cake if you want."

"Go! I can take care of myself."

Standing by her room door, I comb my hair with my fingers. "And we'll talk about Lilly today. I promise."

"Go!"

I spend a second to check my appearance on a wall mirror.

Then, while running to the door, I holler, "By the way, don't burn down the house!"

As I drive out, I find a dog staring at me from the other side of the street. I drive closer, checking the mutt out. It's a boy, very skinny. Definitely a stray. Perhaps Wolf Girl is a dog magnet, too, because I haven't seen him before.

I lower my window, calling the mutt. But he runs away.

12

MORGAN

Bake a cake or burn down his house?

After having lost touch with civilization, I am still aware that it's rude to destroy the nest of my host who has welcome me with open arms, and more.

So, I'm going to show him gratitude with my homemade cupcakes—succulent, fluffy, and delicately sweet.

Just like him, I guess.

I touch my cheek, still feeling the tickles from his chest hair. That's the difference between a good night's sleep and a medi-ocre one. And dare I say, that's what separates men from boys—physically, anyway.

I don't exactly know what I did to him in my sleep—how embarrassing. Or inappropriate. But he never called me out. The only thing I know is he broke my nightmare. The dark hilly forest around me shattered as if it was made of glass. Like nothing had happened, I felt layers of softness caressing me, then swaddling me like I'd been sleeping in my own bed.

While my clothes are in the dryer, I venture back to the kitchen. Whistling the tune of "Color of The Wind," I peek into the oven. There's no cupcake pan here, not that I expect Ty to have one, but I think I've managed just fine with a regular tray and my handmade baking paper cups. Look at the mix rising!

The absence of a cupcake pan doesn't mean Ty's kitchen isn't well equipped. It's a modern kitchen with high-end equipment and cookware, including a professional coffee machine I'm sure was responsible for producing that amazing hot cocoa last night.

And true to his words, his pantry and fridge are stocked with so much food, I wonder how much the man eats!

I wipe my hands on Ty's T-shirt I'm wearing, dragging my feet across the kitchen floor to get to the pantry. They're still sore, but Ty has wrapped them so expertly that I don't feel the need for a walking aid. Hell with those crutches! These slippers are giving me extra cushion, so moving around isn't much of a chore.

After a short deliberation with myself, I decide to stick with vanilla buttercream for the topping. 'Versatility is key, Morgie.' I remember Mom's advice. I have experimented with many flavors, but she was right.

I start whisking the cream. Mom would've loved Ty, perhaps a little astonished by how far he'd gone to take care of me. Above and beyond, serving without limits. I only need to look down to see proof of it. That man has a touch of a saint.

I dip a finger into the cream, tasting it. My tongue is dancing.

Just like the snow-white goodness, I feel light. I've had a restful night, and I have someone to lean on, someone who wakes me from my nightmare. And I'm baking. *I'm friggin' baking!* Two years of running, finally, I'm doing the thing that I always regard as the ultimate home comfort. My life has certainly gotten its flavor back.

I gaze out, catching a couple of wrens flying over the veggie patch. Ty opted for a huge window instead of a backsplash, giving an illusion that you're out cooking in the garden. The birds land on the fountain—swallowing small gulps of water, then dunking themselves for their afternoon bath. I could stay here forever.

I generously top the cupcakes with cream, then sprinkle them with small fruit slices. For the best one in the batch, I carefully place cranberry parcels to make a heart. Will he take the hint?

I kissed him last night—my second kiss with him. His response was a lot more than just stunned, unlike the first time in Venice. Last night, or early this morning, rather, he *enjoyed* it. He let it linger. I wouldn't have called him an asshole if he had followed it up with a move that said, 'I want sex.' But he didn't. He's such a gentleman that he didn't.

Would I have said yes if he'd asked? I trust him with my life. There's no reason I wouldn't with my—

"Tyler has a girlfriend!" a boy sings, loud and clear. He must be the boy Ty is babysitting today.

"Shush! Don't say that."

That's definitely the boy and man. I gulp back the chuckle from my mouth, acting cool as if I didn't hear a thing.

"Tyler has a girlfriend!" the boy keeps singing as the front door opens.

But who's coming into the kitchen is not the boy nor the man.

A huge gray and white canine charges on while the frantic voices of Tyler and the boy blare in the background. "Jasper!"

It could well be a wolf—and it jumps straight at my centerpiece. In one bite of his jaws, the cranberry heart cupcake is no more.

"Bad dog! Bad dog!" the boy shouts in horror.

Ty gapes, observing the Great Dane chewing merrily, then licking clean the cream from its mouth and the floor. The former Navy SEAL is speechless—I'm not sure if it's for the dog's actions or for turning his kitchen into a mini bakery. After a few moments, he grasps the dog's leash.

"Come on, Jasper! Come on!" He keeps pulling, but the mutt doesn't budge.

"Let me," I offer.

Seeing me dragging my feet in his slippers, Tyler's expression is between amused and apologetic. "I'm so sorry, Morgan. This dog is a menace."

He reaches out to me, transferring the leash. Oh my, those forearms! I didn't take notice last night. Now, as the sun is shining, their sheer size astonishes me. Those protruding veins, the curves of his muscles—as far as I remember, they didn't look like that two years ago. It must've been all the SEAL and Red Mark work all these years.

The dog leans on me, rubbing his head on my T-shirt.

"Jasper, sit!" I command, and the dog sits tall. I then tug the leash gently and start walking. "Come, Jasper. Come."

Tyler whistles in amazement. "Now, Noah, that's how you handle a dog."

"Where do you want him? The backyard?" I ask.

"Um... the garage. For now. If he's left in the back, he'll destroy my plants."

"Fair enough."

Controlling Jasper turns out to be a breeze, but controlling my bandaged feet inside Ty's oversized slippers while towing the big dog is a challenge. But I keep going.

"She's good," the boy comments despite my inelegance.

"Yeah. Observe. Well, you don't have to walk like that, though."

"I heard that!" I turn my head and throw a smirk at Ty.

He cackles as he follows me. "A Bigfoot and a Dane. Hey! That'll make a good nursery rhyme."

"Shut up!"

Ty leaves Jasper with plenty of toys, a bowl of water, and some treats. "I'll take him for a walk later." He closes the garage door, then turns to me. "So, you didn't like the crutches?"

"Obviously not," I purr. "I prefer these slippers."

"They suit you." Bigfoot is written all over them.

Chaos squashed, we all head back to the kitchen.

"Jesus, it smells so good in here!" Ty draws a breath, inspecting his kitchen.

My attention turns to the boy. "So, you're Noah?"

"Yes."

He must be the famous Noah Forbes, the son of Ivy Connor from her previous marriage. "Nice to meet you. I'm Morgan."

"Hi Morgan, I'm sorry about your cupcake."

He's a sweet kid, a handsome one too. I wouldn't mind stealing him for a day. "Don't worry. I still have plenty more." Too bad the one that I've put my utmost TLC on has gone into the dog's stomach. "Come on, help yourselves." I invite them to a few pieces.

"When I said *bake a cake*, I didn't think you were going to do it for real! But this is seriously good." Tyler's eyes flirt with me.

"Now, don't start calling me 'Cupcake,' okay?"

"Well, I was thinking 'Sugar.'"

"That's even worse!"

We both laugh while Noah frowns, apparently trying to figure out what's so funny. The boy decides to steer the conversation. "Tyler said you worked with wolves."

"Yes, I did."

"At the zoo?"

"No. Wild wolves, mainly in Yellowstone."

"That's so cool. Maybe that's why you're so good with Jasper."

"Maybe," I say. "But the key to controlling a dog is leadership."

The boy twists his lips, apparently processing what that entails.

"Stand straight, stay calm. Remember, you're the boss," I elaborate. "Praise the dog when he does the right thing. When he doesn't obey, you don't need to yell or talk. Just yank his leash a bit. Or say a sharp 'no.'"

"I see."

"It takes practice, but you'll get there." I glance at Tyler, who's silently telling me it's easier said than done.

The afternoon goes quickly. After Tyler and Noah take Jasper for a walk, Mark and his wife arrive to pick up Noah. I opt to stay hidden from view. Still wearing Ty's oversized tee, my hair unbrushed, I'm certainly not ready to face the boss of Red Mark and the former attorney general of Montana.

"She's shy." I hear Ty defending my no-show decision.

"That's okay, let her be," It's a woman's voice. It must be Ivy. "But do tell her these cupcakes are phenomenal."

"I will."

"Ty's girlfriend is real pretty," Noah says. "He calls her Bigfoot."

I can hear everyone laugh. That boy!

As they're saying their goodbyes, I peek out. What a lovely family. Even Jasper looks to fit right in. The Dane seems calm when Mom and Dad are there.

I welcome Ty back. "Mark's wife is heavily pregnant, I see."

"Six months."

"Six months? Her belly is huge!"

"They're expecting twins. A boy and a girl."

"No way! That's so wonderful! Noah must be excited."

"He is. He's been telling me about his bro-bump talks."

I'm twenty-one, and my life is more turbulent than the

average woman my age. But it doesn't stop me from reacting to this pregnancy talk. The thought of me baking a different kind of bun somehow tickles my belly.

What kind of trouble am I in? I've been hormonal before—I mean, period type of hormonal—but never like this, as if my maternal instincts have suddenly surged. I guess I'd never been this close to a man.

"I heard what Noah told his parents," I hint. "They weren't buying it, were they? That I'm your girlfriend?"

He laughs. "No. They know a relationship is the last thing on my mind."

"Huh. So you're not even looking?" I try to fish out a clue about who that pretty woman was at the bar last night and my own chance with him, not that it's my priority.

"No."

A straightforward answer.

Is my disappointment warranted? Or have I simply lost focus on why I'm really here?

He adds, "Work keeps me busy."

"Just like last night?"

"Yes. Just like last night."

"You were at the hospital. But you weren't hurt, were you?"

"One of my colleagues fractured his ribs. We rescued a girl, a fifteen-year-old. She was groomed by a manipulative man, acting like he loved her. And she wasn't his first victim."

"That's terrible. Men like him don't deserve any freedom!" I get upset on the girl's behalf. I guess the nation should be grateful that Ty chooses duty over love. And so should I—because I'm here to find Lilly.

Tyler seems to be engrossed in his own thoughts, but soon he breaks the silence. "Hey, you know, I keep seeing this dog wandering around. He watches me a bit, then he's gone. I'm sure he's a stray."

The news mops out the leftover girlfriend thought and my silly vision of a bun in the oven. "What kind of dog?"

"Short hair. Gray and brownish."

"Skinny?"

"Yeah."

"That's Gravy! Is he still there?"

"No. I think Jasper scared him away. You know the dog?"

"We had a dinner date on my first night here. We shared a pot pie."

"How romantic."

"That dog did well to find me. If that's what he's here for."

"His one true love?" Ty teases.

Just like how I kept coming back to him.

After being cared for, protected, and *loved*—truthfully, what he gave me last night was nothing short of love—what woman can ever resist him? If she can, I want to know how. Because what I see is an impossibility that I'm helplessly succumbing to. This man has turned my heart upside down, inside out.

"I'll call you when I see him again." Tyler strides closer to me. "You wanna sit down and talk about Lilly?"

"Yeah. Let's." I pause. "Although, I wouldn't mind cleaning up a bit and getting changed." I pout at the flour and cream stain on my clothes, along with Jasper's fur clinging all over the fabric.

"Of course. Do you need another of my T-shirts?"

"No thanks. I've done my laundry."

"Take your time. I'm all yours."

I pad to my room—*I'm all yours* playing in my head, over and over.

13

TYLER

"Morgan?"

She's certainly taking ages to get ready. Not that I'm trying to rush her. I just want to make sure she's okay.

No one's in the bathroom. So she must be in her room.

She is there, sitting on the edge of the bed—spine straight, hands clasping together. A familiar posture. Her long hair drapes over her bare shoulders. She has changed into a tank top and a pair of jeans.

"Morgan?" I shuffle myself next to her. I use the same shampoo, but the coconut scent is milder and sweeter coming from her hair.

"Sorry, Ty. I don't mean to waste your time."

"No, you're not. We don't have to discuss Lilly now if you're not ready."

She unclasps her hands, revealing a pea-size pendant attached to a thin chain. "From Mom. I've always kept it safe in my bag. I didn't want to lose it when I had to run and duck and tumble."

"It's beautiful." I observe the shiny black rose pendant.

"Lilly has a matching one. So, if you see a fourteen-year-old girl wearing this necklace, that'll be her. Well, I hope so, anyway."

"We'll find her."

"You see, the rose has five petals. They're made of onyx." She puts it up closer to me. "Lilly might have her own interpretation, but for me, the biggest one is Dad. And this is Mom, almost as big. But truly, she should've been the biggest—she called the shots in the family."

"Why am I not surprised?" I raise my eyes to her.

She chuckles. "But there it goes. Dad is always the biggest. Then this is Hudson." Her finger quavers on top of the middle petal, and she points with her nail. "And this is me and Lilly." She skims the remaining two petals. "Could you?" She hands over the necklace to me.

"Sure."

She lifts her hair, exposing her delicate nape. I swear it's her natural scent that I'm sensing right now, and it triggers a lot of chemicals in my brain to fire all at once. What would happen if my lips landed there? Just below her hairline?

I don't want to embarrass myself, but my hands fail me when I attempt to fasten the chain. My fingertips brush her skin like a pair of drunken spiders. After a few fumbles, I manage to secure it.

I would admire her adorned chest, but the pendant falls too close to her cleavage. I decide to praise her without even looking at it. "It looks great on you."

She takes a deep breath, ducking to admire the pendant herself. Then she slants her face to me. "Let's do it."

"Come on, then." I tug at her arm.

We saunter along.

"Do I smell hot cocoa?"

"It comes standard when you and I have a chat."

Her mouth hooks a smile, her intense gaze tempers. We sit on the same sofa as last night, as if resuming where we left off.

"Tyler. First of all, I'm glad you kept safe in Afghanistan," she opens.

"I still have your coin, by the way."

She lets out a light laugh. "I thought you would."

Her face shines when she shows me a photo of her and Lilly in front of the Roosevelt Arch at Yellowstone.

"You said Lilly is fourteen now?"

"Yes. My parents were desperate to have another child after me, but they had two miscarriages. Lilly was a miracle. They weren't even trying." She wipes some fibers off the photo. "Lilly and my parents visited me on my last assignment. It was about six months before that disastrous night. Lilly was almost twelve in this photo."

They look adorable together. "I wish I had a sister. Well, my mother certainly did."

"I could be your sister," she innocently says.

That's a thought. But no. If she's meant to be in my life for the foreseeable future, I want her to be more than just a sister. Way more.

A vision of the rose pendant dangling above her cleavage flashes at me.

Jesus!

I'm not the type who'll hesitate to make the first move. But with Morgan and her situation, I can't. And my brain doesn't seem to get the message. Or is it my heart that interferes?

I answer her, "My sister? Don't think so. You're my Wolf Girl."

Morgan then takes out the sketch, which she showed me briefly yesterday. The more I analyze it, the more I'm astonished by the detailed strokes. "This is amazing. You said your best friend drew this. Was it the one whom you sent that letter to from Venice?"

"Yes."

"See! Told you you'd see her again."

"Well, I haven't."

I feel silly for assuming. "Sorry."

"I spoke to her, though, on the phone. After my aunt had failed to turn up at our designated meeting point, I went crazy. I was sure I would be next to die, and I just had to hear my best friend's voice for one last time."

She shuts her eyes, stroking the rose pendant vigorously.

I can't bring back her lost family, but I swear I'll do anything to keep the rose alive. Whatever I have to do to make her feel like she has a family again, I'll do it.

I'll find her sister.

I'll reunite her with her best friend.

I swear it on my life.

After moments of silence, Morgan continues, "Ava told me then that she saw my sister, and being an artist, she sketched the scene almost immediately. I asked her to send the sketch to a post office. It was too dangerous for her to see me."

"You'll see her again, I promise." My thumb and index finger grip the sketch. "So, Lilly... this is how she looks now? And your friend saw her with this man?"

"Ava has a photographic memory, so we can rely on this. One hundred percent. As you can see, Lilly looks like Lilly. And we can safely presume the man looks exactly like this."

I still remember writing her full name on the envelope. *Ava West.* "Did she report it to the police?"

"No. We didn't trust anyone. Besides, she said Lilly looked to be content following him. There was no sign of force. So they could be protecting her? But I doubt it somehow. I know this is my sister's face Ava had sketched, but she looked flat, blank."

"Like she had been brainwashed?"

"Yeah."

It's common for children to succumb to harsh treatment, persuasion, or even torture until they become someone else entirely. Morgan isn't wrong to observe Lilly's expression, and I believe her. Out of anyone in this world, Morgan would be the one who knows her sister best. "This is a start. We've got something to work with. When was the last time you saw Lilly?"

"The morning before my house was burned to the ground when my parents were killed." She hugs the cocoa cup in her hands tight, huffing quickly.

"Take your time, Morgan."

"I drove her to school. Then, I went to work at my university lab, finishing early because I had an interview with NatGeo. I earned my Bachelor of Life Sciences with honor, and I loved filmmaking, so I thought I should give it a go."

I smile, picturing her in her element. "You graduated at nineteen. That was impressive."

"Thanks. I loved animals too much. It was almost an obsession," she admits. "I was accepted into an accelerated program in high school. That allowed me to enter college early, and then I took more credits and summer classes while juggling my 'wild' life in Yellowstone." She chuckles, shaking her head softly as if not believing how she managed it all. "I just couldn't wait to be a biologist."

I cock my eyebrows in amazement. "That's dedication. No doubt the wolf population would've thanked you for it."

Her lips quirk. "Still, that NatGeo interview was tough. I had to convince the panel that I had what it took to contribute to their winter shoot at Yellowstone. I knew they had doubts because of my age."

"A wolf documentary?"

"Partly. They called it the three-dog shoot—wolf, fox, and

coyote," she explains. "I guess I'll never know if I was successful."

Gingerly, she puts the cocoa cup away, then her hands form a fist as she continues, "I came home just before dinner. As soon as I opened the door, Mom tugged my arm hard. Frantic. She wasn't the panic type, but she couldn't hide how dire the situation was. She kept saying I should go. I asked about Dad, and her face just crumpled. She then shook her head. I knew he was dead." She sniffles.

"I'm sorry, Morgan. Do you need a break?"

"I'm okay."

"Go on. I'm listening."

"Then Mom gave me the backpack. I still have everything that she packed for me. She also gave me a set of coordinates— our rendezvous point."

"The house in North Cascades?"

"Yes. Soon, we heard people coming. She simply shoved me out through the back, whispering, 'Just go. And find Lilly. Go! Run!' Whoever was outside was now inside. She shut the back door, and I ran. When I got to the street, I saw my house engulfed in flames. So ferocious, I knew she wouldn't have survived."

She rubs her face, clamping her mouth as if wanting to keep air inside her lungs. It's as if something is tugging her. She falls onto me. My hand lands on her back, keeping her in place. She won't call for a break, but I'm giving it to her.

After a few inhales, she carries on. "Then I met you in Venice and got to the rendezvous point. I was so happy to see my brother there."

"You and your brother were close?"

"I was close to him when we were kids—he was two years older than me. He was the one who'd give me his own ice cream when I dropped mine. Or swapped toys when I thought his was better."

"Like I said, I only heard about you and your sister's disappearance. I never knew the details. But tell me, I remember the press always said the 'Blackwell sisters,' but I never heard about your brother."

"He'd been far away from us, so he was never missing. He left home when he was sixteen, traveling the world, doing his own thing."

"So your brother was overseas when your parents were killed?"

"Yes. But he got the message."

"So your aunt would've received the same message?"

"I think so."

"Obviously, your parents had planned for this emergency."

"Yeah. But I don't know why. They were a couple of LAPD cops."

"Cops?" So that's how she knew about my Glock 47—which she called 'a cop gun.'

"Yes. So now you see, I couldn't have been a criminal."

I smirk a little. "Did your parents or aunt tell you anything about who might've taken Lilly?"

"No."

"Did your parents discuss any unusual case with you? Something that may have put you and your sister in danger?"

"No. But anything was possible, I guess. They worked in Major Cases. When Hudson and I reunited in that North Cascades home, we discussed going to LAPD for help. But there was a reason Mom and Dad wanted us out of California. That was why we never went to the police."

"Makes sense."

"Sometimes, I told myself that Lilly might've been saved by a stranger. And somehow, I was glad she wasn't with us in

North Cascades. Being so young, she couldn't have endured what my brother and I did."

Her head dips forward into her palms as she tries to compose herself. There's something about her brother that shakes her like this—like she was having that nightmare.

"Morgan." I squeeze her shoulder.

She shakes her head. "I'm fine." She sniffles. "Where was I? Um... Lilly. Yes. Lilly. She hadn't been saved—that was just wishful thinking. Because she was young, she easily hid and transported around. But she's not safe. She's safe when she's with me."

"What do you know about the man who wanted you? Scarf-face, didn't you say?"

"I saw him coming out of my family home, stalking the surrounding area while it was burning behind him. He was searching for me. He knew I'd escaped. I don't know his name, so I call him *Scarf-face*. I'm sure he was that third man you saw in Venice—sunglasses and scarf."

"Scarf-face. I see. So, how long have you been running on your own?"

"Almost a couple of weeks. Since that Tacoma ambush. I learned not to take the conventional way. Whenever and wherever I could, I took the back way, the unexpected way. It doesn't matter if it's longer, as long as I feel safer."

"That's smart and brave, Morgan. I'm proud of you. And I'm sure your parents are too, wherever they are. And your brother."

"Maybe. But I won't be able to do this without you."

"You'll never be without me, Morgan."

Whoever Scarf-face is—whatever he's hiding behind the cloth—I will find him!

"All right. Now let's find Lilly," she asserts.

"We'll go to Red Mark first thing tomorrow. No doubt you'll remember more, and you can tell us all about it."

"Okay." She straightens herself. "So, we'll be talking to your bosses?"

"Yes. Mark Connor and Sam Kelleher. They're good men. They'll help us." I then glance at her feet. "You think you'll be able to walk?"

"Yeah."

"Do you need me to buy you a new pair of shoes? Perhaps two-size larger?"

That earns me a hearty laugh from her. "My feet aren't as big as you think, Ty! I think I should be fine. I have a pair of regular sneakers in my bag."

"I'll get rid of those bulky bandages and put thinner band-aids on the big blisters."

"Booyah! Bigfoot no more."

The news draws a smile from her pale face, followed by a huge hug coming my way.

14

MORGAN

"Gee, you should really open a bakery." Tyler goggles at the two dozen freshly baked strawberry cupcakes. "But you know you didn't have to do this, right?"

I stare at them, too, wondering why I woke up at 5 a.m. this morning and headed straight to the kitchen like I had been programmed to. "I guess it's my way of calming my nerves."

He rounds his chunky arm around my shoulders. "We'll be fine, Wolf Girl. Though I'm sure the guys will appreciate it."

"Have I made enough?"

"Morgan, sit down."

We sit on 'our sofa.' "Ty, if I'm lost for words, you'll help me?"

"Of course. I'll be there for you. And so will my bosses. When I say bosses—they're my superiors, highly experienced, and you can talk to them like you talk to me. They're on our side."

"I just don't want to act or sound stupid—like wasting their time."

"You won't."

I puff out air. "Yeah, I'll be fine." I shake off my silly nerves.

"By the way, why's the company called Red Mark? I presume 'Mark' is for Mark Connor?"

"Yes. And Sam's middle name is Redley, nicknamed Red. Hence Red Mark."

"I always wondered." I pause. "So, if Sam and Mark are your bosses, you're like a commander of some sort?"

"Well, I just got promoted to Head of Operations. There wasn't such a position before. I mean, Mark and Sam used to do everything when Red Mark was just a two-man band. Then, they started recruiting more staff. I was their first. I trained with them for months before going full-time. And now we've got support staff and about a dozen men on the ground. Someone will need to lead those men and manage the missions."

"You were a SEAL. Why the training?"

"Red Mark missions are like no other. We deal with young people. And with the nature of their circumstances, it takes a different kind of mental toughness. It's empathy, it's discipline, it's care. Plus, you have to learn to be diplomatic when working with other agencies like the police or sheriff departments."

"I see."

"At times, the pressure can be harder than in the battlefield. When young lives are involved, everything gets more delicate." His index finger and thumb gesture a small distance as if illustrating the delicateness.

"You never choose easy, do you?" I comment. "First the Navy SEAL, being a sniper, now Red Mark."

"It's just my calling. It's in here." He taps his heart. "My job isn't just about rescuing the kids but also about minimizing their traumas, especially with the little ones. Often, they don't show how frightened or stressed they are. You've got to read them very closely."

I give him an admiring gaze. Not many men are equipped to

do this kind of job, and I'm thankful that our paths crossed. The ocean had chosen us for this.

He angles his head as if saying there's more. "Sometimes, though, the hardest thing about what I do is the parents. Things can get hairy with them. They may run out of patience and take things into their own hands. They may not tell you the truth or hide things from you. They may get abusive. So you must know how to react to any eventuality."

"I guess that was why I stuck with animals."

"Huh," Tyler scoffs. "It doesn't mean you have it easy, Wolf Girl. Come on, we should get ready."

"Yeah."

I put on the only dress I have in my pile. Mom used to say, 'Always pack a little black dress wherever you go.' And she did, and she was right. I don't have a shiny pair of stilettos to go with it, but the sneakers will have to do for now—which, thankfully, is still reasonably white.

Ty removed the bandages on my feet earlier this morning, and now only a few thin plasters remain—negotiable for me to put on my footwear.

I plod to the bathroom, ready to put on my make-up for the first time in two years. My lipstick has gone out of shape, and my powder and eyeshadow palettes are cracked, but I'm not leaving this house looking like a village baker. My life has gotten its flavor back. Now it's time to recolor it.

But temptation stops me in my tracks.

Tyler's door is open, and my nose unashamedly follows the scent of his cologne, instructing my feet to do the same.

I gasp.

Holy wolf and coyote.

This isn't the time to indulge. I should start making myself pretty, but I'm being teased and seared by the magnificent scene I shouldn't have seen.

Tyler is perusing his wardrobe, I'm sure contemplating which shirt to wear.

Damn! Look at those well-sculpted traps and sturdy waist. His eagle-and-trident tattoo is still the only one on his back, but as he reaches up to unhook a shirt, I can see a small, inked inscription on his left inner bicep. I can't quite make out what it is.

As he keeps moving, his unzipped pants droop below his hips. I've seen him in surfer's shorts and even boxer shorts, but there's something about a man half-dressed—and half-exposed man-ass.

And Tyler's ass is something to behold. So sinful that I can't help feeling the heat between my legs.

He starts putting on his shirt, jiggling his ass to tuck the hem under his pants, unaware of my scrutiny.

Before the heat turns into a flame, before I invite disaster, I remove myself and head into the bathroom.

I tie my hair into a ponytail and then apply the make-up.

A voluntary smile surprises me as if the reflection in the mirror isn't me. In a good way. It's how I used to look when I was safe and surrounded by my family.

I touch my necklace. I miss wearing it. Now that I'm no longer alone, I can. I've got a man protecting me, so I'm not going to lose it.

"You ready?" I hear Ty outside.

"Yes." I meet him in the hallway.

My plight isn't over. I stand speechless. He's wearing a full suit, smelling like the ocean breeze, his beard neatly trimmed, his hair slick. I've got to find a way to fend off this temptation with a capital 'T,' or it will get out of hand.

Seconds pass, and I realize that we're *both* speechless.

It's Tyler who breaks the silence. "You look stunning."

"Is that your work uniform?" I quip clumsily.

He smiles sideways. "It's just how we do it at Red Mark."

Now I feel giddy, thanks to the vision of me surrounded by handsome hunks in their suits. "We should go." I march ahead of him, but I know he's watching me.

"Your feet feeling okay?"

I stop, twisting back to glance at my companion, who struts like a model, a man, and a protector in one. "Still a little sore, but it's like you'd been partying all night with heels, that kind of sore."

"Okay. Party all night sounds negotiable."

Despite the okay, he holds on to me and helps me get into the car. He loathes my royal bodyguard novel, yet he's treating me like the princess in the story. The man overflows with caring instincts and does it naturally—however or wherever he got that from.

We make our way downtown.

"You look stunning," he repeats as he drives. He's been glancing at me, not out of concern. I'm sure he genuinely wants to imbibe in the new me.

"Thanks."

"If you, um, need anything, we can go to the shops after the meeting."

"Yeah, sure."

"Cool," he says. "Not every day you go shopping with a SEAL. Well, an ex-SEAL."

I giggle. "I'll make the most of it, don't you worry. By the way, can you fight in that suit?"

"Of course I can, sweetheart," he says guilelessly.

Damn me.

Something more than heat has just disturbed my crotch.

He makes a turn, passing the Montana State Capitol building and then the park where I had dinner with Gravy.

"We're almost there," Tyler announces.

In my head, I keep practicing what I should say to Mark Connor and Sam Kelleher. I don't know why I'm still nervous, but they're the Hercules of all things rescue and protect—so I have the right to be.

I need to set something straight before I'm in a room with them. "Look, Ty. I'm going to pay you and your company, okay? This isn't a favor."

He frowns. "Just like you paid me the first time?"

"I guess." I did leave ten thousand dollars in his bag before we parted ways in Washington. "I had to make up for the boxing match you'd missed because I believed you would've won."

"Did you know how much the prize money was?"

"No idea."

"Two and a half grand."

"What can I say? I'm a generous tipper."

Tyler shakes his head playfully. "Is this your way of saying you want us to stay professional?"

It's like a fist has just landed on my chest.

Do I want us to stay professional?

I'd been isolated in remote areas with support crews and other researchers. Some of them, I must admit, were quite attractive. But I'd never felt such connection, gratefulness, and passion—yes, passion, that's starting to get out of control—like I have with Ty. I couldn't even handle seeing him getting dressed. No doubt we will spend time on the road, in hotels, for the next... however long, until we find Lilly. How am I going to handle that?

To my defense, though, what young woman wouldn't fall for such a formidable man? With such a big heart? After being at the receiving end of his kindness and care, who wouldn't fall in love with Tyler Hunt?

If I were in an ordinary situation, when love is the only

aspect I need to consider, it would've been different. I would've jumped in. The hell with staying professional!

But I'm on a mission. My sister is my priority. Not love. Not passion.

Paying him may switch my mindset that nothing should happen between us. He and I are just a transaction. I hope that will put enough restraint on my heart.

I explain, "I don't want to take advantage of you, Ty. And Red Mark."

"You need to speak to Mark and Sam about money."

"I will then," I confirm as the Red Mark building looms in the distance.

Tyler puts his palm on top of my hand, melting my nervousness.

Hope surges, along with anticipation of what's to come. I've been planning this since the day I found out about Tyler's involvement in the organization. Now it's real.

The touch of his hand is now not of care—it's a promise. And what can be truer than a SEAL promise?

15

TYLER

My eyes are still on Morgan as I swipe us into the Red Mark main conference room. Her silence and the quietness in here prompts me to cast a lingering look at her.

I've seen her in a bikini before. But that black dress somehow accentuates her figure more—her trim waist, the stunning curve of her hips and ass. Her skirt stops at her mid-thigh, revealing her impossibly long legs.

And that wolf tattoo—it makes her even more like a vixen.

"I guess I don't look so pedestrian now."

Damn, she notices. And she doesn't seem to mind.

"Never pedestrian, just badass wild," I comment. Truly, she never looks pedestrian. She's always special, whatever she's wearing.

I pull up a chair, the second out of the four parked on one side of the table, offering it to her. I will sit next to her, and Sam and Mark will be on the other side, facing us.

"A gentleman in and out of the office." She sits down while passing a side glance at me.

I don't know what she's done, but her eyes are killing me.

With the shades she has drawn around her lids, her brown eyes look even bigger, as if it were possible.

Footsteps approach, and soon, the two co-founders of Red Mark enter. I introduce them to Morgan.

"Nice to meet you, gents," she shakes their hands.

"Please, sit down," Sam says. "I take it that you were responsible for those artful pieces of patisserie?" His head tilts toward the lounge downstairs.

Morgan smiles shyly. "It's a hobby of mine. I'm glad you guys like them."

"They're a hit!" Mark chimes in, his eyes discreetly observing her. "Didn't I see you at the Thirsty Fox the other night?"

"Yes. I was there."

Mark Connor and his eagle eyes.

Then Sam offers, "Oh, would you like a drink? Coffee, tea?"

"No, thanks. I'm fine," Morgan replies.

"Mark is crazy about hibiscus tea if you're into it?" Sam teases.

Morgan chuckles. "It's healthy, I know. But truly, I'm fine."

Mark places his hands on the table. "Miss Blackwell—"

"Morgan. Please."

"Morgan. Tyler has sent me a few things about Lilly. But I'd like to start with your parents."

"They were LAPD detectives, worked in Major Cases."

Mark nods his head slowly. "Did they ever tell you about specific cases? Or people?"

"No. They never discussed work at home or with the children."

"Look, Morgan." Sam moves forward in his seat. "Your parents were FBI informants."

The news hit me like a hurricane. I can't imagine what goes on inside Morgan's head.

I reach out to hold her hand. She's not shocked—she's fired up.

"Why didn't I ever think of that!" She frowns. "That explained the interstate assignments, the long trips. When Lilly and I were young, when my parents had to travel, they left us with our aunt. Sometimes weeks on end."

"We believe their deaths, the disappearance of your sister, and your brother's death stemmed from this."

For the first time in this meeting room, Morgan turns pale. Her breathing hitches.

Her brother. There's something about her brother that shakes her.

"Morgan, we can take a break if you need one," I suggest, still holding her hand.

"No. I'm fine."

"Tyler is right," Mark agrees, appraising her.

She takes a deep breath. "No. Please. We should continue."

"Okay," Mark says with conviction. He and Sam never hesitate to call off a meeting with family members of the missing when they don't think they can handle it. Mark obviously knows she has what it takes to carry on.

Morgan sits tall. "Before that night, when my parents died, Lilly went missing, and men started hunting me. Mom and Dad were away for about two weeks. I don't know where, though. Before they left, they argued about whether one of them should've stayed home with me and Lilly. In the end, they both went."

"We tried to get information about their last assignments, but the FBI has been tightlipped, and I doubt the LAPD knows much," Mark explains. "We'll keep trying. We'll get to the bottom of this, but in the meantime, we should focus on Lilly."

Sam takes out a copy of the sketch. "Your best friend drew this when she was in Florida?"

"Yes. She was in Tampa for a vacation, and she saw my sister."

"How long ago was this?"

"About a month ago."

"Have you seen this man before?" Sam points at the figure beside Lilly. In the sketch, the man is putting his arm around the girl as if he was a friend.

"No."

"He wasn't one of the men who pursued you?"

"I don't think so. Before I got to North Cascades, there were always two men dressed in black and a man wearing a scarf across his face—whom I knew was calling the shots. I called him Scarf-face."

"Scarf-face. Fitting," Sam comments.

Morgan adds, "I'm sure Scarf-face isn't that man in the sketch. Scarf-face is thin, fair-skinned. I know this sketch is black and white. But this man here, he clearly looks Hispanic."

"Good observation," Sam acknowledges, studying her as if trying to find where it came from. "We've sent this sketch for analysis by our facial recognition team. We'll keep you updated. But I must ask, has there been any demand? Ransom money? Exchange of information? Anything?"

"No," Morgan replies.

"I guess when they decided to take Lilly, the kidnapper would've known that your parents would be dead. Demanding ransom would've been useless," Mark argues, to which Sam responds with a 'you're a smart ass' glance.

"Is there anything you can think of, Morgan? Perhaps something trivial that your parents might've mentioned?"

She shakes her head.

Mark suddenly straightens up. "Morgan. I have to ask you this."

"Mark," Sam warns, shaking his head.

"Your brother. Some investigators—"

"Mark!"

I wheel my chair closer to Morgan, who's wringing her hands.

Mark continues. "Please, Morgan. Can I ask this question?"

Morgan leans forward. "Please do, Mr. Connor."

"Some investigators suggested that your brother was behind all this because of jealousy. I want to hear what you think of it."

She takes a deep breath. Tears coat her eyes, but she carries on. "Hudson would never hurt me or Lilly. Or my parents. It's true that Lilly and I got way more attention from our parents. But he was never jealous. He lived an independent life. It was his wish." Her lips quiver. "He died defending me, Mr. Connor."

Mark presses his lips together. Damn, the man himself is close to tears. I wonder what he knows. He certainly has faith in Morgan's strength, perhaps more than Sam or I was prepared to give her. "Thanks for answering, Morgan."

"They want something from me, Mr. Connor."

"And what would that be, Morgan?"

"My parents left a sum of money for me. Two million dollars," she reveals. "Hard cash."

We gasp.

She kept it hidden well.

"My grandparents were wealthy property developers. That was inheritance money from them. I'd happily give it up if I can get Lilly back," she continues. "Unfortunately, I don't think that is what they want either. Besides, my parents gave that money to a Meredith Bennett. I'm sure they'd gone the extra mile to cover the trails." She places an ID on the table.

I ignore the ID, focusing on her face instead. "So, you're Meredith Bennett, too? Besides Emma Schiffer?" I know she's not very fond of those names.

She shrugs nonchalantly.

"Who knew about the money?" asks Sam.

"The whole Blackwell family did. But I guess no one knew it ended up with me," Morgan answers. "Mr. Connor, Mr. Kelleher. My mother left me with cryptic messages." Then she puts her attention on me. "They're in those books, Ty. Including that silly royal bodyguard romance."

I scoff. That explains her so-called eclectic taste of reading. "Okay."

"I lugged them everywhere for a reason. Mom gave me a reference grid, pointing to the page numbers, line numbers, and the locations of words in those books. I found out about the money from some of those messages. I've got others, but I really don't know what they mean."

"Would you be willing to share them with us?" Mark requests.

"Yes. I'll write them down for you."

"Who knew about those messages?"

"No one. I didn't want to bombard my brother or my aunt with more secrets that might've made them targets. Like me. But I guess they were Blackwells, so they were always targets."

"So the kidnapper doesn't want money, and they killed the rest of your family. That means they want *you*?" Mark says.

"I think so. They believe that I know something."

Morgan leans back, glancing at me.

"You okay?" I whisper.

"Yeah."

Sam and Mark turn to me. Sam asks, "Where do you want to start, Ty?"

"We always follow the lead, sir," I say. "I'd start with Florida."

Sam agrees then turns to Morgan. "Morgan, do you mind if we talk to Tyler for a few minutes?"

"Please," she says.

"I'll get Cora-Lee to keep you company," I tell Morgan. "She's the head of tech and our command center boss. You'll like her."

She nods with a smile, then gets up. After a few steps, she pivots. "By the way, Mr. Connor and Mr. Kelleher. Tyler is a dear friend. But please invoice me the full amount for the work, including all disbursements. And if you need a down payment, please charge me now. Treat me like your other clients."

"We can talk about that later," Sam says.

"It's not because I can. I mean, my parents left me plenty. But my payment to Red Mark will no doubt help your company help others."

"Thank you," Mark and Sam utter almost at the same time.

AFTER INTRODUCING MORGAN TO CORA-LEE, I'm back in the conference room with Sam and Mark.

"Funny you mentioned that you saw Morgan at the Fox the other night," Sam nudges at Mark. "Cass told me there was a girl at the bar, definitely not local. And hear this, Cass thought she had eyes on you then." He points at his partner.

"Don't be ridiculous!" Mark dismisses the banter.

"Well, of course my wife told it as it was. She told her you were taken."

I'm dying to hear what Cass knew about what 'that girl' thought about me. But Mark gets us back on track, saying, "All right, Sam. Morgan isn't here for love. Let's focus."

Sam eyeballs me. I think he was saying all that to get my reaction and to finally ask me, "Have you two got anything going on?"

I take a breath. "No, sir. She's just a friend."

"You said you met her in California?" Mark asks.

"Yeah. Two years ago."

Sam, who has been spinning his chair, stops to look at me straight. "You sure about this, Ty?"

"I must admit I haven't searched anything on the Blackwell case. But I believe her."

"It's not that I don't believe her or that we don't trust you. We want to protect you," Mark says. "I'm gonna do a background check on her to make sure she is who she claims she is."

"Mark is right," Sam supports him.

Much as it pokes me deep down, I understand where they're coming from.

"I'm fine with that."

"So Lilly has been missing for two years, and she was seen in Tampa about a month ago," Mark says. "Here's the thing. Scarf-face is after Morgan, and Morgan is after Lilly. If Scarf-face has kidnapped Lilly as bait, why the chase? If he wants something from Morgan, why hasn't he just told her as it is? *I've got Lilly. Give me what I want, or else.*"

He's right. Something else is at play here.

Mark adds, "Just like Morgan, Lilly is a very attractive girl. I hate to say this, but a lot of rich men would be willing to pay a high price for her. In saying that, if what Scarf-face is after is worth a lot, the earnings from trafficking Lilly would be minuscule in comparison. It wouldn't be worth the hassle."

"I agree, Sir. I'll look into it. But for now, I still need to pursue our lead in Tampa."

"Agreed, Ty," Mark affirms. "Whatever is happening behind the scenes, your priority is still Lilly."

"Yes, sir. And, well, since I'll need to be interstate, I won't be able to perform my duty here in Helena. I must take a leave of absence."

"This is your mission as much as Red Mark's. Not because of the money Morgan is paying us, but because we're family."

"You do whatever you have to, buddy," Sam says. "Mark and I will hold the fort."

"Thank you."

"So, who would you like?" Mark asks.

"Boss?"

"One of the guys should come with you."

"With all due respect, sir. I have to do this alone."

"No, Ty."

It only takes me a second to pull the team roster from my memory. "Ben is still recovering, and he'll be needed in Billings with the three recruits. Mr. Kelleher and Micah are on the Missoula case. The rest of the team are all assigned to cases in Helena. So all of Red Mark men are tapped out. And I don't mean to exclude you, Sir." I look at Mark. "But it would be wrong for me to take you away from your wife and Noah."

Sam scratches his chin. "Florida..." His other hand knocks at the table in front of him. "I'm not going to promise you anything, but I'll talk to Jack. He has vast knowledge of kidnapping cases in the state, and he knows a few friends we need."

I've only heard Jack's name in passing, although I know a bit of his story. He's Sam's Marine brother who was kidnapped as a boy and was presumed dead after more than ten years of no leads. But thanks to his brother's persistence and determination, they were reunited a few years ago.

"Are you sure, sir?" I also know that Jack has just lost the woman who rescued him, a nun from a Florida monastery.

"I can't promise anything. We both know he's still grieving —although it's been too long in my book. He needs a kind of push that goes straight to his heart. And I think Lilly's case will do just that."

"I don't want to put him in danger, sir. Physically or emotionally."

"I know. I'm his brother, Ty. So, the answer may be a no. But I'm going to persuade him to do this—because he'll be with you."

"I understand."

"Well, let's prep. And if I find anything, I'll let you know," Mark says.

Sam taps my shoulder hard. "Go on, don't keep her waiting."

16

MORGAN

Cora-Lee Rancic is a tech girl who defies stereotypes. She doesn't wear glasses or don some geeky outfits or exotic piercings. She's probably in her early thirties, originally from Serbia. She looks impeccable in her pants suit and perfect make-up. Her dark curls have some blonde streaks, combed neatly back in a ponytail. From what Ty has told me, she's a genius, but when she greeted me for the first time, I felt instant warmth and her down-to-earth demeanor.

"Hey, thanks for the cupcakes. They're absolutely delicious," Cora-Lee says then nods at my arm. "Love your tattoo, by the way. Is that why Ty calls you 'Wolf Girl'?"

"Yeah. And I studied wolves."

"Huh. I can guarantee that you're the first wolf expert who has set foot in this office."

I chuckle. "I feel special."

"Hey, you *are* special!" she asserts. "Full disclosure. As Red Mark's head of the command center, I know about your case."

"Perhaps you know more about my parents than I do. How could I not know that they were FBI informants?"

"Because you were too busy following wolves and their mating patterns."

I laugh. This woman has a quirky way to calm me. I've certainly come to the right place.

Cora-Lee rests her hand on my shoulder. "It's natural that sometimes you don't know things about your family until your neighbors or your cousin's cousin mentions them."

"I guess."

"Because all you know about them is just—love. Don't be too hard on yourself. Besides, if you were an FBI informant, chances are, your family isn't supposed to know."

"Thanks, Cee. Can I call you that? Everyone seems to call you Cee."

"Yeah. Cee is good," she replies, then gets up to take another cupcake. "Damn! They're all gone!"

"I'll make some more for you next time."

She returns to her seat. "So, you know Ty from California?"

"Yes. He saved me."

"That's what he does."

"We parted ways. Then things went from bad to worse for me, and after all these years of running, I managed to track him."

"You *tracked* him?"

"Yeah. He's my wolf, I guess."

Cora-Lee smiles, full of thoughts. "You're good."

"I bumped into him at the hospital a few nights ago."

"Oh, it must've been after they rescued Tia. Ben, one of the team, was injured, and Ty stayed with him."

Of course he did. "And then I bumped into him at a bar. The Thirsty Fox. It seems like the official hangout place for the guys?"

"You could say that," confirms Cora-Lee.

"You weren't there?"

"I had to leave early. My cat was sick."

"Oh…"

Cora-Lee shifts her position as if thinking about something lighthearted. "Hey, did you try the Fallen Angel while you were there?"

"No. I had a few shots of whiskey."

"You should try it. It's the best ale in Montana."

"Thanks for the tip. I'll try it next time."

"If you want a stronger one, the illegal one, there's this brew called the Valley Wolf. I'll get it for you."

"Maybe after all this is over. Right now, I can't afford to get smashed."

"So, how did you meet Ty in California? Did he like rescue you from something?"

"I was pursued, and for some reason, I just gravitated toward him. He almost mowed me down with his surfboard."

"Huh! He surfed?"

"He was a complete stranger, but, I just trusted him."

"That's Ty. He's sweet. I mean, people say a SEAL can never be sweet. But he is."

"Interesting choice of word."

"I mean, he takes care of everybody. He knows when his colleague's son or daughter is sick. He knows when I'm in people-repellent mode. I'm a geek by nature, in case you don't know."

I consider her choice of words. "People-repellent, huh? So Ty hides you?"

"He shoos people away from me. Nicely, of course. One of the little things that make him sweet."

"Perhaps you're right."

"I have a word to describe most people here."

"So, how would you describe Mr. Connor and Mr. Kelleher?"

"Well, Mr. Connor is stoic. Not my word. Everyone calls him that, including his wife."

"He asked me the toughest questions in there."

"A good sign."

"Why?"

"That means he thinks you're tough. And that's one hell of a compliment from Mr. Connor."

"Right..." I sigh, shoulders back, chest up. "And Mr. Kelleher?"

"He's charming."

"The 'good cop' kinda person?"

"Umm... maybe not. He can be deadly when provoked."

"I shall not try!"

"Then Ben Winter—I'm not sure if you've met him, but he often partners with your Tyler."

My Tyler?

Cee carries on, "Ben is fierce. He's the only non-military on the team. He's a Taekwondo master who always speaks his mind."

"I see. And how would you describe yourself?"

"Ah, a great question," Cee praises. "Um... hmm... nerdy."

"I think you're brilliant." I won't use the word cute as a button, although she is in my eyes. "And you're more extroverted than you think."

"Thanks, Wolf Girl. And I'd describe you as... tenacious."

I cock my head, comparing the word with what I feel inside. She's not wrong. "That means a lot."

"Well, I was going to say 'stubborn.' But that's not very nice, is it?"

I laugh. "You are brilliant, Cee."

I hear faint footsteps, and I immediately turn around.

Cee cocks her head. "God! You're just so in tune."

Indeed, it's 'my man.'

Tyler is now standing behind my chair. "Thanks for keeping her company, Cee. I hope she's not challenging you as she did me."

"No. We've been having a rousing conversation."

Tyler rounds my chair, then bends down to whisper, "I need to talk to you."

"Sure."

Cee looks over us. "Maybe you could do it over cheeseburgers and Fallen Angel?"

"Not a bad idea," Ty says. "And then we can pop to the shop?"

"I can't wait," I reply.

"I'll leave you two to plan your day," Cee says, getting up. "Nice to meet you, Wolf Girl."

Tyler frowns. "I thought that was my pet name!"

"We're not exclusive yet," I quip.

"Snap!" Cee interjects cheekily as she walks away from us.

17

TYLER

Preparations for our Florida trip are underway.

Red Mark is my work, but they're also my family. And it's proven by the fact that Mark and Sam were willing to go the extra mile to protect me. Running a background check on Morgan was a good call. I would've done the same if I was them.

I trust my gut. But at the same time, I'm a man. I could've been blinded by the beauty and desperation of Morgan Blackwell and believed everything she said without questions.

Now, I can move on with confidence.

Wolf Girl is *the* Morgan Blackwell, who has been missing for two years. Her photos and the story about her interview with NatGeo checked out. I even found out that she was, in fact, successful. She will be over the moon when I tell her.

Hudson Blackwell, her brother, was also the man I saw welcoming her in North Cascades. And the infamous wolf tattoo—I brought that up even before Mark or Sam asked me.

Earlier today, I got news from Jack Kelleher. He has agreed to help and partner with me in Tampa. In fact, something comes through in my email inbox.

"Fuck me..." I murmur as I open the attachments. Jack hasn't mentioned it, but I'm seeing something that may answer one of the many questions we have. "Morgan!"

No answer.

"Morgan, you wanna see this."

Whatever she's doing!

I pad to the back of the house. The smell of lavender gets stronger as I approach her room.

My God.

I stand mesmerized at the door.

Morgan is facing the mirror, brushing her hair. I must admit, the first time I saw her in Venice, her hair was wild. Now, the strands shine like a bundle of silk yarn ready to be woven. It's grown a lot, down to almost her waist.

And that body.

The girl bought many things from the shop the other day, and we spent a while in the lingerie area, but I never paid attention to what she put in the basket—or I was too embarrassed to.

Now I know at least one item. A jade-colored satin nightie. The straps are very thin, the skirt barely covering the bottom of her ass cheeks.

Bless me... how am I going to get through tonight without taming my hard-on?

I've been training all my life since I decided to be a SEAL. It's no secret that military training is more about mental toughness than physical fitness or battle skills. I'm supposed to be able to face anything without emotions, separating head from heart. But my principle to keep romance at bay is standing on shaky ground when Morgan is around.

What should I do with her? What should I do with *me*? Tonight, tomorrow, and beyond?

Maybe my mind is in crisis, the residue of seeing Daisy moving on right in front of my eyes.

But that's not it. My yearning for Morgan has got nothing to do with my ex.

The truth is, I haven't gotten over my Wolf Girl.

"May I come in?" Finally, I can bring myself to announce my presence.

"Hey," she greets me, letting go of the brush. Her glorious hair swings as she turns to me.

"I've got something to show you."

"Sure." She pivots, grabbing a matching robe from the bed on the way, covering herself.

Damn. That robe looks so much better where it was. And perhaps that nightie would be, too, lying next to it.

"Have you found more stuff about me?" she teases. I had told her about Red Mark doing a background check on her.

I smirk. "It was protocol, okay? Don't take it personally."

She pats my shoulders. "I did the same to you, Ty. I researched you and Red Mark before convincing my brother to get us to Helena."

"So we're good?"

"Of course."

"About your research... Tell me again, how did you find me? You didn't even know my last name, and I know I'm not the only Tyler in Montana."

"Well, you went through my things in Venice. I did the same when you slept. Not your wallet, because you had it on you. I saw the name embroidered on your uniform patch."

I cock my head. "I *have* underestimated you."

She winks at me proudly. "So, what were you going to show me?"

I usher her into my study. It takes me a few seconds to decide whether to walk ahead of her, behind her, or next to her.

But wherever I am, I can't escape. All I see is her body swaying beneath the loose and thin satin clothing.

In the end, she decides, walking just ahead of me, flaunting her sexy mounds.

I'm so in trouble!

"Come, sit down." I pull up a chair next to mine and slide my laptop toward her, a photo on the screen.

She squints. "That's the man on the sketch!"

"Yes. Eduardo Callas. He's a known people trafficker, and he's based in Tampa."

She covers her mouth. "Oh my God!"

"Jack is on the case. Hopefully, we'll have a location by the time we arrive."

"Jack, Sam's brother. So he's going to meet us in Tampa?"

"Yes."

She rests her elbow on the desk, her chin on her hand. Her eyes wander sideways when she asks, "Is he as handsome as Sam?"

"Morgan, come on. You've got me, isn't that enough?"

"You don't see James Bond with just one girl, do you? Why can't Morgan Blackwell have two hunks on either side of her?"

"What has the wild done to you, Wolf Girl?"

She grins happily. "James Bond... I can't remember the last time I was at the cinema. I used to go every weekend. Anyway!" She blinks as if reminding herself what we're doing. It seems that I'm not the only one who's distracted. Even more dangerous. "So, Jack, he's not a Red Mark, is he?"

"No. He's a Marine, although currently he's on leave. The nun who brought him up passed away a few weeks ago."

"Oh... are you sure it's wise to involve him?"

"He's agreed."

"And... what did you mean by 'a nun who brought him up'? What happened to his mother?"

"You see, Jack was kidnapped when he was seven."

She gapes. "He was?"

"Sam was twelve at the time, and he never stopped looking for his little brother. The grief and frustration that he went through were the main reasons he became a missing children rescue specialist."

"Wow... I never thought."

"But his persistence paid off. He found his brother," I reveal. "Jack managed to run away from his kidnapper, although he had no memory of who he was at the time. A nun from St. Leo, Florida, took him under her wings—and so became his mother."

"It must've been so hard for the both of them."

"Sam thought your case would be a good distraction or pick-me-up for Jack. He felt it was time for his brother to get back on his feet doing something instead of just isolating himself."

"And you said Jack himself has agreed?"

"Yes. He has," I reply. "And there's something else." I zoom in on the video.

"Shit..." She holds her breath, turning the screen back toward me. "That's Scarf-face!" She points at the figure in the background, right at the edge of the frame.

"So we know Eduardo Callas has a connection with him."

"My God... Ty..."

"When was the last time you saw Scarf-face?"

"Not since I left Cali. But somehow, I felt his presence when we were attacked in Tacoma." She huffs, stopping short at saying 'when her brother was killed.'

I spin her chair around, tapping her cheek so she pays attention to me instead of the laptop screen. "Morgan?"

"I didn't see Scarf-face, but I sensed he was there when my brother was killed."

"Okay." I'm glad she manages to say that without breaking down.

"And, again, I didn't see him, but I swear he was there when I had to get to a town for some supplies. South of Spokane. I was still driving then, but that was too close. So since then, I was hardly out of the wilderness."

"Hang on. Hang on." I shake my head repeatedly. "You walked to Helena from Spokane?"

"Pretty much."

Jesus! That's more than three hundred miles. And that's via the main road. If she had woven through the mountains and forests, that would've added at least fifty. "No wonder your feet gave up!"

"My whole body almost gave up, Ty. But I couldn't give up."

I press a palm on top of hers. "I'm glad you came to me."

"Me too."

"Cee has confirmed our plane and crew. They're ours for the next four days. They'll follow our plans."

"Thanks. You know I requested a private jet, not because I'm a diva, right?"

It was her idea, but I know the reason is secrecy. The company we hire the plane from regularly caters to diplomats and the Secret Service, so our journey won't be tracked, and it'll save us from having to show our faces to the public. It'll barely put a dent in her two million, but I know the word diva or princess or prima donna will never be attached to her.

"You'll always be my Wolf Girl. Never a diva."

Her mouth hooks a small grin. "So, did you find anything else?"

"No. That's all for now." I appraise her. "How's your side? I haven't checked in on you about that."

"It still stings when I move a certain way." She shows it by twisting her torso a little. "But I can feel it's healing."

"Good. We'll change the bandage again before we leave tomorrow. It's late. We'll pack in the morning."

Morgan rises, standing right in front of me. I get up to meet her. First, her cheek arrives on my pec, then her chest projects. Then her arms snake around me.

And...

Did she just?

She hitches one shoulder up with a restrained smile, sparkles in her eyes. "Good night, Ty."

18

MORGAN

When you still trust a man after he ran a background check on you, that means you've managed to separate feelings from facts.

Tyler had told me openly about Red Mark digging into my records. It did annoy me at first, but that affirmed he's someone who'll always have my back without doing things behind my back.

Battling thoughts send me tossing and turning under the covers.

The fact that I'm paying him hasn't changed my mindset at all. The more I tell myself to 'forget about it,' the more my heart rebels.

He's the one.

It's now or never.

Perhaps I'm simply freaking out about tomorrow. I could try to counter it by baking yet another batch of cupcakes.

But that's not it.

Be a woman and tell him—because he didn't frigging take the hint!

He let me walk into this room by myself, turning into his bedroom like his work was done for the night.

I swing my legs off the bed, pondering one last time if this is need or want—lust or sensibility.

He was surprised that I had walked from Spokane. Thinking about it now, it was a miracle that I'd survived. My body had given up a long time ago. The thought of Lilly fueled me to keep going. But hope had taken me here. The yearning for a safe place.

Now that I've found safety, I'm seeking a different kind of safe.

I *need* Tyler for me and no one else. The timing may be contestable, but the need is as private as it is important to me. I need to share it with him before tomorrow.

I run a hand over my chest and belly. The silk of my nightie caresses me back. I should be a woman and tell him. Lying here without him just feels wrong.

So wrong.

I tiptoe to his room.

I don't know if he always leaves his door open, but I'd like to think he has done it for me—so he can hear me if I need him.

"Tyler..." I whisper, standing in his doorway.

He gets up and urgently strides to me. "Nightmare?"

The speed of his response takes me back. But that's him. He'll come to my aid at the drop of a hat. "No. I just can't sleep."

He takes my hands, as if taking me for a dance. It's subtle, but finally, the energy he oozes has changed. It tugs me to him. Or perhaps I've simply helped myself.

"You're cold," he remarks as my face touches his bare chest. "Did you lose that extra blanket?"

I bow my head, unable to answer.

He murmurs, "You want me to stay with you?"

"Maybe."

Obviously not convinced with my answer, he offers, "You're welcome to sleep here. Well, if it helps."

I stare at the shuffled sheets behind him. It must be even warmer under there if we lie down together.

I nod, although avoiding eye contact with him. We've been together in bed a couple of times now. Out of need. But on the eve of our mission, and thanks to my own agenda, I feel like there's a forest fire starting within me.

Tyler makes an attempt to straighten the bed, but I'm too quick to jump in.

The linen is full of his scent, coated generously with his body heat. He can't blame me for claiming the spot.

I take off my robe.

Clothes were never important when I was on the run. But when you're with someone, yearning for that person, what you wear matters.

Since I stocked up, I've felt more human. And the touch of luxury from this lingerie on my skin makes me feel like a woman again.

With a smile on his face, Tyler joins me, sinking into the mattress and adjusting his position a few times. Closer to me.

A spurt of delight disturbs my crotch. By this time, he should have figured out my intentions. I'm sure I smell like sex all over.

"You won't let me fall, will you, Ty?"

He erases the last few inches between us, snaking his muscly arm under and over my waist. He's so careful he manages to avoid my wound. "I'll hold on to you. Don't you worry."

Lying next to him is not enough.

I crawl over his torso like a lizard, desperate to get on top of a sunbaked rock. I move my head a couple of times, trying to find that perfect position. I don't mean to complain, but I fail to stop myself from huffing.

An unexpected chuckle flies out of his mouth. "You notice,

huh?"

Yes, I do. He has trimmed his hair.

"Your body, your hair," I reply, feeling the soft—and thinner —layer of hair on his pecs. Truly, Tyler—hair or no hair—is still the only man I want to be with. And the hand that keeps hold of my waist tells me we're on the same wavelength.

Trying to find a perfect position himself, he shuffles his shoulders, lifting his other arm. I peek at the second tattoo stenciled on his inner bicep.

I squint, relying on the light coming from the outside to read it.

It's a known Latin saying, and I can make out the words without reading all the letters. *Homo totiens moritur quotiens amittit suos.*

Who did he lose that he had to carry it with him?

"I didn't see this tattoo when we first met," I comment. Although I now remember his graveyard expression when we were in the water. Had that got anything to do with it?

"You weren't that observant."

"You had it then?"

"I've had it for a long time," he rasps. "Perhaps you were too busy imagining me with hair."

"I had a lot on my mind, and that certainly did not include your body hair," I grunt. "What does it mean anyway?" I pretend not to know.

"Come on, let's go to sleep."

So he doesn't want to discuss it. Perhaps after we've found Lilly, we can explore what's behind that reluctance and that sad tone.

I shift my head one more time, perching my chin below the curve of his pec, my hand covering his nipple. "I'm glad I found you, Ty."

He places his fingertips on top of my hand. "I'm glad you're here with me, Morgan."

"Here, or *here*?"

"Wherever, with me."

"You know, Ty. Since you dropped me off at North Cascades, I hardly had any pleasant thoughts. *Who killed my parents? Who took Lilly? Do I want revenge?* It was awful."

He tightens his hold on me a bit.

I add, "Unlike thinking about you."

"So you were thinking about me?"

"Being on the run is a lonely place," I lament. "Did you think about me?"

He takes a deep breath. "Sometimes."

My head rises and falls following his chest movement. It wasn't a convincing answer, but perhaps *sometimes* is good enough—considering he might've been with another girl, or other girls, between then and now.

Silence falls, and it lingers. The fire within me abates. I'm disappointed, but it may be a sign for me to drop my intentions and start doing what I should really be doing. Sleep.

Just as I think he will let himself drift off, I hear his low voice. "I'm not one to keep mementos. Yet I still have your Yellowstone coin. That tells you something."

"It kept you safe. Admit it."

"Not really," he chortles. "Training keeps you safe. Being vigilant keeps you safe."

I dismiss his explanation. "I know, Ty. I know."

He pulls the sheet higher to cover my back, then he inserts his palm under it, placing it in between my shoulder blades and rubbing my skin. "I did think of you, Morgan. I always wondered if I would see you again someday."

The revelation wakes my longing, and I can't help showing it to him. My hand reaches for the side of his neck, and I caress it like a lover does.

Tyler shifts himself, suppressing a groan that may say he likes it. "I became good at separating my SEAL life from my everyday existence."

He makes it sound easy. I wonder how he had not turned into a machine. Maybe he did at some point.

"In battles, I had no room for emotions." His voice strains. "My brain, my body, my whole capacity as a human being simply converged—laser-focused on the task at hand, on the mission, or I could get myself or my comrades killed."

The hand holding my waist moves down, following the curve of my hip as he carries on, "But once I was back in the compound, confined to my tiny bed, trying not to replay the day's proceedings, sometimes emotions help."

I lift my head, trying to read his expression. Then I hear a soft chuckle. "Especially when you try to block out the chorus of a dozen men snoring."

I can imagine!

"My point is," he adds. "Emotions kept bad thoughts at bay. Good emotions, that is. But it wasn't from thoughts about my family or my girlfriend. I tried not to think about them. I mean, I loved them, but it wasn't the emotions that I needed in those situations."

I shift myself up, and my heart kicks up into a rhythm—one of anticipation, hoping for more of his vulnerability to show—even though I may hear a thing or two about his then-girlfriend.

After all, I came into his room, and not just to sleep. I'm about to pass the point of no return. What I'm going to do tonight will be irreversible. I need to strip bare this man's heart before I do his body.

"What emotions were you seeking, Ty?" I keep stroking the side of his neck. The new growth of his beard tickles my palm.

"I don't know what they were exactly, but they just came out every time I—" His hand now moves up to my neck, almost mirroring what I'm doing to him. Soft, a little unsure. But as if he has convinced himself, he presses a palm on my cheek, appreciating me. "It was the calming emotions I got every time I thought of you."

My face dips in a sigh, my lips so close to his. "I'm glad."

"I was with a girl then. But I never meant to cheat on her or anything. Because I knew my thought was impossible—it was just for a few seconds of comfort."

His hand is now wrapping the back of my head, the other stroking my spine—lower and lower until he reaches the small of my back.

His lips advance toward mine. He doesn't have to do much to reach me.

Heat rises, searing my lips. Everything in me breaks into pieces. Every fiber in me begs me to yield.

How does one keep it professional when you're being touched like this?

When you're being kissed like this?

I don't need reminding—that honesty I found years ago is still there. He doesn't have an agenda but to be with me. With the ferocity of his move, his honesty is renewed, not in a shy way.

Tyler presses harder, his tongue teasing my lips.

He asks, not demands. He cares, not intrudes.

I don't leave him knocking for too long.

The sensation of his twirling tongue inside me feels like a touch of a cloud. He's creating a calm, and it's not one that hides a storm—he's that steady. A storm isn't what I'm searching for tonight. He needs to take me there with all the gentleness that he has.

Perhaps feeling my chest tightens, he pulls back, giving me a moment to catch my breath.

"How many liars have you kissed since we parted?" he quips.

"None," I answer with pride.

"Does that mean you didn't kiss at all? Or did you find an honest man or two?"

"You still have no idea what I've gone through, do you?"

He takes a moment to appraise me. His caressing fingers tell me he's reading me, for me. "I just can't believe a beautiful woman like you hasn't caught the attention of another, well, I'd say suitor, but in your case, I guess—another protector? How did you go on by yourself?"

"Because I didn't want to be caught. By anyone. You were the only good guy in my book."

Tyler pulls me back in, and his lust escalates. I reach for the hem of my nightie, rolling it up, tugging it over my head. He welcomes my move with a touch of his palm, softly kneading my bare breast while his lips never leave mine.

"You're magnificent, Morgan," he murmurs over my gaping mouth. Just like his touch, his voice exudes his considerate and patient nature. He doesn't hesitate to increase the intensity but never rushes it—deepening my trust, binding me to him.

"You have a man's kiss." I rub his bulge. His boxer shorts can barely contain his hardened flesh.

"You want *this man*?" he groans, pulling the elastic band of his shorts down past the contour of his hips.

"I've been with too many boys. You're my first man, Ty."

He straightens his back, nudging me to sit on his lap. By this time, the sheets on top of us are shuffled to one side, draping almost to the floor.

I paint his chest with my palm, coasting down his abs. He takes the cue and frees his manhood. Just like his limbs, it's thick, veiny, and sturdy.

I don't even bother to hide my delight. That is a beautifully-carved cock. At the base, his testicles sit firmly between his thighs. And as if I'm reaping my reward, my gut sings at the sight of his generous coat of pubic hair.

I press his chest, asking him to stay there as I voluntarily crawl down until my mouth reaches the head of his penis.

"Morgan…" His pelvis prances as he groans erotically, clearly relishing me licking his gleaming crown. Sweet. Not the buttercream kind of sweet, but musky sweet, turning me on like a dream man.

My mouth slides up his shaft, taking him in as far as I can. His flesh in my throat, this is the closest I've been to him. But it's more than that. My body rackets because of what I'm going to do. I'm proud to be a woman, and there's a time when every woman has to make a choice. It's overdue, and with this man, I cannot wait.

I let his cock go, and Tyler pulls me up, telling me he still wants my lips.

We kiss again—I think this time he's trying to gauge where I want him. And I tell him as it is, whispering, "Lay on top of me, Ty."

He shifts himself sideways, making space on the bed for me to lie on my back. He then rolls on top of me, propping himself with his elbows.

I push my fingers into his curly fringe. "Tyler."

"Yes, Morgan?"

"When I said you're the first man, I meant it."

"I believe you."

"I *really* meant it."

"Morgan?"

"I'd fooled around with those boys, but I'd never let them —" I hold on to his forearms. "We never… I'm still a virgin, Ty."

"Morgan… sweetheart." He holds me, sliding one arm around

my waist and the other caressing my back into my hair. He's still the same Tyler Hunt—solid, full of heat—but his grip is delicate, as if he's been entrusted with a fragile treasure. I've been forced to be tough and independent, but the softness of the contact makes me feel like I'm precious and worthy of his protection.

"You're my first."

"You trust me that much?" his voice breaks faintly.

"I only want to do this with you."

"I've got you." His hold grows into a possessive embrace. It's a kind that signals he won't let any other man come near me—for romantic reasons or not.

Tyler finally lets me go, as delicately as he did taking me. He then descends on me, pressing kisses against my flesh with emotions that can only come from his desire to care for me, to please me. I part my legs, and he reaches for my panties, slowly rolling them along my legs. Then, he rubs himself against me. My skin croons in gratefulness, savoring the tickle from his body hair.

His hand discreetly extends into the drawer of his bedside table. "You wanna be on top?" he offers, sheathing himself.

"No. I want you on top."

He tosses me a reassuring smile—*I've got you.*

I'd been warned by my friends back then not to make your first time a benchmark of what sex was like—or could be like. Some said it was vanilla, some said it hurt like hell, and a lot told me it was like blind leading blind.

But I'm with Tyler. Granted, he's an experienced lover. He has never boasted about it, but he doesn't have to. His touch, his confidence, and his consideration tell me he knows women. Moreover, my visceral instincts drive me to him—following the rainbow between my heart and his—so my body has already felt comfortable with him.

"If you don't like anything I do, just say it, okay? If I hurt you, say it. Promise?"

"Uh-huh." I'm too tense to compose an elegant answer.

He massages me as he makes his way down.

I jolt, feeling his finger touching my opening.

"Is it okay?" He starts playing with it.

My fingers have been there before, trying to teach myself what it would be like. But having his circling my pussy, parting the lips, while maintaining fierce eye contact with me, he has the right of passage. So naturally, like God himself has granted it to him.

He then retracts himself down, brushing my front with his hair in the process. This time, he enlists his tongue to pleasure me—at a different spot.

My legs snap close, not anticipating the titillating sensation from under my skin. No one has told me a woman is sensitive there.

Tyler looks up at me, gauging my reaction. He uses one hand to rub my nipple as if trying to calm me down. It works. Until he starts lapping me up again.

"Ty! Ty!"

Realizing I'm a little too animated, he stops. Just in time before I burst out in tears for the sensation I can't bear.

He meets me again face to face—his eyes fiery, as if asking me permission to do more. His genitals are only an inch away from the top of my pussy, but he continues with his fingers, sliding them in and out, trying to find the spot inside this time. Every spot he touches spurs a reaction from me, so I'm not sure if I'm helping or confusing him.

But the man is already on fire. His impatience shows, but he reins it in.

"I want you," I remind him, and with that, I hope he gets my hint that his impatience is welcome.

The movement of his hips gives a cue that he's about to enter me. But his eyes stay focused, and his hand is back to holding me steady. Like that, he has his guardian look on.

"Relax, sweetheart," he says, perhaps feeling me holding my breath.

Gradually, I feel the tip of his length moving in, replacing his fingers that have been guiding me all this time. He nudges my legs to part wider, and with a little lift of my butt, he glides in so slowly it feels like a ritual.

Rightly so, this is the sacred moment when Tyler Hunt is inside me. I moan and contract from a tingle, one that stands up from the other sensations assaulting my core.

"You okay?" He pulls out a bit. And thanks to his unbelievable control, he manages to soften his shaft just a notch.

There's a reason why it hurts—it's a moment that changes you as a woman. Yet there are more reasons why it is so satisfying. When you do it right, with the right man, the hurt is beautiful.

I sigh out a 'yes,' my eyes on him and him only.

With that, he pushes in again, this time with more rigor, letting me buck and deal with the pleasure however I wish—as if saying, 'Time to let you fly.'

Making love is a matter of the heart as much as it is the body. Maybe because I adore this man so much, or it could be my naivety at the forefront, but every contact feels like I'm about to climax.

He's not in the military anymore, but to me, he's still my SEAL. I'm not a princess, but he sure makes me feel like I'm his queen.

Tyler glides long, in and out with prudent speed, so I feel him. He moves with purpose and with results. The repeated moves rouse me—it's like a skillful skier carving the mountain slopes, choosing his way carefully, leaving beautiful trails in his wake.

My lower abs press in, and my breathing speeds up. It's not snow that he's carving. It's my sanity. Balls of fire form in my core—how am I supposed to stop them? Or am I meant to?

Before I can decide, Tyler pulls out.

I whimper when the last part of his flesh leaves my entrance. The sensation of my pussy stretching and letting go in quick succession takes me by surprise.

"You're still okay there?" he checks in.

"Uh-huh…" I huff.

He clears hair off my face, smiling at me, allowing me to regroup. "Talk to me, sweetheart."

"I'm fine." Call me naïve, but I'm sure I was about to come then. But what about him? "Am I good for you?"

"Morgan, there's nowhere I'd rather be than here with you. You're magnificent. And tonight, it's about you."

"It's about us."

He steals a peck on my lips. "You're right. But *you* have a slightly bigger slice this time. Just tonight," he teases.

I lift my butt, placing my opening right in front of his swelling cock crown.

He enters me again. Every nudge and prod guides me to the point that I'm able to flex my core to fit him. It doesn't take much this time. It's unmistakable. This is what people call 'the edge.'

I whimper as my hips tighten. Tyler pulls out slightly again, but my pussy clenches even tighter. I think he may have wanted to make it last, but I just can't.

He obliges, staying inside me as his mouth reaches for my nipple, sucking it, licking it. Just being in bed with him had gotten me wet—how am I meant to survive his deliberate attempt to stimulate me?

Tyler hugs me with both arms this time. Clearly, I'm not meant to survive this, I'm meant to ride it with him.

"I'm gonna cum, Morgan."

I bury myself in his chest, absorbing his heat, sweat, love, and tenderness.

He releases with a long moan, calling my name as if he doesn't want me to forget him. Who says it's impossible for a woman to enjoy her first? Anything is possible when you're with this man.

I might've gotten lucky—Tyler has the physique and technique to please any woman he wants—but it's the way he reads me and responds to me that makes tonight sexually satisfying as much as it is emotionally fulfilling.

He hurls himself to bed, and soon, my body folds toward him. He strokes me generously, serving almost every inch of me. While I'm still catching my breath, he steals a few kisses on my cheek, sometimes nibbling my ear as if telling me he's still with me.

I involuntarily chuckle.

"What?" he murmurs.

Perhaps he thinks I'm happy to get it out of the way. But really, this isn't about losing my virginity—I haven't lost anything. Making love to Tyler solidifies my deep and exclusive connection with him. It's a spiritual bond that I've never had with anyone else.

I play with his chest.

"What is it with you and hair?" he queries.

I only hum, unable to think, let alone talk. But as I explore his body further, a bumpy patch on his left shoulder compels me to sit up and peer into his skin.

"Hey... hey... don't." He brushes off my discovery.

"Is that...?"

"Morgan, what did I say? Tonight is about you. Not me."

"Ty… is that a gunshot scar?" I remember reading an article about 'a bodyguard' being shot multiple times trying to defend the attorney general. My hand soon expands the search, and I find another spot on his side. "And this too?"

"Morgan, just drop it."

"I sure hope you aren't close to using your nine lives."

"I'm not a cat, sweetheart, but what did I just say?" He takes my hand away from his scar and kisses me, sucking my lips, stopping me from saying anything more.

I lie hopelessly on his shoulder while he keeps caressing me, sending me to purr like my nine lives are safely guarded.

After a while, he slowly slides away from me.

I hum in protest, sensing his escape.

"Sorry. I thought you were asleep. I'm just gonna go clean up, okay? I'll be back."

I peek as he grabs his cock, pulling the filled condom out.

I watch his ass swaying all the way into the bathroom. He then runs himself under the shower. The thought of his wet body lathered with berry-smelling soap pushes me to stay close to him, so I join him.

He lets me stand under the shower, pouring liquid soap over my breasts and spreading it all over with his wide palms.

My arm coasts to his backside, pinching a cheek.

"Hey!" he growls, then tickles me. "Huh! So you did pinch my ass earlier?"

Yeah. The hint that he didn't take.

"I just want to be with you."

He traps me in his embrace, kissing the crown of my head. "You'll never be without me, Morgan. Don't forget that."

Shrouded in his muscle, guarded by his vigilant mind, he won't give fear a chance at me, and he certainly won't let any nightmare come near me tonight.

19

TYLER

"I've packed everything," Morgan says to me in a spirited voice.

She's certainly a different girl this morning. I've seen the effect of orgasm on girls, but that is on another level.

Maybe it's her makeup, but her cheeks glimmer as if she'd just been in the sun. And holy smokes, that red lipstick.

I still remember how those luscious lips looked, wrapped around my—

I must've done something right that she's glowing like this. But somehow, a part of me whirs with questions. Because the effect of last night's orgasm on *me* is so strong that it may just be wrong.

"I've left my books in your library," Morgan informs. "I hope that's okay."

"Of course."

"Now that I've got a proper suitcase, I can be a proper tourist. I won't have to stick out like a sore thumb carrying a filthy backpack."

"I really hope you won't ever need that backpack again."

I raid the fridge and prepare my morning smoothie. My head is split in two—one side rehearsing what I'm going to discuss with Jack once we land in Tampa, the other recalling how last night panned out.

And the split isn't fifty-fifty. My brain has decided to dedicate most of its capacity to think about last night.

Fuck.

"Hey, you okay?" Morgan asks, rubbing my arm.

"I'm fine." I keep the blender running as she looks on. My eyes don't dare wander, locking my sight on the green semi-liquid spinning and shaking inside. I have to repel her energy somehow.

But Morgan has another idea. She rams herself against my back playfully, encircling me with her delicate arms from behind. "I can't decide if I prefer you in a suit or naked." Her voice is low, and one of her hands runs over my tie all the way down to the tip, stopping only when she reaches just above my crotch.

"Morgan, please." I wriggle myself free from her.

"Huh... someone woke up on the wrong side of the bed."

I pour the smoothie into my usual tall glass, then turn to her. "Come on, Wolf Girl. Time to get serious."

"Okay." She steps back, keeping her distance.

"Hey, I think I saw your Gravy earlier." I take a sip of my smoothie. "Poking his head out, observing from the corner of the street. But as usual, he ran away when I approached."

"I'm gonna check him out. Maybe he's back."

I watch her jeans-clad ass swinging as she paces to the living room. My mind is so full of her, how am I going to get through the next four days? I hope Jack's presence will bring back my sanity—and focus.

Since when did I rely on another man to sort myself out?

But before I can even take the first step to take back control, I feel something on my belly. Cold and sticky.

"Oh, fuck!"

This is why I usually have my smoothie first before changing. Why the hell did I flip my routine this morning?

Morgan runs back into the kitchen. "What's wrong?"

Soon, she laughs.

"Not funny, Wolf Girl!" I snap, hopelessly staring at my green-stained shirt and pants. "Gah!"

"Let me help you clean up." She grabs a kitchen towel.

"No. I've ruined my clothes." The goo has even seeped through my underwear! "I'm gonna have a quick shower."

"I can still help you," Morgan insists.

"Please. Be a good girl and wait here." I dart to my room, pushing the door before she can reach me. But I leave it ajar, saying, "Go and check out Gravy. I'll be there in a minute."

She relents, but that's not the end of it.

I strip myself naked and step into the bathroom. Never mind my soap. Her smell is still everywhere, reminding me of the shower with her last night that went on longer than I anticipated.

I stare down at my hands. The bubbles won't let me forget. And the emotional entanglement stemming from my chest is so real I can almost see it tethering me to her.

I've had a few girlfriends, but I've never experienced anything like it. When I was with Morgan, it was like the whole me was inside her. I could feel everything she felt. And it didn't take much to move her.

Every man needs a woman's touch. Call it a physical, psychological, or sexual need. But I think men do because we have our demons, and we need the strength of a woman to help us cope one way or another.

Venice Beach had left a scar in my heart, yet I had kept going back, trying to mend something that could never be unbroken. But with her in it, Venice had transformed, as if it'd been painted a different color.

I'm her partner. I fulfill her needs as much as she does mine, like a pair of trapeze artists taking each other's hands in midair.

I've got her—and that gave 'manhood' a whole new meaning.

I close my eyes, replaying her every wriggle, every writhe, and every moan as I lathered her in this very shower. Her post-sex sensitivity seemed to have no expiry. She even let me rub her pussy then. The water in my hand turned pink for a few seconds, reminding me how privileged I was to be her first.

Jesus Christ.

I turn the tap off, catching my breath as if my aching cock is already inside her sweet body once more.

What if she's right there on the other side, lying in my bed —naked, slick, ready for me?

I dry myself as I open the door.

There's a bark in the distance. Perhaps Morgan has finally found Gravy.

Then, a scream slaps me like I'd been hit by a bolt of lightning.

"Morgan!"

What the hell have I done?

20

MORGAN

"Ty!" I scream.

It's a fucking trap! The man who drew me out by trying to bash Gravy turns out to be Scarf-face's man. Although Gravy manages to get away, now I'm being dragged toward a blacked-out van.

My heart stops seeing who's in the driver's seat.

Whatever I've got to do, Scarf-face cannot take me.

"Ty! Help me!" I can't keep the fear out of my voice.

Where the hell is he? He's been in the shower for ages!

My kidnapper tries to gag me, releasing a hand off my arm. I use the opportunity to push him away. He soon abandons the gag, and with full force, he wrestles me from behind, lifting me, ready to throw me into the van.

Suddenly, a roar.

"Let her go!"

It's more than a roar. It's thunder strong enough to split the atmosphere. It's Tyler when he's mad.

My assailant turns around, shooting at Ty relentlessly. I haven't forgotten the sound of bullets hitting flesh when my brother tried to shield me. This time there are two men aiming at Ty—the man who's holding me and the driver of the van.

Tyler has barely run a towel over himself, but he has turned into a war machine. As if the spray of bullets was just water, the former SEAL keeps charging ahead, and with just one shot, he hits my kidnapper's head.

I run to my man, hiding behind his towering body.

The van drives off behind me. It hasn't gone far before Tyler unleashes another shot with pinpoint accuracy. The front tire is blown, sending the van to a screeching halt.

Seeing movement behind the vehicle, instinctively, Tyler dives on top of me. Bullets soon rain on us as Scarf-face tries to flee. But Tyler's bullet halts the man's run. He drops to the ground, and his head lies motionless.

"Get inside!" commands Tyler. His eyes are that of a tiger.

"I need to see it for myself!" I insist.

"Get inside!"

I reluctantly go back to the house while Tyler, one hand holding his gun and the other sustaining the towel to cover his genitals, marches toward the corpse.

My chest cage is overrun with nervous shudders, watching him remove the scarf. He then up and quickly pivots to join me.

"Is he dead?"

"He is, but it wasn't him."

"Are you sure?" I push myself past him. I need to inspect that corpse with my own eyes!

But Tyler catches me, biting out his anger. "He might've put on weight and gotten a good tan in Florida, but that isn't Scarf-face. His pointy chin couldn't have suddenly turned rounded."

Of course he's a fake! Scarf-face isn't the type who gets deep into an attack. He always observes from a distance.

I throw myself into the sofa. My side is so pinched that I squirm for a second.

"You okay?" He pats me all over. "You hurt?"

"No. I'm fine. Are you?" His expression has changed. Those tiger eyes are angry—and somehow, that anger isn't for the attack.

"I'm gonna get dressed. You stay here, okay? Don't peek out. Don't do anything."

He then calls the police as he plods toward the back of the house.

When I find him in his room, he's done with the call, slumping at the edge of the bed, his face buried in his hands.

"Ty, what's wrong?"

He shakes his head as he tightens the towel around him as if his body is not for me to see. "I'm sorry, Morgan. But last night can't happen again."

"The hell, Ty?" He's blaming me for all this? "You regret it? So all of those emotions that you boasted about, they were all lies?"

"No—"

"Oh no, no." I cut him off. "Let me guess. Last night was a mistake?"

"Emotions are one thing. But sex is something else. This morning was my fault—okay? Not yours. My fault."

"So it was just sex?"

"I didn't mean that, Morgan. Last night meant the world to me. But we're not in Blissville. There aren't rainbows and stars —only bullets." He stands up, then paces along the room. His teeth grit. "I'm a man. I thought I was strong, but I'm not."

"Ty, we're both in this. Scarf-face clearly knows where I am. But it's not your fault. We can still do this together. We can't cancel us."

"Being with you—" He sighs painfully. "It just took over me. I've failed to train my mind that you're not just someone I have to protect."

"You're making me feel like shit, Ty."

"As long as you're safe, if you feel shitty, so be it," he insists. "Promise me last night will never happen again, or I'll assign you to someone else."

"Tyler?" I can feel my face cringe. "What happens to 'You will never be without me,' huh?"

"You're paying Red Mark for this job. I mean it. If you can't promise, someone else will be in charge."

"Now you're reminding me that I'm your client?"

"Damn right. So act like it. Last night never happened and will never, ever happen again."

His anger has subsided, only to be taken over by despair. I know what he did to me last night was genuine. Perhaps it's too genuine, and he's not prepared for the consequences. So it wasn't just me who experienced 'my first.' Seeing how agitated he is, I bet I'm the first who makes him feel this way.

He adds with a quiver, "I was thinking of you in the bathroom just now that I'd forgotten I was supposed to protect you. Now, that was *my* mistake! Please don't let me repeat it. If anything happens to you on my watch, I won't forgive myself, Morgan. I mean it." His stare compels me to take a step back. "Now, please, I need to get dressed."

The door shuts behind me as I swing my legs in frustration. Tyler had defied the impossible last night, yet I've been brought down by reality—the man isn't ready.

Silent cries rip through the lining of my lungs. The pain is sickening, but I remind myself it won't be as bad as the pain of witnessing his death.

I grab Ty's car keys.

I told the lynx in that forest to stay away from me. I should've done the same with Ty. People who got close to me just kept dying. It will be a matter of time before it's his turn. I know he can't get me out of his mind with just a flick of a switch—sex or no sex. But I don't want to be the distraction that leads to his demise.

I reverse the car along the driveway and then pull into the street.

From the rearview mirror, I see him.

"Morgan!" he cries out.

His open shirt flaps in the wind, his cheeks tighten, and his limbs swing as if powered by an engine—I've never seen anyone run so fast.

"Morgan!"

But he's too late.

No matter what he thinks or feels, last night was never a mistake. Love is never a mistake. I'm running away from him because of a reality I didn't see coming. He was my protector. I'd always wanted him to be. Like it was natural, like he was born to do it.

But that also meant he might lose his life so I could live. It wasn't what I signed up for.

Being one with him last night was the kind of irreversible that I will cherish forever. But sending him to the grave is an irreversible act that would end my world.

He's capable, he's well trained, he's made to face danger. But beneath all that, he's a man with a heart that can stop beating. People depend on him—his Red Mark comrades, they're his family even if they're not related by blood. And those kids out there, lost, far from their family with no one even close to finding them—they're the ones who truly need Tyler.

I can't cut short a life so precious.

This is my fight. And just like how my life is meant to be, I'm doing it alone.

21

TYLER

"Morgan!" I keep running, fooling myself I can catch a four-by-four tearing the street at fifty miles per hour.

Huffing, hands on my knees, I finally give up.

Dammit, Morgan!

I've hurt her, I know, but she should've just grown up and listened to me.

Whatever it is, I've screwed up.

I lead men. It's my job. I repel their egos all the time, but dealing with women's feelings turns out to be impossible.

I pause, thinking about my options.

"Kevin!" I run to my neighbor's house.

The sixty-year-old Army vet is standing on his porch, his rifle at the ready. No doubt, the neighborhood is aware of the shoot-out. "Tyler, are you okay?"

"I need your car."

He briefly goes inside and then comes back to me with a key. "Take it."

"Thanks, man!"

The police have arrived. A few of the officers have already

approached the body of the man who dressed up like Scarf-face.

I keep going, zooming past the police cars crowding around the messed-up van, ignoring their signal to stop.

A second later, my phone rings. It's Helena PD Captain Zander. He's Red Mark's ally in the police force, and it used to be Sam or Mark who liaised with him. Now that I'm the head of ops, it's my responsibility. He's a good guy, but at the moment, he's very low on my priority list.

I answer his call anyway. "Yeah."

"Ty, my man says you're fleeing the scene. Something you wanna tell me?"

"I'll give you my report, Zander. But here's what I can tell you right now. I'm working on a case. The two dead men on my street were after my client. She's run away because of them, and I have to find her."

"Okay. You do that. I'll talk to Mark."

This is why I call him a good guy. He understands our operation, and he's not one to hound us for deviating from protocols every now and then.

I'd like to back myself that I know Morgan, but trying to think like her has proven difficult. The first option she has right now is to fly with our chartered plane without me. Well, technically, it's her flight. She paid for it.

"Cee," I call Cora-Lee at Red Mark. "However you do it, get Helena airport to stop our chartered flight."

"Right away."

"The tower might not like it, but you've just got to try."

"I've got this, Ty."

"Stay out of trouble, okay?" I warn her. Cee is a computer whiz. I can see her going the back way to get things done for me. I just want to make sure the word 'hack' isn't on her mind today.

Reading Cora-Lee is like interpreting sets of zeroes and ones—hard but readable. In contrast, trying to understand Morgan is like navigating a room filled with tangled threads.

When I get to the airport, the plane is still on the tarmac. The pilot and crew are ready, but there's no sign of Morgan.

Fuck me!

I should've known. I didn't even need to read her. *She* had told me about her strategy, that she often took the more discreet routes, even if it meant a longer journey. With the current situation, it can mean anything! If I've lost her in one of the national parks in Montana, I'm finished.

Cora-Lee calls as I return to my car. "You found her?"

"No. She's not there."

"Well, you may not want to hear this. But perhaps she didn't want your company—or protection. If that's the case, there's nothing you can do, Ty."

The Red Mark tech is right, but there's no way I'm going to let Morgan fight this alone.

"Cee, what's the next best thing a wolf biologist would do to disappear, apart from going into the wild?"

Although Morgan is recovering well, her feet are still not a hundred percent. Besides, time isn't on her side. She won't go on foot.

"I don't know. Maybe hitchhike?"

"I don't think she'll do that." I close my eyes, picturing her.

"Are you sure she hasn't flown with a commercial airline?"

"I doubt it." I keep thinking. It takes me a while to picture her without her backpack. *She's lugging a suitcase.* I put her in different scenes, different transportation modes. "The bus! Cee, contact all bus companies in Montana and see if someone named Emma Schiffer or Meredith Bennett is one of their passengers. She has to go to an airport at some stage."

As if I can smell her trail, I keep driving south. The vision of her pings at me like a beacon. She wouldn't have chosen Helena as her departure point—it's too close. The next possibility is—

"Ty, your car has been spotted," Cee reveals.

"Don't tell me. Butte bus station?"

"How do you know?" Her voice curls. I'm sure she's frowning as if I'm playing tricks on her.

You can take a bus from Butte to a lot of places. It's far enough from my house that she might've gambled I wouldn't look there. At the same time, it's close enough that she could disappear quickly.

Cee carries on, "But there's no passenger by the name of Emma Schiffer or Meredith Bennett."

"She might have another name. I'm on my way!"

The station is less than two hours from my house, so there's a big chance that I may have already missed her. But I should be able to get information on which bus she took.

There's one bus that's still loading passengers.

Is that her?

I sprint toward the vehicle, ignoring people's grumbles for cutting the line. I scour the inside, trying to locate the girl who attracted my attention.

I huff in despair. She looks like her, but it's not her. How could I even have mistaken her for Morgan?

"Hey!" the driver calls out. "You got a ticket, man?"

Just as I turn my head toward him, in the background, I see a face in the window of another departing bus.

"Morgan!" I shout.

My car is on the other side of the building, but I've got to stop that bus. I run inside the station, calling to one of the people behind the counter. "You've got to stop that bus!"

"You're the police? Show me your badge."

"No, I'm not with the police, but someone is in that bus, and she's in danger."

"Stop the bus. Get the driver to turn around." A voice of authority compels me to swivel. "Mr. Hunt." The man approaches me.

There are two possibilities. Either this man has received a word or two from Red Mark, or he's as desperate to get his hands on Morgan as I am.

"Who are you?" I ask. My hand is ready to pull my gun.

"I'm on your side, Mr. Hunt. I'm the station manager."

I turn to the operator, who has just called the driver to stop. "Don't let any passengers out!" Then I face the station manager again. "How did you know my name?"

"Tia Grant's case. Her mother Betsy works here. She told me what happened to her daughter. I know you saved Tia, Mr. Hunt. I trust that you really needed to stop that bus."

I gulp, my heart calms just half a beat. "Thank you."

"This way," the man leads me to the returning bus. "Open the door, let the gentleman in," he orders the driver.

And there she is, her face as furious as an erupting volcano.

"Miss Emma Schiffer," I call, extending my hand to her. I don't know what name she used to get on this bus, but I bet that's the name she hates the most.

Lips pressed tightly together, eyes wide like an angry pug, she stands up, collects her backpack, and follows me out.

"Piss off!" she gripes as I try to grab her arm.

I insist on holding her. "Don't say anything until we're in the car."

I leave my neighbor's car in the parking lot and head to my own instead, led by Morgan. I'll get someone to drive the old man's wheels back to Helena.

Morgan knows better than to make a scene and gives me my car key back. She then dives into the passenger seat quietly.

"Don't you ever, *ever*, do that again!" I warn.

"I have the right to go!" she thunders. "You don't have a say in what I do. Got that?"

"Oh, I do have a say." I take short breaths, recalling a dire mistake I made. Venice, eleven years ago. One that has defined my life ever since. "Look, I've lost someone because I had let things slide, staying silent, doing nothing, letting go. I'm not going to make the same mistake with you."

"It was a mistake to find you."

I know my anger only fuels hers. But what I'm feeling inside is not anger. It's fear. For the first time in my life, I feel it. And the only reason I do is because I've never loved anyone as much as I love her.

"Morgan, let me protect you while we try to find your sister. Isn't that what you wanted?"

"I will find my sister. Alone."

I shake my head, unable to fathom her stubbornness. "You're just pissed because you think I regretted the sex."

"Wasn't it good, Ty? Come on, man up and say it! But the truth is, I ran away not because you regretted the best moment I've ever had with a man." She takes a breath, straightening herself. "I can't afford to take casualties."

"You think you're better than me?"

"I know the situation better than anyone. I've lived it in the past two years."

"Gimme some credits here. I was in the Navy for almost a decade. I was a SEAL for half of it. I'd fought alongside the best. I'd faced enemies who were ready to blow us to pieces. And that hasn't stopped—I'm with Red Mark, and I fight just as hard."

"I don't dispute that."

"This—rescuing and protecting—is what I do day in and day out. And I'm committed to doing it for you, for your sister.

But don't think being on the run makes you more capable than a trained sailor. Drop the stubbornness, Morgan. Grow up!"

"Listen, Mr. Steadfast!" Her voice travels like a bullet.

I let the bullet hit me while frowning at her choice of calling me. Really, Mr. Steadfast? "What, Morgan?" I keep up my—steadfastness.

Somehow, she mellows. "Look. It's not the sex, okay?" She takes the time to look me in the eye. "Seeing you so close to death…"

"Trust me, Morgan, I'd been a lot closer to death than I was this morning. You've seen those scars."

Her shoulders slump, her face stricken. "Ty, you're not helping."

"I got those scars because I tried to protect others. But may I remind you, none of them was more precious than you are. I've told you. If anything happens to you, I won't ever forgive myself."

"Yes, I've seen those scars on your body. It was like reading your career history. But seeing the event unfolding with my own eyes? God, Ty. You have no idea! You're not the only one who won't forgive oneself."

"I'm not gonna give you any choice, Morgan. We'll go through with this together, whether you like it or not. You can't fire me."

"Oh well, I can!"

"I'm your man. You chose me. I can't separate emotions from the mission because it's you. And I know I won't be able to change it. *We* won't be able to change it. I just have to adapt. And I promise you, I will do my job as much as I will take care of your heart."

Her head bows, her lips part. "If I were your client, I would be firing you now. But you said it yourself: you're my man. Maybe the right word is divorce."

"Not even marriage is more binding than what we have. Come on, admit it!"

She closes her eyes, and her expression almost mimics the agony on her face when she wrestled with her nightmare.

I touch the top of her hand. She stays still.

"I heard those bullets, Ty," she murmurs. "Hissing past my ears. And I know it's impossible—but I saw those bullets like missiles seeking their target. Their target was you. *You*. Those bullets were going to tear your flesh, rip your organs, take you away from me."

She withdraws her hand from under my hold, and slams it over her lips, trying to stop herself from crying.

"Hey, listen." I soften my voice.

"People were dying around me, Ty." She shakes. "My brother.... Hudson... he died because of me."

"No, that's not true, Morgan."

"He wanted to take it slow, but I urged him to get to the airport so we could fly to Helena. We were out there like sitting ducks."

"There was a reason you thought it was the best way. Time was of the essence. I would've done the same. You can't blame yourself for that, sweetheart." I know it's easier said than done. But guilt is a bitch. It eats you alive, but I'm not going to let it destroy her—not like me carrying mine for over a decade.

"Well, maybe you know how it feels. You've been on many battlefields. You put aside your emotions, didn't you say?"

"Yes. But it caught up on me."

"I was bathed in his blood, Ty," she sobs. "He shielded me while those bullets hit his back."

"I'm sorry. I'm so sorry, Morgan." I round my arm to get me to my side, but she wriggles herself free.

At this time, I've almost forgotten that she's only twenty-one. I told her to grow up. And she has. She had no choice but to grow up fast, and she's done a damn good job of it. But inside, she's a girl desperate for a shoulder to lean on.

"Those dying people were my family," she gulps. "And you, you're my only family left. And you were about to do it for me. Taking those bullets. I couldn't go through it again."

"I'm sorry I've been too harsh on you."

"While you were in Afghanistan, I kept checking the casualty list—praying that I'd never see the name Tyler Hunt on it. I checked it every day. Every. Fucking. Day." She sniffles.

This time I pull her into me, and I'm not looking for her permission. She's shaking in my embrace, but she's never weak. My Wolf Girl is the steadfast one. And now I see how deeply she cares about me. She was right all along. This isn't just about the sex—this is all of her that she surrenders to me.

"Please forgive me," I murmur, kissing the crown of her head.

"You're my only family, Ty. That's how I see you."

"I am your family, Morgan. And whoever you need me to be. I am that man."

This time, she lets everything out—her sobs, her tears, her howls. A part of me wishes I could take all those away from her. But I bet she had never had a chance to cry, let alone grieve. She needs this, and by the veracity of her hold, I know I'm the only one she would ever open up to like this.

I cradle her as she collapses. "I'm here for you, Morgan. And I'm telling you, I don't regret last night, and I'm humbled by everything you've given me. I said what I said because no one else has ever meant as much as you to me."

After a deluge of emotions, she loosens her grip on me. She's no longer shaking. "I can't lose you, Ty."

"No," I whisper to her. "You leave, you'll lose me. You stay, and we'll go a long way. I promise."

22

———

MORGAN

Emotions spread through me, settling in my heart and sending peace and contentment. 'We'll go a long way,' he said. And that's just what I need to restore my faith in the chaos. I have found my true partner.

I tighten my arms around him once again, not ready to let him go just yet.

Meeting Tyler had taught me how to separate boys from men. Now, being in his arms, after a heart-to-heart that has melted us both, he has shown me what separates great men from ordinary ones.

"I guess this is the consequence of having feelings." I end our hug.

"And what is that?" He tucks my hair behind my ear.

"That you simply can't live without the person you have feelings for. They stay, Ty. How did you do it when you were on deployment? You weren't single then."

"No. I wasn't. But when we were out there, we tried not to think about our wives, girlfriends, or families. But you could never train yourself to forget."

"No. You never forget." I shake my head, trying to imagine how hard it must've been. I shift myself toward him, wanting an answer to something he mentioned earlier. I've got a feeling it's the same person that compelled him to inscribe the Latin saying on his body. "Who did you lose, Ty? You said you lost someone because you let things slide."

He lets out a suffering sigh. "A dear friend. But please, I don't want to talk about it now."

"Okay." I understand. The man needs space, and I'm happy to give it.

"How have you dealt with your loss, Morgan?"

"I haven't," I concede. "Memory is the worst and best thing about being alive. I don't want to forget, yet I do. But life can change in an instant. I guess we've got to have a system that keeps reminding us how it happened. How I lost my parents, my brother, my aunt. It's still destroying me. I can't go through another loss like that. And right now, you're the only possible loss that will end my world."

He rests his face on the side of my neck, breathing into my skin as if trying to comfort me. "I will never let you hurt like that again. You hurt, I hurt, Morgan." His chin lingers on my shoulder as he whispers close to my ear.

After a moment, he lifts himself, his fingers parting my fringe. But no words.

"So, where to from here?" I sigh.

His face is tinged with discomfort. "Last night changed me, Morgan."

Now, I see his statement in a different light. "Tell me, Ty. Be honest with me."

"I feel like I'm going into battle with skills I haven't acquired yet."

"The sex is still bothering you?"

"No. It's not the sex. It all goes back to feelings. How do I numb them?"

"I don't want you to numb your feelings for me. That's not what I want."

"What you want is for us to find Lilly. Right now. I'm talking about right now."

"Yes, but—"

"As a SEAL, I was great at compartmentalizing things. I want that back, but with you by my side."

"We can do this, Ty. We're not distractions to each other. We're each other's strength."

A smile paints his face, and it's getting wide. "Tell you what. We protect each other. That's the only thing we can do."

"Yeah, all right." Although I have no idea how to protect him.

"You've survived all these years not just because of your physique or defensive skills but because you're smart and know how to control your emotions."

"Well... until you."

"Point taken. Regardless, now that we're aware we can't put aside our feelings toward each other, we'll embrace it. I know you can show us how, Wolf Girl. You're strong that way. So I trust that you will be a great protector of mine."

If he puts it that way, I might be able to pull this off. "Deal. I protect you."

"And I protect you," he says.

It sounds equal, but I know he will be doing the heavy lifting.

Sensing that we're about to leave soon, I look around, extending my neck to try to see over other cars.

"Hey." He squeezes my hand.

"I'm not planning to run away if that's what you're thinking."

"No," he denies, appraising me. "Protective instincts starting to kick in?"

I chuckle. "I guess."

He then assesses me. Serious. "Do you think you're being followed?"

"No. It's just—automatic. Looking left and right, forward and back. I don't think anyone followed me here."

He seems to agree.

"Although I'm still jittery about going back to Helena and getting on that chartered flight," I explain.

"No one knew where that plane was heading."

"I know. But what if Scarf-face smells something about a canceled private flight?"

"I've got an idea. You trust me?"

I cock my eyebrows, giving him a yes.

He makes a call. "Cee, Ben is due to leave for Billings tonight?" He pauses. "Ask him if he fancies taking himself and the team there, executive-style." He listens in, then ends the call with a laugh.

"You're volunteering the plane to take the Red Mark men? I'm all for that."

"And, we can catch our flight from Billings. A reset. A clean slate."

"Good plan, Tyler Hunt!" I praise. "And we can spend a few hours bonding while driving to the airport?"

"Even a better plan." He turns to me, reaching for my lips.

God bless us. That honesty is the best a man can give you. But as our mouths dance, deepening our contact, heat starts to spread between us.

I nudge my head back to draw a breath. He quickly cups my chin as if not wanting our lips to part too far. In the end, he moves back too, just enough so he can look into my eyes.

"I don't want to spend a day without seeing those eyes," he mutters.

The corner of my lips lifts. He may be talking about my eyes, but heavens above, those brilliant blue eyes are paralyzing me. The color of Venice water. The first things that emerge in front of me out of the ocean, ones my heart readily took as a sign of safety.

"And that smile," he adds.

"No, you won't."

He runs a finger under my chin as he finally lets go. "Ready?" He turns on the engine.

"Yeah. Let's go."

He takes his SUV slowly, pulling into the street. Curiously, he keeps his speed down, eyes hopscotch between the rearview and the side mirrors. After about half a mile, he speeds up.

He's not taking any chances—he has to be sure no one's tailing us.

"So, where were you going?" he asks casually.

"Billings."

Curiosity fills his gaze. "And, what was your name this time? I knew it wasn't Emma or Meredith."

"Ty, don't." My attempt to be serious quickly falls to pieces.

"Come on. Humor me."

"Audrey Baker."

Tyler throws his head back, shaking with laughter. It takes him a while to settle himself, and then he says, "What did you do to annoy your mother, Morgan?"

"I wish I knew, Ty. I wish I knew."

Tyler rubs my arm, giving me a quick kiss—perhaps an attempt to stop me from getting emotional thinking about my mother. But I'm okay, really okay.

"So, what was your plan after Billings?" he probes.

"I was planning to fly to Vegas."

His face lights up. "Vegas?"

"Yeah. I figure it would be relatively easy to disappear from there. I don't think Scarf-face would've guessed that."

"No. No one would've!"

I glance at him. Boy, I bet he's glad that bus didn't leave with me on it.

23

TYLER

As expected, Jack is waiting for us when we land in Tampa. The Kelleher trademark handsomeness is there on display, although he's taller than his older brother Sam. There's a whole six-foot-six of him! And I've been told Sam takes after their father while Jack is the spitting image of their mother.

"Tyler Hunt, welcome to Florida." The thirty-two-year-old Marine shakes my hand. I haven't met the guy before, but the handshake feels so familiar. I could be back in San Diego, and this man in front of me could be a Marine Lieutenant who has just welcomed me to his briefing.

"Great to meet you, Jack." Standing close to him, I can almost say that he's Ben Winter 2.0, perhaps with a bit more charm. When Jack smiles like that, there is a bit of Sam in him. "I'm sorry about the delay." I glance at Morgan, who's holding her smile.

"Not a problem," Jack says.

"This is Morgan Blackwell," I introduce my partner in crime, rounding my arm around her waist. Not that Jack is showing any interest in her, but just a nudge to say *she's mine*—I can't help it.

"Nice to meet you, Miss Blackwell."

"Please, Morgan. Nice to meet you, too. The delay was on me. Thanks for doing this for us."

"Pleasure is all mine. This way." Jack leads us to his car. "Just so you know, Eduardo Callas is one of the most wanted in Tampa and Florida in general. One of his associates was arrested last week. He got caught trying to smuggle two boys out to Honduras."

He has been speaking to us in a typical military tone, but his voice dulls a bit when he conveys the last message as if it reminds him of his own ordeal.

Jack resets himself. "Meanwhile, Callas has been under the radar. When that happens, usually he's planning something big."

"Anything on Scarf-face?" I check.

"Unfortunately not. I must admit, when you told me about that figure in the background, I was shocked. We'll find out who that mysterious scarfed man is, but let's focus on Callas—he was the one seen with Lilly."

"So, do you know where Callas operates from?" Morgan asks.

"Good question. I did find a couple of locations that you need to look at. For now, let's get you two to your hotel."

I'm not sure how much Sam has briefed Jack about our travel style, but his younger brother seems to understand what it means by 'no expense spared.' He has chosen a boutique hotel—classic Art Deco, so glamorous we may bump into a few celebrities.

Delight paints her face. After two years on the run, she deserves this kind of luxury.

Following our check-in, Jack leaves us as he takes the room next door.

Morgan and I plod around, surveying the room. "Certainly an upgrade to what we had in Venice," she banters.

Indeed. This room is a suite—it has everything except a grand piano.

"We've got to discuss plans," I say to Morgan. "Do you mind if I invite Jack in here?"

"Of course not. Call him. I'm gonna take a quick shower."

"You've got everything?" I observe the pile of clothes draping over her forearm.

"Yeah. Don't worry. I won't come out naked."

I give her a side glare. In response, she pokes her tongue out. She's such a tease like that!

Jack comes in with a folder.

"I really appreciate you doing this, Jack."

"When Sam told me about Lilly Blackwell, I had no second thoughts whatsoever. I want to help." He puts the folder on the dining table, then glances at my holster. "Do you shoot left-handed?"

"Yeah. I was a sniper in my SEAL team. A left-hander makes a better shooter."

"Huh!"

"And lover," I quip.

"I like you, Ty. Don't make me change my mind."

Suddenly, I hear Morgan call. "Ty, could you pass me my lotion? It's the skinny green bottle with 'aloe' on the label. It should be in a small bag inside the suitcase."

"Sure. Hang on." I rummage into the overnight case and find the object in question. "Here it is, sweetheart." I pass it on to her hand as she opens the door slightly. I can't help peeking in, and I can see her blowing a kiss to me.

"So she's your sweetheart, huh?" Jack smirks as I rejoin him.

"Yeah."

"You must know her well. It took you less than two seconds

to find what she was after. I've heard about women and their things."

"I just got lucky," I chuckle, staring at the bathroom door. I can smell the aloe vera seeping out. "She's gone through a lot," I tell Jack. "I really hope we find her sister soon."

"Sam told me. I wouldn't have guessed. She seems... feisty."

"You have no idea!"

Jack pulls up a chair. "So, has Sam told you about me?"

"That you were kidnapped as a child?"

"So he did." He taps his fingers on the table. "That's good. Because I wouldn't be able to tell you that myself."

"I'm sorry about Sister Laura."

"Thanks. She was really good to me," he replies quickly. But then he pauses, apparently mulling over another question. "Does Morgan know?"

"She does."

"Good. Good. We're a team. I don't want my past to be treated like a secret. And just so you know, pity isn't welcome."

"No good man deserves to be pitied. But I must ask you personally, Jack. You're going into a territory that smells a lot like your past. You may even be dealing with the same organization that was responsible for your kidnapping. You sure you're up for this?"

"Straight to the point. I like it. And I'm telling you straight, Chief." So he knows I retired from the Navy as a Chief Warrant Officer. "I'm a Marine. And Marines don't do jobs half-ass."

I pat his shoulder, acknowledging his commitment. The rivalry between SEALs and Marines is often told from the wrong perspective. Yes, we're competitive bunches, but we have enormous respect for each other. And since the first minute I saw him, my respect for this man is instant.

He carries on. "I'm not afraid to return to my past. How do you think I know about Callas and his hideouts and whatnot?"

"How?"

"For every hour I'm not on duty, I've been tracing my steps back to the time when my life stopped. I've made it my mission to find the man responsible for destroying my childhood. And in the process, like you said, I am immersing myself in environments that smell a lot like my past."

"Don't you just want to let go?

"You sound like my brother. I know he wants to protect me. But I can't, Tyler. I can't." He whips his head, looking away. "Anyway, we're not here to talk about me."

The bathroom door clicks open. Morgan strides out and immediately notices the folder Jack brought in with him.

"So what's the plan tomorrow?" she asks.

"Morgan," Jack says. "There's something I want to tell you about the sketch."

"Go on," she presses.

"Callas and his men, when they take in a girl, they treat her like a slave. I'm sorry to be blunt, but that's how it is."

"I understand," Morgan trembles.

"But this." Jack points to a copy of the sketch. "For him to be side by side with your sister like this, there's something more."

"You think Lilly ran to him willingly? She would never do that!" she protests.

I tap the top of her palm, telling her I believe her.

Jack continues, "I'm not saying she did. I mean, this sketch is amazingly detailed, and you can see her face is far from happy. I'm just saying there may be another explanation," he argues. "I've been scouring through many kidnapping cases to find my own story, Morgan. Some things will surprise you beyond what you can comprehend. You need to keep an open mind."

"As long as we find her," she determines. "Explanations can come later."

"So, where are the two locations?" I ask.

"There's a farm just past the monastery. My sources told me Callas owns it. We haven't seen any movements, but it doesn't mean there's nothing there." Jack presents us with the photos of the farmhouse.

"Okay." I keep pondering.

"The other location is an apartment two blocks from here. It's also owned by Callas. A luxurious pad. Two bedrooms. Allegedly, he uses the place for meeting new buyers." He lays out the photos of the apartment next to the farmhouse set.

I inspect all the pictures.

Jack looks at me intensely. "What are you thinking?"

"If Lilly was not taken to be trafficked, Callas might've let her stay in a decent accommodation. Let's start with the apartment."

"Good thinking, Chief."

Morgan hums positively, apparently agreeing with my call.

"Callas' ring is super-efficient, super sensitive to police's presence. They'd rather hide and wait than take chances. I haven't told anyone at the Tampa PD except the captain, whom I trust one hundred percent."

"Good."

"You've got an hour."

"An hour?"

"It's not a terribly big place. It should give you enough time. If you find nothing, you get out of there quietly. Clean. As if you've never been there."

"And if I do?"

"You get Lilly out. Get yourselves to safety. Then give me a sign, and I'll deal with the police."

"An hour..." I mumble, trying to work out my course of action.

"Eduardo Callas is a very dangerous man. You won't want to stretch your luck."

"I understand, LT," I call out, using his current rank.

"I'm coming with you!" Morgan says. "Lilly will only trust me."

"Morgan, as soon as Lilly is safe, you will be the first person to see her. I promise," I say.

She groans, shaking her head.

"We've made a pact, Wolf Girl. Protect us by staying here with Jack. Or I'm calling this off."

She doesn't like it, but if things get hairy in there, I don't want her to be caught in it.

"Fine," she finally relents.

"I'll go out at first light," I decide.

Jack leaves the room.

Eyes half closed, Morgan plods to the bed, curling up under the sheets. She's one tired girl.

I slink down next to her, and as usual, she rests her head on my chest, purring away. I survey the decorated ceiling and vintage chandelier. I should be with her on a romantic getaway in this hotel. But I remind myself once again—I'm her protector.

UNDER THE SOFT light of dawn, I make my way to Callas' apartment.

Since Sam contacted him about Lilly, Jack had spent days surveying the apartment, and he managed to catch the code to the front door. Thanks to a suspected cleaner who was too slow and casual in punching in the keys.

For such a big man to be invisible, I'm pretty impressed with his strategy, although he simply winked at me when I asked how he did it. At the same time, I wonder if this surveillance business has become his obsession. I understand why my boss is a bit concerned about his brother. But just like any of my partners, I've got Jack's back—whatever he does.

I pad sideways through the hallway, my back to the wall. One, to minimize the noise, and two, without any lighting, I need to use it as a guide.

The hallway leads me to a large room. Convinced that the room is empty, I turn on my flashlight.

This place is a palace, all right, but it's as ghostly as an abandoned hotel.

I keep my Glock pointed at the space in front of me, ready for anything.

It's a living room. All the furniture seems to be in its place, and the curtains are closed with their tiebacks neatly folded. I skip the other rooms and head into the kitchen. Clean. Like a showroom. Fridge is empty, glasses and plates are on the shelves. I doubt anyone lives here or even uses the space regularly.

I keep scanning as I explore the rest of the apartment, stopping at the first bedroom. The bed is covered with a white sheet, and the closets are empty. The bathroom is bone-dry, no smell, no nothing.

The sunlight starts to break as I approach the second bedroom. I might not even need an hour after all.

But something keeps tugging me from my gut—like a hunch telling me the next discovery is only around the corner.

I stay in the bedroom and systematically check the space. Just like the other, I can't find anything.

I pause, taking a breath—sticking with my gut.

Why does it feel different? It's not because the bed is made or because the décor feels feminine. This room feels like it has been holding someone's heartbeat.

I open every closet door once more, every drawer, every shelf. I trail my hands along the walls, combing for gaps, hollow spaces, or loose sections.

Nothing.

Until I stop next to a bedside table. There's something under the tip of my shoe.

I step away from the object. It's the end portion of a chain spilling out from under the table.

I stoop low, shining my torchlight through the gap between the table legs.

"Lilly..." I reach for the chain and pendant—a black rose pendant, exactly like Morgan's.

Dammit! Now I wish I had more than an hour.

After securing the precious jewelry in my zip pocket, I rush to double down on my search. There's got to be more!

Back in the living room, something catches my attention. It's traveling along the floor, no bigger than a marble, but it's light and airy. It's a ball of fluff, probably from one of the rugs, rolling back and forth, blown by a soft breeze. There's air coming from behind one of the shelves.

I run my fingers along the outline of the shelf, and something clicks. It's a door leading down to some kind of basement.

"Fuck me..." Someone must be living down here to create such a strong smell of... life—although a concerning one.

I descend one step at a time. There's a bend at the end of the stairs. That makes me believe it's more than just a basement. I think it's a tunnel—maybe leading to the adjacent building?

After running unchallenged for about thirty feet, a steel sliding door stops me in my tracks. It's heavily padlocked.

I give it a knock, trying to gauge what kind of response I'll get.

It's silent, apart from—

No way!

Whimpers.

Girls' whimpers. Desperate, hopeless, painful—I've got to go in!

I shoot the padlock and haul the door to slide it open.

No matter how many battles you've won, no matter how much you've gained or lost in the process, you'll never be prepared for a scene like this.

Ten girls are lying or sitting on mattresses that may be as damp as the sewer. Hell, this place smells worse than a sewer! Some of the girls stay still, and some of them shift themselves toward the wall, hugging themselves. Leftover food is scattered on the floor, along with a few bottles of water. In a corner, there are a couple of buckets, which I'm sure are the only facilities these girls are allowed to use.

"Don't be scared. I'm not gonna hurt you." I control my breathing despite the angry heat rising in my chest. At the same time, I stay alert, studying the terrified faces. "Lilly? Is one of you Lilly Blackwell?"

I'm met by shakes of their heads. I don't think she's here. These girls are way younger than fourteen.

"Please help us." The voice is no more than a whisper. I'm surprised the girl has the courage to speak up at all.

"I'll help you, I promise."

I scan the space once more, thinking how I'm going to get these girls out. Two of them may be able to walk with me, but the others are either looking too scared or too weak.

Silence takes over—all eyes are on me, anticipating my next move. Now, I hear thumping noises right above me. It could be the cleaners that Jack mentioned. But judging by the girls' demeanor, I know danger is coming.

"Don't leave us!" another girl begs.

The protocol is if I don't find Lilly, I should get out cleanly without anyone seeing me. I will call Jack and get him to get the police in here, but how fast will they come? There's no way I'm going to leave these girls to chance. Whoever is coming, they'll take them away. They'll hurt them. I am their chance for safety and freedom.

"Fuck!" I grumble. No cell reception.

The footsteps are getting closer. My only option is to face them here. I back myself to take them down as long as the girls stay calm.

I venture further from the steel door toward the stairs, and as soon as a reception bar appears, I make the call.

But something brushes the side of my leg. A small figure slides past me. With a scream so loud, I'm sure whoever is up there now knows something is going on down here.

"No! No!" I call the girl, chasing her up the stairs.

I only have half a second to calm her and to get through to Jack.

24

———

MORGAN

"Tyler! Talk to me!" Jack answers his phone. I eyeball him, and he immediately puts it on speaker.

"Call the police. There are ten girls in the basement. I can't do it alone."

"Basement? That place has no basement!" But Jack doesn't go on about the new discovery. "Stay on the line, Chief. I'm calling the police with my other phone."

Jack makes the call while on his other phone, Tyler curses, "Shit! They're here!"

I hear his breath coming out of the speaker as if he was with me. Then, relentless gunfire. I feel like I'm choking on my own teeth. Maybe it's a good thing—with my throat filling with nervous clumps, I'm not giving myself a chance to talk to him in hysteria. It's not going to help him.

Tyler's call cuts off.

"Jack! You've got to get to him!" I shake his shoulder despite his figure dwarfing me.

"No. Tyler will kill me in my sleep! You're my priority here."

"Tyler is *our* priority. Trust me, Jack. I'll be fine here."

His eyes flare as a groan vibrates in his throat.

"Jack, go!" I order.

He snatches his gear and rushes to the door. "Stay inside, close all the curtains. Keep your phone close."

"Go!"

My fear of Scarf-face and the dreaded feeling of getting caught are nothing compared to the not-knowing. Not knowing what the hell is going on with Ty. The only thing I can do now is to trust him. As he's repeated several times—he's capable, he's well trained.

I sit on the bed, my hands clasped as if I was praying.

While all windows in my room are closed, this art-deco building has a generous number of windows along the hallway. And unlike modern hotels, the doors here aren't airtight.

A shadow moves, disturbing the sunlight coming through the gap at the bottom of the door. It could be housekeeping doing their morning round. But after being on the run for so long, you know when you're being watched. You feel it when you have dodgy company.

Someone is pacing in front of my door.

I've got to get out of here, somehow.

I part the curtains of my window, checking for any presence outside. There is no adjacent building where someone can see me directly, and down below, it's a garden. We're on the second floor. I'm sure I can find my way down.

I grab Tyler's cap and put on my sunglasses. I open the window warily.

Here's another thing about Art Deco buildings. They have tiers, flat and straight, which make them the perfect stepping stones to get to the bottom.

There's a concrete canopy that runs about half the width of the side wall, providing shade to the walkway under it. I make myself as skinny as possible, then scale down the window ledge onto a protruding chevron decoration. It's like a rock-climbing wall, only I don't have a safety net.

Finally, I make the jump onto the canopy. I'm sure I'm now close to the first floor. I crouch to the ground, observing a balcony beneath me.

A man in a chef's uniform is having a smoke. That door may lead to the kitchen.

The chef snuffs out his cigarette with his boot, then heads inside. I jump onto the balcony. It turns out the door leads to a staff locker room. Like I belong there, I smile ay people, pushing my way through the narrow corridor to get to the main area of the hotel.

And I'm out.

I increase my pace, going toward the location of Callas' apartment but keeping on the other side of the road. Police are already there, and my God... there are a lot of girls being ushered out. Ten-year-olds, maybe—and there's no sign of Lilly.

After assessing my surroundings, I slip into a park to get a different vantage point. I move from tree to tree, but soon something halts my step.

A man is crouching behind a hedge. The man isn't doing his morning Tai Chi. He's handling a rifle and is aiming at someone on the other side of the road.

Ty!

I speed up, although I remain stealthy. On the way, I pick up an oak branch that has fallen onto the grass. The man is so focused he doesn't even sense me. And I don't give him time to. I whack the back of his head, and he drops to the ground without even twitching.

I take a few steps back, hiding but keeping watch of the man. I call Ty, trying to locate him behind the passing traffic.

A red sedan whooshes past. The speed! Is that the way people drive here?

"Morgan? Are you okay?" Tyler says on the phone.

"Yeah, I'm fine." I hold on to my cap as breezes sweep through the park.

"You don't sound like you're in a room... Morgan, where are you?"

"I'm at a park opposite you."

"Jesus Christ! What did I say?" he grumbles.

"Ty, just get your ass over here."

He grumbles some more, but I can see him powerwalking in my direction. As soon as he's close, I give him a small wave.

I nod at the unconscious man, still on the ground, and his rifle is on a tripod.

"Jesus... what the hell?"

"He tried to shoot you, Ty."

He quickly secures the man's wrists with flexi-cuffs.

"Come on, we've got to get out of here." Ty takes me in his arms. "You're okay?"

"I'm fine."

We make our way out of the park. His hold is relentless. I glance at his sun-kissed face. Only now, I realize I've honored our promise—that I'll protect him.

We stroll hand in hand like any other couple on the street as if recreating Venice.

In the meantime, he calls Jack. "We've got a fourth man out at a park opposite. He won't be unconscious for long."

I listen in, and I hear Jack reply, "Get back to the hotel. Get Morgan."

"Not necessary."

"What? Are you on drugs?"

I scoff. "She's with me."

"I'll be damn!" Jack mumbles over the speaker. "And I take

it she's got something to do with making that fourth man unconscious?"

Ty and I look at each other, and he rubs my shoulder—*I'm proud of you.*

"Told you she's feisty," Jack comments. "I'll get our things from the hotel. Call me when you're ready to meet up."

"Yeah." He then hangs up.

"I saw those girls. So, Lilly wasn't there?" I ask nervously.

"No. I'm sorry. But I found this."

It's her necklace! I grasp it and hold it close to my chest. "You didn't miss any secret door, chamber, or anything?"

He shakes his head regretfully. "No. Sorry. Your sister had been there, but she's gone."

"We were too late."

"Your friend saw Lilly weeks ago. Chances are, she's been taken elsewhere."

This is the closest I've been to my sister. Yet something pounds at me hard from the inside. "Do you think she's dead?"

"No," he asserts. "If they wanted her dead, they would've killed her along with your parents."

He's right.

We keep walking.

"What happened at the hotel?" Ty asks.

"Someone was waiting outside our room," I explain. "I knew I had to leave."

He holds me tight. "Did he see you?"

"No."

"Then how did you get past him?"

"I didn't. I went out through the window."

"You what?" His eyes get big.

"I've been on a run for two years, Ty. I know a trick or two."

"Come here." He pulls me into a corner and gives me a hug. "You saved my life. Thank you."

"I need you." I part my lips, nipping his playfully.

As we continue walking, I notice Tyler secretly wincing, his hand on his stomach. The man will always put others' needs before his. But it's time I let him know it doesn't always have to be the case. Adrenaline might've kept him going, but every man needs real fuel.

"Hey, you haven't had much to eat since we got here. You wanna grab a bite?" I suggest.

As if blotting out his tiredness, Tyler tosses me a big smile, obviously thanking me for thinking of him.

25

TYLER

So we're back to square one. But that isn't necessarily a bad thing. Now I know for sure Lilly's disappearance has a different objective—its own narrative, separate from Scarf-face and his mission to get something from Morgan.

Morgan scans the café. After apparently running out of things to observe, she settles her gaze on me. How I want to wipe off that disappointment coating those brown eyes.

She ruminates, "What Jack said about the sketch is really bothering me. I know Lilly isn't the type who would go with someone, even if she was duped or forced. And for her to travel this far?"

"Well, judging by the behavior of her sister, I don't believe Lilly would've done that either. Stubbornness runs in your family—I'm sure of that."

She scoffs with pride. Then she asks, "Ty, how about the farmhouse?"

"I doubt she's there. And now that Callas knows we're onto him, I don't think that farmhouse will mean anything to us."

"You're right."

"Something is amiss. If it's a puzzle piece, it's certainly a big one. Scarf-face is central to all this. He connects California and Florida. Callas may just be a tool to get what Scarf-face wants."

My phone buzzes in my pocket. It's Jack.

"Hey, where are you?" he asks.

"At a café called 'Rare Bites.' Corner of North Florida Ave and Wood Street. Any updates?"

"The police are still processing the apartment and that basement. Another squad is raiding the farmhouse. We've got to find another lead, Hunt. Lilly's not here."

"I know. You coming?"

"Yeah." Jack then ends the call.

"What do we do now, Ty?"

"Go back to Helena. Let's regroup. We'll find another lead. We've got to."

She slumps back in her seat.

"Hey, this isn't over." I rub the top of her hand.

While munching my sandwich, I go through the CCTV footage that Jack had sent when we were still in Helena. Callas and Scarf-face. The more I look at it, the more I question it. Something's not right. Or odd, at the very least.

A waitress approaches our table, serving my dessert. "One flan pudding?"

"Ah, yeah," I answer, salivating over it.

"That is what you call a pudding!" Morgan comments enthusiastically.

"Well, we can order another one."

The waitress smiles regretfully. "Sorry, that's the last one."

"Have it, sweetheart. It's yours."

"No. No." She pushes the plate back to me.

"Come on, let's share. You start."

She dips her fork, but her attention lands on a red car passing us.

"What is it?"

"No, nothing."

She lifts the piece of flan in slow motion, putting it on her tongue carefully as if we were shooting a commercial.

"Hmm..." She cringes. Not the reaction I anticipate. "Well, I know cakes, and this doesn't taste that good. Looks can be deceiving, I guess."

"Are you sure you're not just being fussy?" I take over the fork, dipping it into the cake.

"Ergh... no, don't touch it, Ty. Really, it tastes like almond gone bad."

A thump attacks the back of my ribcage. "Spit it out! Spit it out!" I yell.

Her color changes. She lets out a heartbreaking whimper, then contorts. "Ty—" she wails, clutching her chest, then her stomach. But she seems to be tortured everywhere. She's not one to exaggerate. If anything, she suppresses pain. Her face is now turning blue as she struggles to breathe. This is completely fucked up!

"Call an ambulance!" I belt as I stop Morgan from falling on the cobbles. "Hang on, sweetheart."

The urge to give her a mouth-to-mouth almost gets the better of me. But I can't risk swallowing the poison. I have to stay alive for her.

She needs oxygen and an antidote, ASAP!

I shield her as she desperately hangs on to me. The lane is quiet, apart from some startled onlookers.

Whoever did this, I'm coming for them!

The poison was clearly for me. She only had a tiny bite of it, but they must've put lots in it, too much for Morgan that she could taste it—and too much for her body to bear.

I feel foul all over.

What would've happened had she eaten the whole cake?

No, no! I can't afford to go through this kind of life-and-death situation again. The first time, it changed my life forever. This time, it may just destroy me completely.

By now, Morgan has given up. There's no sign of her struggle.

"Morgan ..." I shake her hand. "Wake up! Wake up, sweetheart! Listen to my voice."

But I'm getting no response.

"I love you. You've got to hang on. Do you hear me? I need to hear you say, 'I love you, too.' I need it. Please... please..."

But she remains motionless, pain frosting her beautiful face.

No. She can't die like this!

Hours have passed. An antidote has been administered, but Morgan is still in a coma.

"Can I see her now?" I ask a nurse. I may sound like a broken record to her, but I can't just sit here and do nothing.

"We'll let you know when anything changes, Mr. Hunt." She passes me by.

There's only so much television, magazines, and coffee can do. Jack is tied up trying to tie loose ends with the Tampa PD. So I've only got myself to talk to.

I rub my arm, thinking about Morgan's question about my Latin sentence tattoo.

Away from home, facing this life-and-death situation exposes a part of me that I've sealed shut since Venice eleven years ago. It's like a grave site disturbed by an earthquake, its soil washed away by a deluge.

I huff like a caged-in bull. What if Morgan never wakes up? And one day I have to decide whether to turn off her life support? It'd be the kind of loss that would send me back into that grave—buried alive until my heart really stops beating.

I shake my head like an alien is wreaking havoc inside my brain.

She'll pull through!

This is no time to fall apart!

But feelings like this highlights how hardy my Wolf Girl is. How had she coped all this time, surviving on her own?

Someone makes a turn toward the waiting room. The pace and weight of their steps catch my attention as if I've heard it before. Of course. Those steps belong to my boss, my ex-SEAL brother Sam Kelleher.

"Sir. I didn't... I didn't know you were coming. Thank you."

"Hey, we're all brothers at Red Mark. I *had* to fly here. How're you holding up? How's Morgan?"

"I'm fine, sir. And Morgan is stable, although still in a coma. She's... ah... I'm sure she'll pull through."

My boss extends his trademark hug—firm, reassuring.

"She won't give up. I'm sure of that," he asserts.

"The poison was meant for me, sir."

"Ty?"

"Hydrogen cyanide—however they put it on that cake. They must've been watching our every move. They knew I ordered that pudding. I mean, that cake was small. I would've eaten it in one bite." I shake my head.

"They couldn't shoot you, so they poisoned you? That was a different kind of low!"

"That shows how desperate they are to get what they want and to stop us from getting to the truth."

"You need to lay low for a bit. I know time is of the essence. But I don't think they intend to harm or kill Lilly. Protecting Morgan and yourself is paramount now."

"I'll try to convince her, sir. When she wakes up."

"Good luck with that," he chuckles. "Hey, can I get your mind off her for a minute?"

"Please do."

"How's my brother?"

"There were nerves, it was obvious. When we met at the airport, he went straight to the point, like nothing else mattered."

"He's a Marine. What can I say!"

"Indeed. He's as good as any Red Mark man, sir. His past is still front and center in his mind, but it never interfered with the mission. In fact, it might've actually enhanced his focus. He didn't try to dodge it when I brought it up. That's my honest assessment."

"Thanks, Ty."

Another nurse walks past. As if it's second nature, my immediate reaction is to stop her and ask the same question. But I let it go.

"Speak of the devil!" Sam calls.

Boots on tiles, it's the Devil Dog Jack Kelleher arriving. "Hey, how's Morgan?" he pants.

"She's stable."

"You've been running?" Sam questions.

"Sam!" Jack rounds his arm around Sam. "Good to see you."

"Good to see you, too, brother." Sam appraises him. "You okay?"

"Tampa PD was a handful, but everything is under control."

"Are *you* okay?" Even if you don't know Jack's story, when Sam speaks like that, you know he's in big-brother mode.

"I'm fine. Really," Jack replies, fishing out his cell.

"What have you got?"

CCTV at the café shows a man distracting the waitress who brought out our orders. Jack then points at a table next to the waitress. "This man is pretending to be a customer. Watch. He's leaning back, relaxed. His arms are crossed, but his left hand—"

Holy shit! The man sprayed the cake on the tray while the waitress was distracted.

"You're right. It was meant for you," Jack affirms. "They want Morgan alive."

Sam replays the clip. "Have the police identified them?"

"They're still working on it."

"And the man that Morgan hit at the park?"

"He was a known mercenary. The police are still investigating who hired him. Probably the same person or people who paid that poisoner."

A lady in white joins us in the waiting room. My two companions almost obscure her slight figure.

I approach her. "How's she, Doc?"

"She's been breathing on her own. But she hasn't come out of her coma."

"Please let me see her."

The doctor appraises me and I let her know I'm really begging. "I'll give you ten minutes."

Ten minutes? I want the whole night and the whole day tomorrow. But every minute is precious.

"Go!" Sam urges.

The moment blurs. I don't know how long I've been walking, which turns I've taken, and which door I enter. All I know is I'm with her now. She's sleeping right in front of me.

I caress her hair. "Can you come back to me?" I murmur. "Open those gorgeous eyes. Please?" Getting through the day without seeing them is like being a walking dead.

Her delicate arms lay on her sides. Maybe I'm not meant to touch her, but I can't help it. "Wake up, sweetheart." I brush the top of her palm.

And tell me that you love me.

I might be making it up, but I swear her lips curve.

I keep staring at her face.

Maybe not.

I stay in my seat, maintaining contact with her. I'm surprised no one has come in to call time. And I'm glad. Because, at the end of the bed, there's a small rustle.

"Morgan?"

She has just moved her legs. Now, her eyelids flutter.

"Morgan, Wolf Girl? Are you awake?"

"Ty... where am I?" Words barely form under her breath.

"Hey, don't talk. You're at a hospital. You're safe."

I scoop her hand, lifting it slightly, then I bend down to plant kisses all over it. It's faint, but she squeezes my hand. Warmth spreads through me. I press the call button to alert staff that she's awake.

The doctor soon arrives. Assisted by a nurse, she runs checks on Morgan and then helps her drink. The doctor observes as Morgan swallows. "I can see it's hurting your throat," the doctor says. "But you're not choking, so it's a good sign. I'll leave the water here. But take it slowly. Okay?"

Morgan nods.

"Can I stay, please?" Once again I beg the doctor.

"Of course, Mr. Hunt. But please let her have her rest. She may feel better soon but don't forget that her body has just gone through a major trauma. I'm sure you understand. If there's anything, just call us."

With only the two of us in the room, I see Morgan's eyes gradually blink open. I smile wide. "Hey, Wolf Girl."

"Ty..." Her hand tightens around my palm.

"How are you feeling?"

"You want me to talk now?" she croaks.

I chuckle. So she heard me before. "No. You don't have to answer. Just know that I'm here."

"I feel like my insides have gone on vacation."

"They had to pump your stomach."

She shuts her eyes, apparently digesting the revelation.

Moments later I hear her voice, still painfully soft. "So they did want me dead. Or was it just a warning?"

I stay silent.

Her eyes suddenly flare. "The flan pudding! The poison was meant for you?" She tries to sit up.

"Hey, stay down, Morgan. We don't have to talk about this."

"Ty! How can we not talk about this?"

"I'm glad your taste buds came to your rescue. Otherwise..." I trail off, remembering it was her who stopped me from having a bite of that pudding. This woman has saved me twice in one day.

She motions at me to come closer and then gradually rounds her arms over me like she's hanging onto me. "I'm glad I'm lying in this bed, and you're sitting next to me. Not the other way around."

I look at her lovingly, trying to shoo away the vision of her pale face when she was lying motionless in my arms. "I'd rather have you in my bed, healthy and sated."

"Actually, your idea is better."

"I really thought I'd lost you," I huff, unable to stop myself.

She chuckles, then clears her throat. "I know my cakes, Ty. You won't lose me because of a friggin' flan pudding."

Pudding or not, I don't want to lose her. Full stop.

She lets go of me, looking relaxed. "I don't remember much. But—did you say something to me before the ambulance came?"

I ponder, weighing up whether I should tell her. My eyes wander for a couple of seconds, escaping her stare. This is no time to talk about my feelings—if I have words to express them. "I just begged you to hang on."

Her hand lifts to cup my chin. "We're not done yet, Ty. It wasn't my time."

She's damn right. Acknowledging her resolve, I press my lips against her delicate mouth. She clamps it, perhaps conscious of how dry they are.

"Let me," I beg.

Her mouth curves up. Perhaps she can't resist me, or she just needs the touch. I think the kiss wakes me up more than it does her.

"You know, Morgan. The first time we met. You weren't the only one feeling alone. I did, too. And your presence soothed me. I'd never forgotten you. Sometimes, I wondered about the what-ifs. But I knew you would've moved on."

She puts a palm on my cheek. "You? Feeling alone?"

"We're not that different, Wolf Girl."

"Maybe. We both have a story, don't we?"

I acknowledge her with a rub on her palm. "I'll tell you it some other time. I just wanted to know how much you mean to me. For now, we have to take care of your heart. I mean, literally." I glance at the vital signs monitor.

She cocks a brow.

"You have to rest, Morgan. It's from the doctor, not me." I shirk responsibility for the order.

She draws my hand over her left breast. I give it a gentle squeeze, glazing her nipple. Then I give her a peck on the cheek, my mustache and beard brushing against her soft complexion. With that, she smiles and closes her eyes.

26

MORGAN

Night turns into morning, and morning back into night. Detectives have been coming and going like my room was fitted with a revolving door.

"So this is how it feels to be a 'victim'?" I sulk, sinking back under the blanket after answering yet more questions from the Tampa PD.

"You're still glad you're in that bed instead of me?" Tyler smirks sideways.

Damn, those creases just make the man even sexier. "That will never change," I emphasize—he's got to know I will take *anything* to keep him alive and breathing.

Tyler rubs his chin. His beard seems to start annoying him. But I stop short at suggesting a shave; he looks far too hot like that to get a trim.

Meanwhile, outside, a commotion brews.

Not again! The patient next door is hurling abuse at the staff, asking for his meal. He's been doing this almost every hour since this morning. Nurses have told me the man suffered from delirium.

I pull the blanket over my head. "I want to get out of here,

Ty," I mutter. I don't know how those staff put up with that every day, and can still have smiles on their faces.

Tyler lifts the blanket off my face like peeling a wallpaper. "We'll wait for the doctor in the morning, okay?"

"Hmm... if I must," I tease. Although I don't know what we're going to do now. It's too early to sleep, yet I don't have the capacity to do anything else.

I press my head.

"Headache?"

"Uh huh."

With just one hand, he covers my whole forehead. Now, that is a perfect warm compress. I coo and sigh, absorbing the comfort.

The noise outside has subsided. Although it's not actually peace for me.

A nurse comes in. "Miss Blackwell, Mr. Hunt, the police detective is here."

"Again?" Tyler's eyes go big, and his comforting hand leaves my head, fisting next to his hip.

Dizziness starts overwhelming me. Anything is better than an interview right now—even a pap smear!

I murmur, "Ty, I'm really not up for it. Please, I don't want to talk to him."

The detective has already stepped close to the door. I think he has come alone. "Good evening, Mr. Hunt."

"Not tonight, detective!" Tyler roars, pushing him away, not even allowing him to catch a glimpse of me. Ty has a high tolerance for people, but this is what happens when he's provoked too far—when his woman is in distress.

"Mr. Hunt, calm down. I just need to ask a couple more questions. It will be quick, I promise." His standard line. Yet, once given a chance, he will go on—just like what happened this afternoon.

"No. You talk to me."

"Let us do our job."

"You have my blessings. So go out there and get those sons of bitches."

"Don't make it difficult for us."

"Oh, I can. I know your captain has ordered you not to make another visit here."

The conversation seems to stall after that warning from Ty.

I imagine the detective's lips would purse like a mouse that has been caught stealing cheese. I know Ty had asked Jack to persuade his Tampa PD contact—the captain—to put an end to these impromptu visits.

But the detective apparently has more than just thick skin. "I need access to Miss Blackwell now, or we'll never catch those criminals."

Or perhaps the detective doesn't have skin at all. The more I sense his presence, the more I think that he's more like a fly than a mouse—buzzing, persistent, annoying.

By this time, I can only see Ty's back. But I know his eyes would've flared, and soon I hear his low growl—like a tank about to flatten a terrain. "You've been hounding her. She's not the criminal." Ty moves closer to the detective. "Here's how I'm going to make it easy for you. Ask me the questions, and I'll give her answers to you."

The corridor goes quiet.

"Detective?" Tyler nudges.

"I just need to know the details of that red car she saw driving by when you were at the café."

"You've asked her that twice, and she's answered. What else?"

Once again, the exchanges stop.

Tyler restarts, "You were just here a few hours ago. I'm not going to let my girlfriend bear the consequences of your incompetence."

"Mr. Hunt, don't make me charge you for obstruction."

"Sue me!" he snarls. "Take a hike, detective!"

Tyler watches on, walking backward as if not wanting the detective out of sight until he's completely disappeared. Then he stands guard at my door.

He returns to my side. "He's gone, sweetheart. He won't talk to you again."

"So he's still onto that red car. He wanted me to slip."

I had told the detective about my sighting of the red car for the second time, but I never revealed that I saw the same car driving crazily near Callas' apartment.

"In a way, kudos to him for sniffing something. But we can't place you at the scene of Callas' apartment—let alone bashing a gunman at the nearby park." Ty gives me a proud look, reminding me what I'd done.

"Whoever was in that red car, they've got to be Scarf-face's men. They saw me at the park, then followed us to the café."

"I must admit, the poisoning was a quick plan. But effective, nonetheless. Well, almost. I don't think that detective has any knowledge of Scarf-face. Jack has been careful with who he involves from the Tampa PD. We don't know who Scarf-face has got his fingers on. Not to mention Callas' sneaky work."

I'VE BARELY SLEPT when I'm woken up by the sound of the toilet flushing. The couch is empty. Somehow, I'm thankful that I'm awake—I could feel my nightmare starting to surface.

Tyler walks out of the bathroom, rubbing his head and yawning. He's wearing a pair of boxer shorts, his shirt unbuttoned all the way.

"Ty..."

"Hey, did I wake you up?"

"No."

"If you don't get enough rest, the doctor may not allow you to go home tomorrow."

I don't answer, instead rummaging his chest behind his open shirt. I'm surprised the ebony coat hasn't gone out of control yet.

"Tell me, what is it with you and fluffy things?" asks Tyler.

I choke. "Nothing. Just a preference."

"The first night you were at my place, I hadn't had a chance to shave. I mean, I never let my hair grow like a yeti, but it was pretty wild that night."

"You hadn't gotten laid in a while?"

"Well, no. But that's not my point." He clears his throat. "That night, you really dug into my chest—then you purred to sleep. I mean, just like that, after such a violent nightmare? Did you like my hair like that?"

My guffaw shakes my sore belly. "Oh, shoot..." I grimace, hugging my abs.

"Sorry, sorry. I didn't mean to make you laugh so hard."

"Ty, I like you—hair or no hair. But, holding you with a layer of healthy coat is like hugging an Alaskan Malamute."

His laughter echoes around the room—deep, like a few bass strings being strummed at once.

"Morgan..." He shakes his head. "I've been called a bear, even Chewbacca. But a Malamute?"

I keep laughing that I almost get used to the pain. "I've touched a real bear's fur—well, a sedated one, when I was helping a Yellowstone bear expert. It's rough, Ty. Yours is so soft..." It is—whatever conditioner he puts on it. "And as for Chewbacca, he's a Wookie, so surely, it's even rougher and clumpy."

His laughter intensifies. I hope he hasn't woken up the delirium patient next door.

I keep playing with his pec hair. "Yours is well groomed, sexy, and manly."

"All right, noted," he conveys.

"By the way, your Chewbacca ex, she wasn't a fan of hair, I take it?"

"Nope. Hair on, no sex."

"She didn't know what she'd missed out on!" I dip further, reaching for his abs. "When you're with me, no hair, no sex."

"Ouch!" He smirks. I know he gets my joke because I will make love to him no matter what. "I haven't known any woman who *loved* hair. Some of my exes didn't *mind* it but loved it?"

"Hair is the product of testosterone, honey. And you've got lots of it—I mean, both the hair and the testosterone."

He shakes his head, still laughing like he can't stop. "Oh, Morgan. Here I am, thinking no one will love me as I am."

"So, what did you do with your exes?"

"I shaved almost daily when I was with my Chewbacca ex."

"Ty, a question for you. Your Chewbacca girlfriend. Was she the woman at the bar?"

"You knew?"

I knew it! I knew there was something happening between him and that woman in the purple cocktail dress. "My radar is finely tuned."

"I broke up with her earlier this year."

"That long? I'm surprised you weren't scooped up soon after."

"What can I say? I was waiting for the right one."

I narrow my gaze. "Why am I not buying it?"

"Hey, I did feel pathetic, you know. Thinking about getting back with her and all that."

"Huh..."

"Can I confess something to you?"

"Of course."

"Remember I went through your things in Venice and found your Emma Schiffer ID?"

"Yeah?"

"I wanted to know if you were older than eighteen."

"Ty?"

"Yes. I know! It was silly. But I thought, if we ever did it, I wanted to make sure that you weren't a minor."

"Did I look that young?"

"You did, and you didn't. I mean, I'm bad at guessing a woman's age. At the same time, with how you talked to me, you seemed wise beyond your age."

"I'm glad it didn't work out between you and your Chewbacca ex."

"Me too."

"The things you do for love, eh?" I wink at him. "One demanded you shave, and the other wants your hair like she would die without it."

"I'll do whatever you want, sweetheart."

"Are you really that easy to convince? I thought a SEAL was trained to be tough, unpliable."

"Being a SEAL has nothing to do with pleasing one's woman."

Maybe so. But I'm upholding my bias. Never mind his ass and six-pack abs, it's well known that a SEAL refuses to fail at anything. *Anything.*

And I guess that was why he said he'd do whatever I wanted. Failing his woman isn't an option.

Ruminating the success of his first mission wakes my craving.

Should I ask him? Will he think I'm too much because the

second time I want sex with him is when I'm lying in a hospital bed?

"What's that look?" he quizzes.

He's too alert to miss my body language despite his puffy eyes telling me he's ready to go back to sleep. Or I simply lack competence in playing it cool. Either way, my cover is blown so I might as well be on the offensive.

I reach for the top of his pubis, playing with the curly strands. "I just want to be with a real man, not a Ken doll." I cup his balls.

He bends down and breathes close to my ear. "What do you want from this man tonight?"

Tyler Hunt takes hints well this time. Not that my hint was meant to be subtle.

His hand moves discreetly from the edge of the bed, climbing over to the top of my breast.

"Ty…"

"Do you want me to help you sleep?" His raspy voice tickles my eardrum and the effect is like a brushing kiss on hungry lips.

"Anything, Ty. Anything…" I whisper, writhing in anticipation as he rubs the blanket against my nipple.

"Let's see what I can do," he murmurs even closer to my lobe, producing searing sensation down the side of my neck. I answer his invitation. My hand inches lower into the elastic of his boxers. But he retracts his abs, warning, "No, no. My dick is off-limits."

He doesn't give me time to complain as his mouth puckers right on top of mine, sucking and nibbling my lips. Meanwhile, his hand kneads my breast, rubbing my aching nipple with the middle of his palm.

I moan as he shows exactly how a real man does it. Still showering me with kisses, his right hand keeps molding my breast. Then, his left arm reaches down under the blanket. With his fingers spread wide, he rubs my bare pussy.

"I bet you never fell asleep with your core pulsing from a man's hand job."

At those words, he teases open the seam of my pussy lips, stirring my entrance ever so gently as if he was reading me a calming bedside story.

Lefties are better lovers. I think he claimed that—yes, it was part of his conversation with Jack in that hotel room, I heard it.

Now I understand why he made his cock off-limits. Because whatever he's doing to me, he's sending me to sleep. He's putting need above want—although an orgasm wouldn't have hurt.

27

TYLER

We're flying a thousand feet over Florida.

Last night could've gone a lot worse had that detective persisted, but I couldn't stand the thought of dragging Morgan through another life-sapping interview. She was recovering from cyanide poisoning, for God's sake!

Morgan puts her seat all the way back, almost lying flat. She can do whatever the hell she wants. This is her plane.

"You can be really persuasive, you know," she comments, her bright smile has returned.

"Did you just notice?"

The doctor at the Tampa hospital backed my plan for Morgan's home recovery, knowing there would be medical professionals taking care of her.

"Somehow, I thought your dad was in the military, and your mom, maybe a teacher?"

"Is that so?" I play with her hair. "Well, they met at Bozeman Hospital. My dad has been a physician there since he graduated med school. Meanwhile, my mom had been going places. She started her nursing career in Boise then moved to Kalispell, and finally Bozeman."

"Well, if it wasn't for your parents, the doctor at Tampa Hospital wouldn't have let me out. And you would still be swatting that fly."

Having been sleep-deprived the past few days, it doesn't take long before Morgan falls asleep.

I take the time to watch the CCTV footage of Callas and Scarf-face again. Something is bothering me. I wish I could remove that piece of cloth every time I see him coming into the frame.

I saw the man wearing a scarf and sunglasses in Venice a couple of years ago—I rounded past him. He was sitting on the sand, hugging himself, so I don't really know how he walked. With the man in the footage...

I replay the video, squinting at his figure.

Is he even a man?

"Hey, what are you looking at?" Morgan asks. She hasn't moved, but her big eyes are no longer shut.

"No. Nothing." I put my phone away. "We're almost there."

Morgan pulls her backrest forward, then gazes out the window. "I still remember the first time I came to Bozeman. Gallatin is one of the most picturesque airports in the world."

"It's my hometown, what can I say! Well, sort of my hometown."

"What do you mean?"

The plane completes its taxi, stopping next to a helicopter that has been parked there.

"Wait here, okay?" I get up from my seat, leaving her question unanswered. I then wave at the chopper pilot.

"You know him?"

I wink before making my way out.

My friend greets me on the tarmac. "Ty, good to see you,"

"Good to see you, Ian." We give each other a sailor's hug. It feels like the old Navy days when we were on board an aircraft carrier. He's the best pilot I've known, and we almost lost touch. Luckily, today, he's here. "Are we good to go?"

"We are, my friend. Where's Morgan?"

"On the plane, probably observing us keenly. She's still weak, although she doesn't want to admit it."

"You need help getting her out?"

"Nah. I've got it." I pat him on the shoulder, then rush back to Morgan.

"You chartered a chopper? For a scenic flight or to get to your parents' farm?" she asks.

"Where's your trust? Come on!"

"I trust you, but this is a bit over the top, no?"

"Sweetheart, you need to get used to being taken care of, okay?"

She tosses me a lopsided smile. "I don't care if we use a horse and carriage, Ty. As long as you're with me."

"He's a friend. He was happy to lend his chopper. Besides, I'm not doing this just to impress you. The farm is a bit of a drive from here. And, we can't afford anyone knowing our location."

"Well, if that's the case." She offers her arms even before I ask. I think she's starting to enjoy her status as my princess. I'll give it to her, just for now. Or maybe—forever. As long as she's safe and comfortable, she can be anything.

I scoop her off her seat and carry her like a child, not letting her feet touch the ground.

"Morgan, this is Ian. My friend and your pilot for the last leg of your journey," I introduce her to him.

"Hello," Morgan says cordially.

"Come, I'll help you get on board," Ian offers.

We seat her at the back, wrapping her in a blanket and putting on her seatbelt.

"Comfy?" Ian asks.

"Yeah," she replies, smiling at him, but her eyes are apparently still questioning whether this is necessary.

I kneel next to her. "Yes, Morgan, this is all part of taking care of you."

"Still, it's—"

I place a finger on her lips, sealing them. "Just sit back and enjoy the view."

"What I meant was..." She leans forward. "It's a bit overwhelming, but it feels good." She draws out the 'good.'

Her puckering lips tempt me once more.

We're back in the air, and I can't take my eyes off her joyous face. She admires the scenery below, lost in thoughts. A one-hundred-eighty-degree change from how she was yesterday. Well, because she's free. And I'll make sure nobody takes away that freedom, ever.

"You're gonna love the farm," I foretell. "They have everything. Horses, cows, chickens, dogs. Even I miss it. I haven't been home in almost a year."

"Wolves?"

"I knew you were going to ask. Well, the farm is well-fenced. Wolves hardly come near it. Sometimes they do, but I can assure you, they're never killed at the property."

"Good. I guess a Wolf Girl is welcome?"

"More than welcome."

"I'm looking forward to it. Although I must admit, I wish I had more time to prepare. I've forgotten how meet-the-parents works. The last time I had to do it, I was sixteen."

I rub her thigh. "My parents are the coolest. And I'm not just saying it. They're very laid back. There won't be any interview or interrogation, okay? If you want to be around them, they'll be delighted. But if you want to be alone, they'll be happy to leave you be." I pause for a second. "Well, maybe not my mom."

"Ty?" Her gaze turns a tad worried.

I chuckle. "She'll love you. She'll want to take care of you all the time. You'll see."

"Like you?"

"Maybe," I ponder. People used to say I was proof that the first son usually took after his mother. "Really, if you feel it's all too much, just tell me. We'll have a quiet time together."

"You know, Ty. For a girl who lost her family in the blink of an eye, seeing the friendly faces of a mom and a dad would be welcome."

"Excellent. On behalf of them, I can claim you're adopted!"

"So, *we*'re official then?"

That gets me thinking. "Since when were we *un*-official?"

"I don't know... we never declared our love per se."

I chuckle to dismiss her idea about the declaration. But thinking about it makes my heart skip a beat. I did say I love her just before those Tampa paramedics haul her into their ambulance. But she's right. We haven't really declared us 'together'—I never thought she'd mind skipping the formality.

She then cringes as if reading my mind or feeling the same. "Not that we need words," she adds.

"If I'm honest, Morgan. To me, we've been official ever since you decided to step foot in Helena and find me." I tuck some wayward strands behind her ear.

Zeal radiates from her stare—that vibe when she's happy that I'm around.

"What?" she queries my scrutiny.

"No. Nothing."

We're hovering over the farm. The dogs are already going crazy, running around, barking. I can see Wolf Girl ditching the blanket, fidgeting in her seat, taking in the reality below. She's got to be able to see most of the animals.

"I always tell people I'm from Bozeman because no one will know this area. But this is my real hometown."

Morgan can barely sit. I know she can't wait to get down.

"You can land there," I advise Ian, pointing at the empty paddock next to the hay barn.

"Mind the dogs!" Morgan warns, to the amusement of our pilot. I understand sometimes it's hard to gauge how far objects are when we're flying over them.

"Ian knows, Wolf Girl." I rub her forearm. "And the dogs do, too. They're used to aircrafts landing around here."

"Hmm... so I'm not your first girlfriend to be treated to a private flight to your home?"

I shuffle the hair on her crown. "We fly in feeds sometimes. That's all."

Her attention soon lands on the ATV moving along the track. The quad-bike vehicle is my parents' choice for getting around the farm.

"That's your mom and dad?"

"Yes."

"That's so cool," she remarks.

Morgan insists on disembarking by herself, and this time, I let her. The muddy ground doesn't seem to stop her, reminding me that despite being a city girl in California, she's in her element here.

My mom doesn't need an introduction. As soon as Morgan is off the chopper, she comes to her, giving her a hug as if Wolf Girl was the daughter she never had.

Dad takes the opportunity to welcome me. "Good to see you, son."

I'm a grown man, but I'll never get over my dad's hug. "Good to be home, Dad."

The two dogs circle us, grinning for a pat, tails wagging almost as fast as the chopper blades. Salt is my old friend, and

Pepper was adopted a year ago from a closed-down farm not far from here. Her name used to be Poppy, but because of the incumbent's name, Mom decided to call her Pepper, and the young dog seemed to respond fine.

"How are things in Helena?" asks the old man.

"Yeah, good. Red Mark is everything I hoped for and more." This time, I bend down, patting Salt, who's been circling around me patiently. "You've held the fort well." I scan the fields around me. They're lush, clearly having recovered from the draught when I last visited.

Dad still works at the hospital part-time so he can focus on running the farm. But it's been tough for farmers in the past few years. He had to lay off a few of his staff, so he has to do a lot of the heavy lifting himself these days.

Dad feels my biceps. "Whatever you've been doing! You're gonna be as big as me soon."

"I'm already bigger than you, Dad," I tease, squeezing his arm. Or maybe not.

"Well, I guess we have different looks."

"What looks?"

"Farmer's bulk looks different from gym bulk."

I scoff, telling him he's being ridiculous.

Meanwhile, Dad keeps glancing at Morgan. "She seems lovely."

"More than lovely, Dad. Come, let's meet her. Well, when Mom finally lets her go." I approach Morgan, my mom still holding her. "Dad, this is Morgan."

Mom loosens her arms, and my girl turns to Dad. "Hi, I'm Morgan. Nice to meet you—"

"Peter," Dad says.

"Nice to meet you, Peter."

"We'll take good care of you." Dad is a softie, but that promise is on another level. I think he's really taken by Morgan.

"Come, I'll drive you to the house." Mom beams, helping Morgan get onto the ATV.

Ian comes to me. "I think I've got all your stuff out." He nods at the bags in the back of the ATV.

"Thanks, man. I really appreciate it."

"Anytime, Hunt. Anytime." He salutes me and runs back to his chopper.

"You boys comin'?" Mom yells over the ATV engine.

Salt and Pepper run over to Mom, ready to follow her.

"Nah. I'll take a walk with Junior," Dad resolves.

We used to walk for hours around here, especially at this time of day. The sun is low, and the hills are soaked in orange and pink hues. The air is cooling, sending the breeze to pick up speed. We used to pluck some wild berries along the way, and when we got home, Mom would be busy making dinner.

While Pepper ends up hitching a ride with Mom and Morgan, Salt runs back to me.

"Hey, buddy. It's okay if you want to follow them." I rub his scruff.

"Look at Pepper!" Dad mutters, watching the young collie licking Morgan's face. "She has never done that to anyone here."

"Well, I should warn you, Morgan is a dog magnet."

Dad chuckles. "At least Salt is still loyal to you."

"Oh, he'll never waver!" I tap at my chest, and Salt immediately jumps into my arms. "That's my boy."

"And I sure hope no wolves have caught the scent of her. I really don't want to deal with them right now," Dad adds, to which I shrug—and hope for the same. "We had storms in the past couple of days." He presses his boots against the mud.

"I notice." I follow his steps, then examine my shirt—Salt's black and brown paw prints all over it. I let the dog down, and he calmly walks beside me.

"You came at the right time. It's going to be sunny and scorching for the next couple of days."

"I brought the weather with me from Florida."

Dad shakes his head. "That's very nice of you. But may I remind you, I'm not a fan of humidity."

I fist-punch his arm while we carry on.

He then restarts, "I spoke with the doctor in Tampa. The poison is out of her system. So that's the good news. The thing is, a lot of patients make the mistake of putting everything behind too quickly. Exerting themselves because they feel fine. Don't let that happen to Morgan. She seems to be the type who might just do that."

He's a good judge of character. I suppose, with the hundreds of patients he has dealt with in his lifetime, he knows.

"I'll be watching her, Dad. Don't worry."

He picks up a twig, throwing it away, sending Salt bolting to fetch it.

"Hey, have you been back to California?"

I scratch my chin. "Not recently. No reason to."

He nods.

"I'm fine, Dad. Don't worry about me."

"Good. Good." He throws his arm around my shoulder, then we walk the rest of the path in silence.

28

MORGAN

I marvel at the rustic stone house at the end of the path as the ATV hits the crest. The rolling hills make a perfect backdrop. The sky is filled with strokes of gradients from blue to pink. This is Montana as I remember it.

"On a clear day, you'll be able to see the peaks of the Bridger Range," Ty's mother explains. She comes from an Italian family, first settled in Chicago in the 1920s. Earlier, she told me her first name is Ludovica, but I can call her Lou.

As we get closer, my eyes wander left and right, taking in the sheer size of the house. Large timber windows dominate the wide façade. The stone works blend seamlessly with the wooden beams and shingle roof. On a sunny day, this house must be bathed in light.

Lou parks at the front porch. I hop off, dipping into the cargo bin towed at the back of the ATV.

"Nah, nah, nah!" she pulls my hand away. "Let the boys handle those."

Of course. I no longer need to pack and run. I have a home for the next—however long Ty is planning for us to stay here.

She opens the door for me, revealing a natural pine smell that makes me want to hurl myself into that comfy plaid sofa.

"This is the oldest part of the house. Peter's grandfather built it. The rest of the house grew larger over time. We couldn't seem to stop having children!" she laughs, leading me further in. "Some parts of the ceiling are low. Mind your head, dear."

I duck, avoiding a few beams, while Lou passes straight through.

She turns to me, giggling quietly. "A perk of being short."

After passing the two front rooms, the house opens up. It's as if I'm entering a cathedral. I spin around with my head tilted back, uttering a quiet 'wow' at the high plank ceiling.

Lou carries on. "The rest of the house is a combined effort between Peter and his dad. Amazing, huh?"

"Absolutely."

"Come. I'll show you your room. Well, it's Ty's room."

"Sure."

She observes me. "Don't worry. You won't be sleeping in a Batmobile bed staring at posters of Christian Bale."

"I was wondering about that." I hold my laugh, not wanting my belly to shake too hard.

"You okay, dear?" Lou asks.

"Yeah. Yeah. Still a bit sore here." I point at the right side of my belly button. I don't know why it feels so effortless to tell her this. She really sounds like a nurse now.

"You may want to have a hot compress before bed. I'll remind Tyler," she suggests, then studies my face. "You're still a little pale. That means you have a lot of recovery ahead."

We meander around the open living area. I can see at least two fireplaces. And do I see a galley kitchen in the far corner? My mouth is salivating. Look at those huge ovens! And is that a roast that's cooking inside one of them?

"All the bedrooms are on the second floor," Lou tells me. "Are you okay to walk up?"

"Oh yeah, of course."

"Now, Morgan, it may sound cliché. But please make yourself at home. And I mean it. This is your home."

I stop at the landing, digesting her statement. This is real. I'm in a sanctuary—beyond the stones and timbers. It's the people who live here that make it a sanctuary. "Thanks, Lou. I really appreciate it."

"You can do whatever you want. As long as you don't burn down the house."

It sounds a hell of a lot like Ty's advice.

Tyler's bedroom is tucked in the corner of the west wing of the house. As Lou remarked, apart from some old photos and books, there's no sign of his boyhood in here. I think they've recently renovated it.

"These are Ty's brothers?" I peruse one of the photos on the dresser. Five well-chiseled faces stare back at me. They're in their farm clothes, posing in front of a barn.

"From oldest to youngest. This is Ty, then Brandon, Carter, Liam, and Archer." She smiles to herself.

I raise my brows, studying the photo more closely. Ty is the most handsome—of course—but his brothers may give him a run for his money. They look to be born from the same mold. Their dad.

Perhaps seeing my reaction, Lou chuckles. "None of them are married. If it doesn't work out between you and Ty, I'm sure any of his brothers will take you." The woman then laughs her heart out.

This is by far the easiest meet-the-parents I've ever experienced.

"I won't tell Ty." I wink.

She lets out one last giggle, then settles. "Ty's one hell of a big brother to all of them. He was always the one who gave a hand or made the sacrifices. Sometimes, he took on too many responsibilities. But it's just him. His father is like that."

"You and Peter have done well."

"Here's the thing, Morgan. I've never seen my son so proud being with a woman. His eyes are always on you. You must mean a lot to him."

"Lou, I don't want to take him away from you, but really, he is more than my world, and I want him for myself. So, apologies in advance." I almost give her a curtsy.

Lou restarts her laugh, rising on her tiptoes to reach out to me. She then gives me a peck on both of my cheeks. "When I said proud, I really meant he's head over heels in love with you."

"I'll take good care of him."

"I know you will."

I put the photo back, and my attention lands on the frame behind it. I'm sure one of the boys is Tyler, but I don't think the other one is any of his brothers. "Who's this?"

"Oh..." Her demeanor changes. "I should take this away."

"Who's that boy, Lou?"

She hugs the photo close to her chest, the back of the frame to me. "Tobias. Ty's best friend. They were inseparable. He and Ty bravely went to California. They were planning to join the Navy together," she reveals. Then, she pivots to examine the bed. "Oh, my, I forgot to take the extra blanket."

"It's okay. I probably won't need it," I decide. "Ty never mentioned about him."

"Oh, he died when they were still teenagers." She steps away from me. "I'm gonna grab a ladder. Hang on a sec."

"Don't worry. I can reach. I'll get it when I need it."

She's barely five-feet-two. I wonder how she gave birth to five beautiful boys, all of them soldier-like.

"Lucky Ty takes after his father," she comments as if knowing what's on my mind. "Being short is kind of okay for women, but for guys? I know my father had a hard time growing up." Lou grimaces joyfully.

"But Ty has your smile," I remark. And her kindness and warmth, too. And perhaps her Italian genes might've contributed to Ty's well-furred body.

She smiles sweetly. "Well, I'll let you settle in. Let me know if you need anything."

"There you are," Ty pops in.

Lou tucks the photo behind her hip. She nods at the top shelf of the closet, gesturing to Ty. "Hey, while you're here. Take that blanket down will you?"

He raises a brow. "That fluffy brown one?"

"Uh-huh."

Ty glances at me, then replies to his mother. "Don't think we need it, Mom, but thanks."

"Oh, Morgan might," she blurts.

Ty holds his smirk. "Don't worry, Mom."

"Well, I'll leave you to it. Dinner will be ready in half an hour."

THE FOUR OF us sit around the dining table, covered elegantly with white linen. A vase of lilies sits in the middle, surrounded by a few candles.

"We used to fold out this table," Peter says. "It was always chaos at dinner time. Imagine five hungry boys and an over-worked man competing for Lou's food."

"I can imagine!" I say, masking my overwhelming emotions. I can't remember the last time I had dinner at a table, surrounded by people who love me.

"You okay?" Ty places his hand on top of mine under the table.

"Yeah."

While the boys are served roast beef with all the trimmings, Lou has prepared a special polenta for me and herself.

"The broth is good for you," she comments.

"Oh, God." Just by having a spoonful, I feel like a comforting and warm force is hugging me. Something that I used to have in my L.A. home. Mom and Dad, and Lilly, and sometimes Hudson when he took a break from his adventure. Some nights, we'd banter, like when we discussed the ethics of resurrecting the woolly mammoth. And sometimes we simply talk about everyday family things like planning a picnic in Yosemite.

"You know what?" Ty bails, looking away from the side of the table where the food I can't eat is placed. "I'll have the polenta too."

"Go ahead, Ty. I made plenty." Lou passes the bowl to him.

"Can't let you eat it by yourself," Ty winks at me.

"You don't have to, Ty. When was the last time you had your mom's roast? Besides, it's not a downgrade, you know. This polenta is amazing!"

"I know, sweetheart. But we're in this together, are we not? Like a man becoming a teetotaler when his wife is pregnant."

I lick a drip of food off my lower lip, and I can see Lou donning a big grin. I wonder how long the woman has been thinking about having grandchildren.

"Err... my bad," Ty gulps, reading the table. "That wasn't a good comparison." He scans all the food in front of him. "And, to be honest, I can't shun that juicy rump."

"Have it, Ty!" I insist. "I won't hold it against you."

"But you know that I'm thinking of you."

"Go on!" I meet his gaze. So innocent, so sincere. That man can say anything, and I'll believe him.

His lips curve just a tad, perhaps responding to my melting-all-over look.

Then I notice Peter shifts in his seat. "I'd like to see what you've been prescribed with, Morgan, if that's okay."

"Peter!" Lou glares at her husband. "Let the girl have dinner in peace."

"Oh, sorry, sorry," Peter says, guilt rising in his face. I think this meet-the-son's-girlfriend dinner is pretty new to him. "But, you know that the best medicine is rest, don't you?"

And plenty of love.

I take in another spoonful of polenta.

We hear Salt and Pepper barking outside.

"I think the badger is back," Peter takes a guess. He then turns to Ty. "Hey, your mom and I were talking about getting a new dog."

"Cool," Ty replies. "Another collie?"

"You should get an Alaskan Malamute," I quip.

Ty chokes on his wine.

"You okay, son?" Peter checks on him.

Ty gulps some water.

"Actually, not a bad choice," Lou agrees. "It's not that we need another farm dog. Well, technically, you can train any dog to be one, but probably we just need another companion that will keep us active."

My man glances at me, still releasing the last few coughs.

After dinner, Ty rounds his arm over his mother's shoulder and kisses her. "Thank you, Mom. Dinner was lovely, as always."

Right there, I can see a boy in him. He's a good son, I'm sure. If a man loves his mother like that and loves me like he does, he's one in a million.

Peter pats his son's shoulder. "You two lovebirds go and rest. Especially you, Morgan." Then he cocks his head toward Ty. "If you don't go to bed, she won't either."

Tyler motions me to go ahead. "I'll be there in a minute, sweetheart."

I pad to Ty's bedroom, then change into my nightie, bracing the mirror.

I barely recognize my own reflection. Yes, I'm skinny and pale, but the flush of happiness that I feel inside seems to have manifested itself. That's what family does to you.

Finally, Ty joins me. "Did my mom tell you the joke about my brothers? That if things don't work out between us—"

"Any of them will take me?"

"Thought I heard that laugh."

"How many times has she said that?"

"Well, I was hardly home. So I only took maybe three girls here to see my parents. None of them worked out. And since all of my brothers are still single, you know they never took a chance on any of my exes."

"They're all handsome."

A shred of discomfort flashes on his face, perhaps wondering 'what if?'

I take his hand, driving it to cover my black rose pendant. "You're the only one, Ty. If it doesn't work out between us, I'll go to that Florida convent and become a nun."

"God! That'd be the worst tragedy. I'd rather you pick one of my brothers."

"Is that so?"

He pinches my chin playfully. "Mom loves you, I know. She always wanted a girl. But five boys later... she gave up. So she always welcomed girls in this house. It was the same joke she'd told my exes. But I know you're different."

"Where are your brothers now?"

"They're scattered all over the world."

"Military too?"

"Two of them. Both in the Navy. My youngest has just started his deployment in Darwin, Australia. The one who benefited from your ten grand in lieu of my boxing match prize."

That seems a long time ago!

"I'm glad," I boast.

"Well, I gave the money to Mom. She knew best how to divvy up the funds," he admits. "Then, my second youngest has just graduated nuke school."

"Nuke school?"

"Nuclear submarine. His specialty."

"Oh."

"And my two other brothers are civilians. One is in Italy doing stone masonry, the other in Argentina teaching English."

"No one went to medical school? What did your parents think?"

"Mom was cool. Dad was a bit disappointed. But he didn't make a fuss of it."

I'm interested to hear more, but I can't hold my yawn.

"Now, that's a healthy sign." Ty draws me close. "Do you still need the blanket?"

"Don't think so." Just being next to the stack of muscle that is Tyler Hunt, the whole bed is warm.

29

TYLER

In true Morgan style, she made the most of Mom's kitchen. Two mornings in a row, she baked. And thanks to Mom's abundant ingredients and bakeware, she was able to create toppings that tasted amazing and looked like art. What tickled my heart, though, was that Wolf Girl was happy as a bee and my mom a notch happier.

But time has caught up on us. After almost a week of country bliss, the restart of our mission is looming.

I'm ready, but at the same time, I feel an unfamiliar weight, and it's no pre-mission jitters.

The CCTV footage that I've been playing and replaying has convinced me that Scarf-face is a woman. Her figure appears right at the edge, but I can see the profile of her face and observe the way she walks. There's just too much femininity in her stance and movements. What bothers me even more now is that I think I have an idea who she might be.

Perhaps the weight comes from the fact that I haven't broken the news to Morgan.

"Ready?" she asks, all geared up for our morning hike. The first time we did it, she was hopping and skipping along the path. I almost imagined her wearing a blue dress and a pair of red slippers. "Can we take the longer route this time?" she requests.

"Of course, sweetheart."

Salt the border collie pokes his head out, insisting he come with me. No sign of Pepper. I think she's content staying inside.

"So, where're we going?" she queries as we saunter along.

"To another meadow." I doubt she'll be spinning in among the tall grass this time or rolling down the hill like nothing would stop her. I kind of want her to be a grown-up.

We hit the main path of the farm. It runs between two meadows, and you can hike to the east, down to the river, or take the longer way up to the west hill.

"Have you talked to Jack?" she checks, trekking with fresh speed. I've got a feeling this is her usual pace.

"Not yet. But I will, after this."

She slows down. "Something on your mind?"

A lot.

But for now, I simply need to be with her. "I'll tell you when we get there." And soon, I tug her back, leading her to a branching trail.

"Hey! This isn't the way!"

Salt, who has been following us, barks as if he agrees.

"Salt, home!" I point in the direction of the house. The mutt barks once more. "Home!" This time, he follows my command. "*This* is the way, Morgan." I keep tugging her until we arrive at the stable.

"Ty!" she squeals like a girl in a candy shop, greeting the horses as she passes the stalls. And proving herself to be an animal magnet once again, the horses flash their equine smiles at her, some of them paw at the ground.

She then pads to the one tied outside a stall.

"This is Zeus. He's the gentlest horse around."

"Hey, Zeus." She strokes his black coat right around the neck, unfazed by the stallion's size. Realizing he's the only one that has been tacked up, she asks, "Where's your horse?"

I give her a smile. So she rides, and she doesn't want to share. But this morning, she's got to do it my way. "Ride with me."

She sends me a perplexed gaze.

I make my case, "So I can hug you, feel you close."

"Tempting," she plays with me. "All right then, if that's what you want."

"Trust me, Wolf Girl, it'll be what you want too." I help her mount Zeus and then pat him. He's my favorite beast on this farm.

"Are you sure he can take the both of us?" she wonders, apparently sizing me up, imagining me on Zeus' back in addition to herself.

"Ready for this, boy?" I whisper. Zeus neighs as I keep stroking him. "Yeah, of course you are." I jump on.

The giant stays steady.

"Wow," Morgan sighs. "Way to go, Zeusy."

I'm not sure about 'Zeusy,' but what can I say? He's my boy.

"Move forward a bit, sweetheart."

She nudges herself toward Zeus' neck, then jiggles her butt as I settle myself.

Bless my balls.

The contact makes them throb with lust, but I quickly tame them.

I kick-on Zeus, and he gently walks along the main trail, then up the hill.

Morgan leans back on me. I welcome her, rounding my arm around her waist, perching my chin on the curve where her neck and shoulder meet. I hold my breath so I can hear hers. Being this close to her out in nature wakes my longing for her.

"So we're gonna talk to Jack this afternoon?"

I guess her mind is still on Lilly, which I understand. "Yeah."

"You sound worried."

I grimace painfully. I don't have the heart to tell her the real reason just yet. Besides, I'm relying on Jack to find concrete proof of my theory. If Jack has nothing, it'll be just that—a theory.

I reply, "Of course I'm worried. It's you and your sister we're talking about here." I refrain from reminding her how close I was to losing her.

"But you don't usually show it."

"You can train your head, but you can't train your heart," I admit, then quickly huff, sensing she's about to start a deep discussion about our next steps—and my state of mind. "Can we stop? Just for now. I want you and me here. Nothing else."

She turns her head toward me and gives me a peck. "It's so beautiful here. How can I say no?"

We hit a steep upward slope. The gravity pulls Morgan's weight onto me, compelling me to hold her even firmer. She rubs her back against my chest. Among the pine trees hissing in the wind, I hear her hum. It's so distinct. It's so Morgan.

The smells of wildflowers and sage grass welcome us as the forest opens. My favorite spot.

I get Zeus to climb up further to the highest point of the farm.

"Oh Tyler..." Morgan murmurs as I help her dismount. She takes in the three-sixty-degree view of the rolling hills and lush pasture peppered with grazing animals. Her hands clasp in front of her chest. "I can't believe the mist still lingers. I guess you can only see it when you're this high. It's amazing."

This is why I call this hilltop my favorite spot. And it's my favorite time of day. The land is still cool, while the air is warming from the sunrise, drawing out the mist. It looks like there's a veil covering the greenery below.

I tie Zeus to a nearby tree and then join her, cloaking her with my body like a coat. Slowly, she grabs hold of my hand. It's a different hold—not the way when she wants to know what's on my mind. It's gentle, as if she's about to make a quiet confession.

"Ty," she whispers.

"What is it?"

"I saw the photo on your dresser. Your mom took it away, but... was he?"

So she's asking *me* for a confession. This is the last thing I expect to share with her in a place I always think of as heaven. "Morgan..."

She turns to me, her back to the magnificent views. All she sees is me in a good light. I haven't planned this to happen, but it's time.

She then whispers, "*Homo totiens moritur quotiens amittit suos.*" She recites the line of my tattoo perfectly.

"So, you knew what it means."

"I'm a biologist, I know Latin."

I chuckle, acknowledging her.

She carries on. "'One dies as often as one loses one's friends.' Was it for him?"

I sigh deeply. "That day when I met you, it was the anniversary of his death. He was my best friend—the best of the best. We'd known each other since we were four. When he died—" I exhale, trying to dull the sharpening pulses behind my ribcage. "He was only three days away from turning seventeen."

"I'm sorry, Ty."

"His name was Tobias." God! When was the last time I said his name out loud? "We called him Shakespeare, or sometimes when we bothered to, we called him Toby-or-not-Toby."

A small chuckle escapes her mouth. "Interesting nickname."

"He liked old English literature that much. He was a calm man, unlike me, who used to be the one who said 'go, go, go' without thinking much ahead. He'd do anything for his friends and family."

"You moved together to California?"

"Ah... California." I pause for a few seconds, recalling our decision to pack up and pursue our dreams. "I won a scholarship to Montessori in L.A. I couldn't leave without him. So Tobias and my parents joined forces and saved enough money to send us both to L.A. We both wanted to join the Navy—so we were hoping to settle in San Diego once we'd finished middle school."

I draw in air but hitch mid-breath.

Morgan leans forward, her hand stroking my back. "Ty, did he..." She stops, apparently composing another sentence. "Venice. Something happened there, didn't it?"

I pull her to a grassy spot under the shade. "Come, sit with me."

I settle my bum down, leaning onto a tree. She slides herself in between my open knees, letting her back fall on my chest, her head on my shoulder.

"Venice was my demon, Morgan. Yet it was my salvation," I stammer. "Back then, Tobias had been my swimming buddy. We trained hard. We wanted to be more than just being in the Navy. We wanted to be SEALs. But I don't know how or where we went wrong."

I rest my cheek on her crown as if asking her to support me. I don't even have to ask.

"He started going out with this girl." I sigh, regret starting to flow out of my gut. I guess I've been burying them all this time. "You know, I had bad feelings about her, but I didn't want to ruin his happiness. We got further and further apart. Little did I know, my best friend had become an addict, and one day, his girlfriend just disappeared."

I tap my head back against the bark of the tree. I even almost push Morgan off me.

"Tyler, baby." She crawls up to me.

I shake my head repeatedly. "Damn me! Damn fucking me..."

She wraps herself around me, gently tugging my head toward her bosom. The woman had told me many times that she yearned for a safe place. Now she's giving it to me.

After a moment, I withdraw from her. "I'm so sorry. Look at me! I'm supposed to take care of you."

"It's okay, Ty. I started this." She lets go of her hold and sits next to me. "We're here for each other. It's not just about me."

Her beautiful brown eyes draw a nod out of me. With her, it's okay for me to crumble. I don't always have to be the strong one. We are each other's protector.

I gulp as the scene from that night plays right in front of me. "One evening, a couple of LAPD officers knocked at our apartment door, delivering the news. Tobias was found OD'd at Venice Beach and never recovered."

Morgan shifts so quickly, before I know it, she's already holding me tight.

My voice breaks. "If only I had said something, done something, tried harder—"

"Ty, stop," she interrupts. "Blaming yourself is a deadly temptation. It can bring down the strongest soul."

I shake my head. "I could've done something more, Morgan. No matter how many times I say sorry, I don't feel it'll ever be enough."

"Who did you say sorry to?"

"To Tobias, his family."

"You don't need their forgiveness, Ty. I mean, I'm sure they felt there was nothing to forgive you for. Do you still talk to them?"

"Yeah. I do."

"Have you ever felt they were blaming you?"

I shake my head. "Never."

"You need forgiveness from yourself."

My blood freezes. Not because I'm about to break down, but because I've finally admitted the answer I'd been avoiding all these years. She said it loud and clear.

I dip my head, acknowledging her understanding.

But with what she herself has gone through, she gets it—it's a nod of 'easier said than done.'

"You know, Morgan. I almost gave up joining the Navy. I thought... *fuck it*! It was a curse."

A painful smile forms on her pretty face. "But you didn't quit."

"No. I owed him. A few days before he died, he talked about us completing the BUD/S training." I glance at her, wondering if she's familiar with the underwater training that every SEAL has to go through.

"Well, that royal bodyguard novel never mentioned it, but I know BUD/S." She winks at me.

I scoff, then continue, "Tobias and I talked strategies and whatnot, promising we wouldn't let each other quit no matter what. He challenged me that the day we got our Trident, we should race, open-water swimming off Venice."

I feel Morgan's thumb under my eye. Am I crying? Almost.

"Go on," she whispers.

"So I did that every year, conquering the Pacific Ocean. Including that day when I met you." The frostiness in my blood thaws as if there's a new stream coursing through me. I'll never forget that beautiful face—well, terrified face—emerging out of the water. "I never felt so alone. Sucked into something black, a bottomless cliff. But then, there you were!"

"Oh, Ty..."

"When you handed me that letter to your best friend, I almost lost my shit."

"You certainly didn't show it."

"Because I quickly pulled you into a hug so you didn't see."

She lifts her arm, loosely hugging me. "We're made for each other, then?"

"I believe so." Now she's here, and I'm holding her for a different reason. A much better reason. "That was the last time I swam in the open water off Venice."

"So you surfed after the swim that day? You looked as fresh as a daisy!"

I chuckle. "I don't like to use that expression."

"Uh... what's wrong with fresh as a daisy?"

"It's my ex's name."

"Oops!"

I shrug, telling her it doesn't matter. "I didn't use to surf after the swim, but... I just felt the need to. The water was too inviting that afternoon." I caress her cheek. It has gotten rosier. Perhaps it's the sun, or perhaps she's just feeling it with me. "The ocean had chosen us."

Before her, I'd let too many in, having a girl by my side just for the sake of company, for the sake of forged safety. But Morgan, she's the half of me I never knew existed or could exist.

"Tell me, Ty. If Venice was a sad place for you, why did you keep going back?"

"I don't know, Morgan. Maybe I tried to honor a lost friend. Or maybe to punish myself for losing him."

"Did you go back there this year?"

"No."

Her eyes shift a little as if trying to unpack my 'no.' She then mutters, "So you've forgiven yourself, then?" She knows the answer. She just wants to listen to my explanation.

"Not quite. But... meeting you, helping you, made me think perhaps I've redeemed myself somehow. Every time I thought of Venice, I thought of you."

"I'm glad." Her face shines, full of loveliness that no one else can possess. "You okay?

"Never better," I murmur, then sit up. I swing my leg over her hip as I gently push her back so she lies on the soft grass. My body shields her, and damn, I can't help myself kissing her.

A thank-you kiss.

An I-appreciate-you kiss.

An I-love-you kiss.

Which she welcomes with equal tenderness. This is how it feels to be with someone without burden.

"Goddamn Tyler Hunt..." she mutters.

And this time, I ravage her lips like there's a heatwave sweeping through the hill.

Her legs part as the weight of my kiss becomes needy and carnal. I make quick work of her shirt buttons.

"So this is why you're taking me here?" She lifts her pelvis just a bit, rubbing it against my crotch.

"What else, sweetheart?"

Lust coats her smile as she shakes her shoulders, ditching her shirt, exposing her breasts, cradled by the cups of her bra. Damn, another piece of lingerie I didn't know she'd bought. But those magnificent mounds belong in my palms.

"Take me again. Like you did the first time." Her eyes spark with wants.

"The first time was special, but I'd say let's take it up a notch." I remove the lacy piece and start kneading her boobs.

She sighs, and I exert a bit more pressure on them.

"I need you to be gentle though," she huffs.

Her voice and stare don't really match her request. But I get it. "Gentle is my business—when you want me to be, that is." My fingers coast to her belly. She's so soft there. It's like trailing on a spread of velvet. I haven't forgotten that she's still recovering from that damn poisoning. This was why I enlisted Zeus' help to get us here. So if she *really* wants gentle, I'll give it to her.

I take off my shirt, then descend on her, leaving a gap between my chest and hers so I'm not crushing her. At the same time, I let my hair do a little bit of the talking. It has grown back —although I've kept it tidy, only leaving it on the spots that she loves to touch.

It's as if I can see all the pores in her skin wake up. She moans. I like the sound of it, like she's about to lose all control.

She suddenly puckers. "But I still need you hard down there."

Have I taken this gentle business too far that she can't feel me?

Not really. She just has too many clothes on her still!

And so do I.

I unbuckle my belt, then hurriedly pull my jeans down. She follows my lead, and I help her get naked.

Now we're talking.

"Don't you worry, sweetheart." I straighten myself up, resting on my knees, showing my hard-on behind my briefs. "I'm fresh and fortified, and I'll fit in you like fingers to a glove."

I kiss her, rubbing my crotch against her pink pussy. Slowly, I pull down my briefs until we're completely skin-to-skin.

My senses know her taste, but being on the ground, surrounded by unspoiled nature I've known all my life, there's something new. She's one with our surroundings, and the scent of nature becomes hers, too.

It's a turn-on like no other.

I rest my dick on her belly while I float over her. She reaches down, caressing it along with my balls as if she worships them. I'm used to having my dick squeezed and handled roughly—straight to the point, *give me sex*. But with such care, I feel her appreciation above the carnal pleasure that I'm used to aiming for.

She's harvesting a connection from me. Her touch is so soft, so feminine. This is Morgan at her truest. Yes, she's one tough Wolf Girl, but inside, she's a gentle presence that will keep me on my knees. For I always need her.

I pause, caressing her cheek with my fingertips, marveling at the miracle of my life. Her. Out of the billions of people, she's with me, sharing things that no other soul in this planet possesses. They're exclusively ours—our bodies, our moments, our fears, our hopes— bringing out the best in us. That's love.

Morgan's mouth parts open, feeling me reaching between her thighs. I run my fingers over the rousing texture of her opening. She's so responsive it's already drenched in her own lube.

The last time we made love, she was a virgin. I'm sure she enjoyed it, but there must've been a lot on her mind then that she might not have taken me in all the way.

This time, I want to feel her body shaken by pleasure she hasn't experienced before. She'd been with boys, as she said, and I'll prove that I'm not a one-hit wonder. I'm a man who fulfills her needs—whenever she calls on me.

I tweak her clit.

Her breasts distend, spread prettily as she bucks, giving me access to devour them, licking her nipples one by one.

I pull a condom out of my pocket. I'd do it without one but I don't feel it's the right time. It's not that I don't want to have a family with her. I'd jump at the chance, but she's still young, I don't want her tied down just because we act on passion. I want her to think about it carefully and plan it.

I let her know that I'm putting it on, and she nods. We're on the same page.

I dip into her, holding back to give her time to settle. "You good?" I whisper.

"Yeah." A sweet smile. It's as if I could catch that sweetness and taste it in my mouth like melting candy. She then wraps her legs around me, forcing me to bury my dick deeper. I feel her adjusting, bunching as if tempering a wild tension. "You feel that?"

My length is hugged from every direction, warmed by her slick flesh like it was glazed with honey. "How can I not?" Hot breath leads my whisper. The love I see gleaming in her gaze combined with the feel of her walls swathing my dick almost rends me in two. "I don't want anyone else, I mean it."

"I'm yours, Ty. Always."

The wind has been blowing against her chest when I sit up, and goosebumps pop all over her bare skin. I blanket her, and she releases the loudest, most erotic moan. Jesus, I've almost forgotten that this woman really loves hair.

"Ty... Ty..."

"Oh, sorry, sweetheart." I prop myself up. I guess I was just too eager to brush her. She's wild like that.

"I love you pressing on me, but... I need to breathe, baby."

"Sorry. Sorry. I promised to be gentle, didn't I?" I expose my guilt, kissing her again. Our mouths dance, and our tongues caress each other. "You wanna be on top?" I check in with her.

"I'm good like this. I need to take it easy, remember?" she quips as if warning me what she might do if she was in charge.

"Okay, let me do all the hard work then."

"That's the idea."

It suits me fine. I know her spots, I know her limits—which I'm going to shred until she can moan no more.

Her head tilts forward as I strike those spots, with my dick or finger depending on whether they're inside or around her pussy. Her neck stays in a strained curve and she gapes wide. "Tyler!"

Her body shudders against me, shifting hot energy onto me.

I push my hard-on further, passing the depth when I was in her for the first time. She squirms in pain. I hold my position, waiting for her next reaction.

She claws at my flesh, pushing her pelvis up to get more of me inside her. Her lips blush in heat, telling me 'gentle' has gone out the window.

Her moans turn into howls when I remove my dick. She's goddamn wet, but so tight that the friction sends us both straining.

I enter her again and then keep thrusting—filling her an inch deeper each time while reaching down to rub her swollen clit.

And she becomes absolutely quiet as her gape shifts heavenward, like the calm before the storm. Her body constricts and her arms snake behind me, pressing hard.

She's riding her climax. And it's a fucking beautiful sight.

Then, just as she starts releasing her breath, I cum.

Her moan returns. Soft. Serene.

"I love you, Morgan Blackwell."

She lets go. Her movements are feeble, perhaps milking the last beats of her climax. Her eyes dance with satiation, and a long breath courses out of her mouth. "I love you, too, Tyler Hunt."

I knew that. Yet, her words wash over me like I'm standing beneath a soft waterfall.

The wind skims over the hill, sending the grass around us

to swish as if cheering us on. The sun highlights the yellowing foliage and turns it gold. This is love, connection, and peace I've never dreamed possible. You can't challenge nature, and you can't change the universe's plan. And I can only smile at what I have in my hands.

My Wolf Girl has saved me many times now. From here on, the responsibility is mine.

30

MORGAN

Tyler clucks at Zeus, ordering the stallion to go past the stable and take us to a paddock near the house. Once we get there, he dismounts, praising the horse. Zeus, the gentle giant. I've never seen a calmer horse.

I softly groan when Ty grabs my waist.

"You okay?" he asks, not letting me down fully. Instead, he's propping me on his shoulders like I was a child.

I'm too high up to give him a thank-you kiss. I love horse riding. Sometimes, my fellow researchers and I traveled on horseback, and I never passed on a safari across Yellowstone. But with Tyler, up on that hill, I tasted what it was like to ride a horse after an orgasm and a few rounds of pounding before it. Right then, I questioned Ty's choice of set-up. But he had an answer. He got me to ride sideways, and I felt like a bride already.

"I'm okay," I finally answer.

He peeks at my crotch. I think I might've jerked it a little. He lifts me even higher as if about to throw me in the air, but he hangs on to me, and just as he's letting me down, he steals a kiss.

Right between my legs.

Fuck, fuck, fuck...

The innocence on his face makes me want to scrunch his body and demand him to pound me one more time. It was pleasure, contentment, and wonder. It's a feeling that hasn't been named yet. And it's only him who can make me feel that way.

My gaze lifts to the hills in the distance where it all happened, breathing in the Montanan late-summer air.

I've been here a few days, yet it only occurs to me. It's so still here, apart from the occasional bird chirping and the whisper of the wind.

But a beep changes it. An electronic beep that I used to hear every day, even every hour, when I lived in L.A., And I seem to have forgotten about it.

Tyler takes out his phone, then raises his eyes to me.

"Is that Jack?"

"Yeah." He throws his gaze at the spot I was looking at earlier. Our spot. "You go inside. Let me talk to Jack."

The worry in his face resurfaces, and as if he knows it's disturbing me, he tries to hide it. I approach him. "What happens to 'us' talking to him?"

He steps away from me, making his way back to the house.

I follow, asking me 'why' with my eyes this time.

"Morgan, come and sit with me." He ushers me to the wooden bench on the porch.

I sit right next to him, not wanting to leave a gap, no matter how small. His hand runs on the bench surface.

"You knew what he was going to say?"

"No. Not really. And he doesn't know what's on my mind either."

"And what is that?"

His jaws tighten. "Scarf-face is a woman."

The hair on the back of my neck stands. "Oh?" I never guessed it. But... I won't rule anything out. Maybe this is why he—or she, rather—has been haunting me ruthlessly. Woman to woman. "How do you know?"

"I've been trying to unmask her in my head. Watching her every move in that CCTV clip, albeit not much to draw from. And I've been reminding myself what I observed in Venice when I caught sight of her, watching the beach searching for you."

"Okay..." I follow his explanation tentatively, feeling like a stone has been tugging at his speech so he can't really make his point.

"I'm waiting for something from Jack. It'll prove whether I'm right or barking the wrong tree."

"Show me," I urge.

He clutches his phone hard. "Let me see it first."

"No, Ty." This time, I feel like the same stone is on top of my chest.

He bites his lip. "God... Morgan. I really hope I'm wrong."

"Let's see it. Right here. Now."

He unlocks his phone, opening a message captioned 'You're right.'

He cautiously opens the video attachment. The setting seems to be a hotel. Art Deco. Perhaps it's somewhere in Florida. A woman and a man approach the front door, their backs to the camera. The way their arms twist against each other tells me they're more than just partners in crime.

Then, before another camera catches them, the woman places a scarf over her face while the man turns his head to shield her.

"That's Eduardo Callas. And that's Scarf-face."

"Yes."

"So, they're lovers."

"Yes."

"And your point, exactly?" I beg him to explain, as I still don't recognize the woman.

"This is the first time I saw the footage, Morgan. But—" He zooms in all the way and rewinds the clip right when the couple comes into view—showing themselves in the reflection of the glass doors.

My whole body freezes. Before I can shut down on the spot, I run away from the scene.

31

———

TYLER

"Morgan!"

"Leave me alone, Ty."

I didn't know she could run that fast. I'm about to catch her, but realizing where she's going, I halt.

The door opens behind me. "Tyler! What have you done?" Mom blasts at me.

Almost at the same time, Salt runs past the both of us and makes a beeline to the paddock, joining Morgan, who has already climbed over the fence. She lets the dog watch her while she leans on Zeus, forehead to forehead.

"Mom... she just needs her space, okay?"

I've seen Morgan breaking down when she described her brother's death in detail. She resisted me then, but I could sense she wanted me to be there. She wanted to fall apart in front of me.

This time it's different. Cold anger is all over her, and it settles like hard cement. Telling her 'I'm sorry' a dozen times wouldn't do anything.

"Since when did you start breaking a girl's heart?" Mom continues griping. "Here? At this farm?"

"Mom, it's got nothing to do with me and her. She has just received a piece of bad news. Very bad news." I gaze at Morgan, who's patting Salt this time.

"And you're gonna let your animals handle it?"

For now. Because the last thing she needs right now is for her man to fuel her anger. I'm charged up. It's so unfair that she has to face this betrayal. But those gentle creatures will absorb her ire.

Neither Zeus nor Salt had been born when I lost Tobias. But those animals are old souls. When I was still in the military, every time I came home, heavy as if my battle pack had been on my shoulders, they knew. Zeus used to do exactly that— what he's doing now to Morgan, nuzzling his nose at her—and Salt would've settled at my feet, wrapping my ankles with his fluffy body.

"Morgan and I are solid. We'll be fine," I assure Mom.

I'm not sure what she sees in me, but Mom relents. She taps my shoulder, saying, "What are you afraid of, son? At times, you just need to do things *with* her, not just for her."

Mom goes inside, and as soon as the door closes behind her, I dash to the paddock. Salt knows I'm coming, but he sticks to Morgan's side like glue.

As I approach, Morgan gets up from patting Salt, and then hangs on to Zeus' rein.

I softly unfurl her fingers from the leather strap, taking her hand into mine.

She lets me. "Aunt Diana," she growls. "So she pretended to be a hero, breaking away from us to distract our pursuers. To secure information. Fuck her! She was using the time to regroup with Callas and be with Lilly."

"She was no hero."

"I saw the date of that video, Ty. It was a couple of days before she killed Hudson."

I pull her to my side. "I'm sorry."

"It all makes sense now. That's why Lilly was never in danger. Diana wants her to be her own daughter. When she took care of us while Mom and Dad were away, it was clear how much she adored Lilly. Saying she wished she had a daughter like her right in front of me. It's not that I was competing for her affection. Hell, no! I just remember it."

Morgan stares at Zeus, then Salt. After a few moments, she faces me, asking, "How did you know, Ty?"

"I'd been suspicious about Scarf-face being a woman ever since I watched the CCTV footage in Florida. Then you got poisoned, and everything went on the back burner. I picked up my research a couple of days ago and found out that your aunt was part of her school's shooting team. She competed nationally and at some stage met with Callas."

Morgan shakes her head. "They'd been lovers since then?"

"I don't know."

"Why did she do this, Ty? She killed my mom and my dad —her own brother! And Hudson... God..."

"I wish I knew, Morgan. There's still a lot to uncover."

"Jack said to keep an open mind. That there would be a lot of unexpected things coming to light. I never thought this would be it."

"We'll get to the bottom of this. And most of all, we'll get Lilly back."

"What does she want from me that she kept me alive? Surely, not to adopt me!"

"There are still so many things we don't know."

"That's why the attack at North Cascades was so precise. As if the people swarming our house had known exactly where the guards were. Because she was the mole!" Morgan sputters.

"Was she with you then?"

"Yes. We ran away together. But she did try to break away

from us then. That excuse about distracting our attackers!" she explains. "But Hudson didn't let her. And perhaps she didn't expect Hudson to come up with that plan to burn down the house, blinding those rogue soldiers with night-vision goggles."

"So she kept on pretending. Perhaps still trying to gain your trust? That was why you said the attackers seemed to unravel after they went inside. That they couldn't even defend their own car."

"Yes!" Her eyes go big. "Yes, Ty! Those attackers didn't expect me and my brother to retaliate, and they didn't have their commander to let them know what to do! Because she was with us all the time."

"Your brother was brilliant. I wish I'd met him."

Perhaps this is the wrong time to bring up her brother. But she smiles with fondness. "He was brilliant. He would've loved you, Ty. He would've."

I squeeze her hand. "Much as I hate how this has panned out, can I ask you something?"

"Yeah."

"Did you or Hudson tell her where you were that day? When you were ambushed?"

"We told Aunt Diana about a spot to meet up the day before, about maybe twenty miles off the stretch of road where we were attacked."

I caress her. "Do you know what this means?"

"What?"

"Your aunt knew exactly where you were going. It wouldn't have mattered whether you were going to the airport or hitting the highway for Helena. She would've known."

Her head hangs down, but she agrees, hugging me tight.

I nuzzle the side of her neck, whispering, "It wasn't your fault, Morgan. It wasn't your fault."

She lifts her head. "Just like it wasn't your fault that you lost Tobias."

I smile at her. "Yes. To hell with guilt!"

"Damn right. To hell with guilt!" She nods resolvedly. "I'm glad Aunt Diana wasn't there when you drove me to Washington. Who knew what sort of surveillance she would've placed around there? And I always said I'd made my way there alone. Otherwise, she might've had you in her crosshairs long before those men attacked us in front of your home."

"Wow... I'd never thought of that."

"Fuck that bitch!" Morgan trembles. "Fuck her!"

"She's a bitch, alright."

Morgan looks at me, nodding, although her eyes tell me she doesn't quite believe I would use that word. "We're gonna get her, Tyler."

"We are, Morgan. We are."

32

———

MORGAN

When Ty guides us to our bedroom, I'm still shaken. My anger has subsided, but it lingers. It will for a long time to come. What Aunt Diana has done is not just a betrayal. It's evil's work. Whenever I remember her face, I don't see her as a human being anymore.

At the same time, I'm shaken by an energy that propels my resolve. I have Tyler by my side. Sooner rather than later, Lilly will be here with me. With me! Her sister. She doesn't belong to that monster!

Still, a tiny part of me wishes that this was all a misunderstanding, that there would be clues or evidence that would come to light, debunking Aunt Diana's involvement. So she loves Callas, and they go a long way back. So she adores Lilly and wants to make my little sister her own daughter.

But those wants wouldn't warrant murders, would they?

I sigh helplessly. If only...

"Jack is on his way," Tyler announces. "Callas has gone under the radar again, but he's got to have his limits. He'll show himself. I can feel it. When he does, we'll be ready, and we'll nail that son of a bitch!" His phone rings, but he carries on to finish his statement. "Once we find him, I'm sure Diana won't be far away." He then answers the call.

He listens for a while, then puts his phone on speaker.

"Hi, Morgan," Sam comes on the line.

"Mr. Kelleher," I greet him. Tyler has explained what he found about Aunt Diana to Red Mark. From the vibe in the room, I know there isn't a twist that will make my wish come true. It's time to face reality.

The question that I need the answer to is: *Why does she want me?*

Sam explains, "Cee has managed to decipher all of the remaining messages. One, it's a server name, and there are phrases in the other messages that make up its password."

"And?"

"Your parents' last mission must've gone very wrong. Details are still sketchy. But it was in Florida."

"Florida?"

"There are mentions of 'diamonds' in some of the documents. I think your parents found something significant. Based on the numbers, we may be talking tens of millions. The FBI still won't tell us anything. But—"

"So my family died, all because of diamonds?" I turn to face a wall, hands pressing it hard. It's made of stone, but it's as if I could move it. "That's why Diana wanted me alive. She thought I had information about those diamonds?"

"Have you ever told her about your mother's secret messages?" asks Tyler, tugging me to sit on the bed.

"No. I didn't want to tell those to anyone. I didn't want to make Hudson or Diana a target like me. And Diana had never pressed for it either. I guess she was very good at controlling herself. She only ever said things like... *you can trust me. Tell me anything, we're family.* Yeah. That sort of thing."

"We don't know the full story yet, Morgan," Sam argues.

"I never heard about Callas being in the diamond business," says Tyler.

"There are a lot of dots that we need to connect. But the relationship between Diana Blackwell and Eduardo Callas has helped our search. We've got evidence that Callas was in L.A. the day Lilly went missing."

"And the day my parents died," I murmur.

"Morgan," Sam starts quietly. "Did you know that your father died of poisoning?"

"What?"

"Hydrogen cyanide, exactly the type used to poison the pudding you ate in Tampa."

"So Callas killed my father!" I tremble. "Still, the blood is in Diana's hands! That'll never change. That's why Mom was hell-bent on getting me out of L.A. Danger converged there." Her voice echoes in the room as if she was here. *Run! Find Lilly!*

"How about Morgan's mother? Who came into their house that night?" Tyler queries as if reading my mind.

"From police reports and from looking at the charred rubbles, we believe more than one person started the blaze. It was most likely Callas' men," Sam replies.

I wring my hands. "And Scarf-face was there to make sure no one came out alive. But she knew I escaped, therefore, I must've had the information she wanted. Hence the chase."

"That was the likely scenario," Sam affirms.

"Well, what else have you got, Mr. Kelleher?"

"Back to the server where we found information about the diamonds. There's a folder that we can't open yet. We need another password. The only word we have out of your mom's messages is 'Redemption' with a capital 'R.' But it doesn't fit anywhere."

I throw a sharp gaze at Tyler. "I need my books, Ty. I left

them on your shelf. I don't know what I'm looking for yet. But I need them. There may be something that I missed."

"Okay. I'll get your books." He nods. "Then we'll figure out what 'Redemption' might mean."

"Let us know what you find," Sam says. "The team here is behind you. We'll prevail!"

The call ends. Ty puts his arm around my shoulder.

"It's time. I can feel it," I grit out.

"You stay here. We'll find the way to unlock that folder."

A helicopter whirs in the distance. Jack.

"That's your minder tonight," Tyler quips. "And that's my ride to Helena."

33

TYLER

I drop by the Red Mark office before I pick up Morgan's books. I need to restock my ammo, gather more gear, and reconnect with the team.

Stepping inside this office makes me realize how much my life has changed. The mission to rescue Tia Grant seems like a lifetime ago, and the following dinner at the Thirsty Fox—I'd believe it if someone told me it had happened a year ago.

Sam and Cora-Lee greet me when I pass by the command center.

"Tyler!" Sam rushes to me. "How's Morgan holding up?"

"She's alright, considering. She's with Jack now."

"Good. Good."

"Hey, Cee."

"Ty, good to see you. It hasn't been the same without you here," she quips.

"Don't listen to her," Sam interjects. "Everything is under control."

I look around. "Where's Mark?"

"Ivy needs to be on bed rest. So he's been staying home with her in the past few days."

"Is she okay?"

"Yeah. Just a precaution for her low blood pressure."

"Send my regards, will you?"

"Of course."

I tell Sam, "I'm gonna get those books. See if we can find something about that folder's password."

"Excellent," he says. "We'll stay here all night, Ty. For you and Morgan."

"Thanks, boss."

It's almost eight at night when I start my drive home. Drizzle marks sprinkle all over my windscreen.

Being away from home comes with the job, but this is the first time I had to leave town for days since I moved into my new house. Things felt like routine before—the house was just a house. But tonight, I stand at the door as if I don't recognize it. Everything is different.

Including that Mercedes parked a few yards from my house.

And the movement just outside my gate.

"Hold it there!" I halt the intruder, pointing my Glock.

The woman squeals. She looks to be in her mid-twenties or thereabout, with curly blonde hair with an athletic figure. "No! No! Don't shoot!"

"Turn around. Slowly."

She raises her hands, quivering. "My name is Ava West, Morgan's friend."

I'm about to lower my gun, but at the height of a mission that has gone left and right in a matter of days, I won't take any chances. I haven't seen Ava's face. "Prove it."

"Okay... okay... I'm gonna give you my wallet, okay? Don't shoot, please!"

She seems genuinely scared. Under the pale light, I can't

really see her expression, but her hand trembles as she passes me her wallet.

I examine her ID, and inside, there's a folded piece of paper. A sketch. A familiar style of drawing.

"That's me and Morgan." Her voice hitches. "I drew it just before my family and I moved house. We used to be neighbors."

I stow my gun, then hand her back her wallet. "Don't sneak up on me like that!"

"Yeah. Yeah. My fault," she concedes. "You must be the SEAL guy. I don't blame you for being thorough."

"What are you doing here, Ava?"

"I need to find Morgan. Is she with you?"

"Yeah. She's safe."

"Where is she?"

"Not here. She's with my parents."

"Oh... good. Thank you."

I scan the street, looking for a sign of someone tailing her. "That your car?" I gaze at the Merc that parks like a sore thumb.

"Yeah."

I open my garage door. "Keys."

I drive it in and quickly close the garage.

Ava explains, "I read something about a Montanan girl getting poisoned in Florida. I just knew it was her. Please, please let me see her."

I've promised myself that I would do anything to make Morgan feel like she has a family. And I know Ava is family to her.

I give Ava a reassuring smile. After how I greeted her at the gate, I'm sure she needed it. "I'll take you to her. But first, I've got to get Morgan's books."

"Huh! Morgie and her books! She's crazy. She used to read one book a day."

"No wonder." I dash to my library and pick up Morgan's pile of books.

Suddenly, Ava giggles. "Oh, Morgie! I can't believe she kept that!" She points at *A SEAL for Princess Paloma*.

"It's the stupidest book!"

"You read it?"

I give her a sideways glance. "No. But—"

"You did!"

I growl. "Come on, we haven't got much time."

"Where are we going?"

"To the airport. I'm going to take you to her in style."

"Um... okay," she mumbles, perplexed.

My phone rings. It's Ian, my pilot friend, telling me that bad weather is coming and his chopper can't fly. I look at Ava. "Sorry, change of plans. We're doing it the old-fashioned way."

"That's fine, too," she giggles.

"Still, it doesn't mean uncomfortable."

"I don't care about comfort, Mr. Hunt. I just want to be with Morgan."

I nod at her thoughtfully. "How did you find my house?"

"Morgan mentioned your name and Red Mark—that she trusted you, and she told me she was going to convince her brother to go to Helena. I was at Red Mark earlier, then I followed you. Well, sort of. I overtook you and waited until I found out which street you turned into."

"You told Morgan that you saw Lilly in Florida?"

"Yes." She perks up. "Did you find her?"

"No. Not yet."

Her head bows. "Oh... Lilly-pilly..."

"But we will." I open the passenger door of my SUV. "Hop in."

Barely a few yards in, there's another movement coming my way. This time, I know exactly who it is. I stop.

"Hey, buddy."

Ava shifts in her seat, trying to catch a glimpse of the unexpected guest. "You can't just leave your dog!"

"He's not mine."

"Oh? A neighbor's?"

"He's looking for Morgan."

"Ah, a stray? Not surprising. Animals follow her—been happening since she was—since I knew her."

Gravy slants his head as if it'll make him cuter. Well, it does.

I flick the passenger door open.

What's Morgan's is mine, so Gravy is welcome to hitch a ride.

The mutt takes a few steps back, unsure what to make of the invitation—perhaps the first time he sees a car seat.

"It's okay, buddy," I encourage him. "I'll take you to her. I bet you've been coming here a lot."

"Come on," Ava encourages. And finally, the dog jumps in.

"Good boy, Gravy."

"Gravy?"

"Ask your friend." I smile and close the door.

The drizzle has turned into a downpour now.

"It'll be a few hours' drive." I grimace, looking up at the sky lit up by lightning. "Maybe a bit longer in this weather."

"However long it takes."

I hit the highway, keeping the speed even at fifty miles.

"So you've known Morgan since you were kids?"

"Morgie was three when we first met."

"Wow... that is a long time."

"We were neighbors, but we stayed close even after she and her family moved to another suburb. We're practically sisters. Even though I'm five years older, we still managed to meet in the middle. It's like I could tap into my inner child around her, and she could be as mature as I was when needed." She stares at the dashboard as if replaying the time they were together. She then directs her gaze to me. "Thanks for taking care of her."

"I love her dearly, Ava."

"I know. Still, I'm watching you."

"Yes, ma'am," I chuckle. "You know Ava, she saved me more than I saved her."

Ava smiles. "You're certainly a step up from her previous boyfriend."

I cackle, not expecting such a remark. "Why? Wasn't he a nice man?"

"They got together when she was sixteen. So he was a boy, really. A mortician's son," she confides, almost in a whisper, as if Morgan was in the back seat. "Don't tell her I told you."

Ava mentioned 'a boy' just like Morgan did. I am Morgan's man. So I'm definitely a step up—by a long mile.

34

MORGAN

Tyler should've arrived by now. There's no sign of any aircraft approaching.

"Morgan, sit down, please," Jack pleads.

"Sorry." I've been pacing back and forth in front of him. I understand if I'm driving him crazy, but my chest is about to explode. If I sit down, it may just do.

I call Tyler again. This time, he answers.

"Ty! Where the hell have you been?"

"Sorry, sweetheart. The weather has been horrendous here. I've been losing cell reception. Chopper couldn't fly, so I'm driving home."

My heart returns to almost its normal size. My lungs gradually receive air again. "Be careful, Ty."

"I will, Wolf Girl. And I've got a surprise for you."

"You had time for that?"

Suddenly, a bark in the background.

I frown. "Whose dog is that? Ty... is that... is that Gravy?"

"Damn!" he laments. He then puts on a slightly different voice. "Gravy, you just can't help it, can you?"

I laugh at his annoyed tone. "So you found him."

"He found me. Hey, listen. I'm going to stop by my friend's place. He's a vet. I'm going to leave Gravy there for a couple of days, okay?"

He's going to quarantine the dog. "I understand, Ty. He's a stray. So, Good call."

"My friend will make sure Gravy is up to date with his shots and all that. When he gives Gravy the all-clear, he can come home to the farm."

Gravy barks again.

"What is it, buddy?" Ty checks in on him. "You'll be treated like royalty. Don't you worry!"

"He's gonna be neutered. How can you say it's royal treatment? Say sorry on my behalf," I giggle.

"I feel sorry for him, too, but it's for the best. Really, this Gravy thing was meant to be a surprise," he apologizes. "But I still have another one for you."

The wind outside whistles. Through the window, I watch the silhouette of trees swaying. Despite the gusts, I wait outside under the cover of the porch.

Jack joins me. "So he's coming?"

"Yeah. He's driving."

"Probably wise in this weather."

I pull the front of my jacket so the layers overlap my belly.

Jack observes me, then asks, "How are you feeling? Still sore?"

"Marginally. I'll be back to a hundred percent in a day or two."

"Good to hear," he says. "Ty was a wreck when you were poisoned. But that's exactly when you see a man at his strongest. He really loves you, Morgan."

"I know. I love him too." Maybe a little more if I want to tell the absolute truth.

"Whatever he does, he wants to keep you safe, you know that, right?"

The sky lights up, followed by the air rumbling. Lightning repeatedly strikes the ground.

"So, this is the real Montana," Jack quips. "Before today, I've only been to Helena. I've never seen anything like it."

"What a show, huh?"

We both stand in awe. With nothing obstructing the sky, we can see big clouds rolling in.

After a few minutes, we hear the pitter-patter that soon becomes a drenching.

Behind the curtain of rain, a pair of headlights loom.

It's such a long driveway here at the farm. It feels like forever before the car arrives at the house. There's an under-cover area that extends from the porch, and Tyler parks there.

"Ty!" I come and hug him, and the roof barely protects us from the horizontal rain. He stands guard next to the passenger door. "You've got the books?"

"They're in the backseat."

"Should we get them?"

He stands in place. "I told you I've got another surprise for you." He finally steps away from the passenger door, opening it and revealing who's sitting there.

My knees wobble. "Ave? Ave?" I cry.

"Morgie!" Ava jumps out, heading straight to me with her arms open wide.

I bawl like my best friend had just come back from the grave. I hold her tightly, so overwhelmed with tears that I can't really see what's around me.

"Morgie, I missed you so much!"

"Ave... I can't believe you're here."

We cocoon each other like we are just one big ball of happiness.

When my sobs subside, I see Ty, smiling with happy tears, pointing at his chest—the spot where my pendant would be on me. I think he's saying that he has brought home one of the rose petals.

Of course.

Ava isn't a Blackwell, but she's my family, and Tyler has brought her back to me. I mouth 'thank you' to him, giving him a look that releases all of the gratefulness within me. He may not know how much it means to me—but, oh hell, he knows! He knows damn well.

He thumps a fist on his heart.

I love you, too, I mouth.

Ava breaks the hug, observing me from head to toe. "My God! You've grown up!"

"We both have, Ave." I laugh with her. But soon, reality sinks in. I should be asking her how life has been treating her. Perhaps there's a new man I should know about, but this is a reunion amid a crisis. "Are you sure you're not being followed?"

"You're asking me?" She eyeballs Tyler. "That man made sure."

I stride to Ty. He knows what friendship means, and he delivers. Unable to utter anything, I simply fall on him.

"I take it that you love the surprise," he mutters, softly kissing my crown.

"One hell of a surprise," I tremble with happiness.

Meanwhile, it looks like Jack has introduced himself to Ava. He even offers his jacket to her, which she accepts with a blushing face. Well, it's dim in here, but I know she's blushing. God, they look so sweet together... could it be?

"It's cold out here, guys, let's go inside," Tyler suggests. His arm is over my shoulder, ushering me to the door.

Jack extends his hand to Ava, holding the door for her.

Lou and Peter briefly introduce themselves to Ava, and Lou makes hot cocoa for us.

"Jack, come with me," Ty calls, gesturing to the Marine to leave us girls be.

Just the two of us in the dining room, Ava and I engage in another long hug.

Then she reaches for her cup of cocoa. "Where did you find your boyfriend? He's friggin' gorgeous!"

"We met in Venice Beach, out of all places. He actually sent the letter to you from San Diego."

"Oh, right... But he's from here?"

"Yeah. He's from here."

"What is it with you and Montanan men?"

"He's not just a Montanan man, Ave. He was a SEAL, he rescues missing children for a living, and as you said, he's frigging gorgeous."

"And you thought Evra was your soulmate," my bestie mumbles.

A weird kind of sensation plays behind my throat. I haven't heard that name in years! "He was never my soulmate!"

"Have you forgotten? *Oh, Ava, Evra, and I are just meant to be. Oh, Ave, he loves wolves as much as I do,*" she mimics me.

"Shut up!"

"If you and Tyler made it to Hollywood, you would be nicknamed Tygan."

We laugh for a few more moments, then the penny drops. "I'm glad you're here with me, Ave. I mean, I have Ty and Jack, but I need all the strength to go through this. We need to find Lilly."

"Yes. I'm here, Morgie. We'll find our Lilly-pilly."

I get up. "I think it's time to call the boys in... well, the men."

"So, who is Jack?" She follows me.

"He's Ty's boss's brother. He's helping us."

"Ty's boss's brother." Ava tries to follow, clutching Jack's jacket that's still on her. "Got it."

"He's a Marine. Single, but I don't think he's looking for love. Yet."

Ava pinches my arm. "Who's looking for love!"

"I saw you!" I tease her. "Anyway, it's a long story. In summary, he knows a lot about the people smuggling network in Florida. So he's an asset."

Ava nods, then carefully says, "Hey, Morgie. Tyler told me about Diana."

I flatten my lips in disgust. "Fuck her, really."

"I almost destroyed his car dashboard when I heard it. Why am I not surprised? I never liked her!" Ava declares. "Remember when Lilly came home from the hospital? You were singing to her while she was sleeping in her cradle. Then, out of the blue, Diana just took her away!"

"I was seven then, so you were twelve. And you remember?"

Ava points at her temple. "Don't you doubt my memory."

I suppose that's true. "I vaguely remember welcoming Lilly home, but Aunt Diana? Not really."

"I mean, who did she think she was? You're Lilly's sister!"

"What did she do?"

"She said you were disturbing Lilly, then she took her to another room. Ergh... she was cradling her so close to her bosom!"

"That's disgusting!"

"And remember when your parents were away? You used to dread having her around."

That, I remember.

We're about to leave the dining room to find the guys, and we bump into Tyler, who's about to go in. "Morgan, sorry to interrupt, but we've got a call from Cora-Lee."

Much as I want to stay with Ava all night, pouring my heart out, we have a mission to complete. I motion for Ty to get on with it, and he puts his phone in the middle of the table.

"Cee, you're on speaker now," he gives her the floor. At this time, Jack has joined us.

"Guys, I've run the possible passwords again based on the phrases and words from Morgan's mother. I think what's missing is a set of numbers. You know, Welcome01, Apple123. It's not that your parents were dumb enough to use such silly combinations, but naturally, a password would contain numbers. And it's not their birthdays or any of the combinations. I've checked."

"I trust your gut, Cee," I reply. "We're going to scour the books once more."

"Good plan, Wolf Girl," Cora-Lee praises.

"We'll call you when we find something," Ty says and hangs up.

I lean forward. "Alright, gents. It's time to get bookish."

We lay the books on the dining table. Jack, Tyler, Ava, and I take a few each.

"Inspect them page by page," I instruct. "See if there's a mark or something. Especially around numbers."

Jack has the honor of handling the royal bodyguard novel. He can't stop giggling as he narrates. "*I will go to the end of the world for you, my love, Beckett says. The young royal falls into his embrace, and with a kiss, she unseals her burning passion.*"

"Get serious now!" warns Tyler, but soon he himself breaks out in laughter.

Hours later, though, we sit in silence, hands under our chins.

"What did we miss?" Ava mumbles.

"So, 'Redemption' comes from this book," I allude, holding up a textbook about the evolution of animals. When Mom handed over the pile, it was the last book.

Ava adds, "The book is about animal's struggles which ultimately contribute to their evolution. Does that mean anything? I mean, you and animals?"

"God..." I sigh. Thank God for Ava—my Chief Life Officer always has an answer. "Shit! *Redemption of Wolf 302*!"

I get a blank look from Ty and Jack, but Ava stands up. "I've heard you mention it before. It was another book, wasn't it?"

"It is a book, Ava!" I confirm.

"Do we need to purchase it?" Jack chimes in.

"No. My mom gave it to me just before my graduation. I think the password is Redemtion302."

"Let's get Cee on the line!" Tyler says without waiting.

Cora-Lee is back on call, testing the password. "Fuck my pants..." She sighs. "I'm in!"

"Hell yeah!" Jack and Tyler high-five each other while I hug Ava, almost shaking her.

"What's in the folder, Cee?" Tyler queries.

For a while, we only hear Cora-Lee's breathing. When I start speculating what she's seeing, I hear her say, "There are no diamonds."

"Cee?" Tyler gets edgy.

"Diamonds is the code for the mission. The folder lists the names associated with the syndicate that has been keeping a large network of people smuggling. Callas is only one of the faces we're seeing in these files."

Jack shakes his head as if saying that sounds so fucking familiar.

"What the hell is that?" I hear Sam Kelleher's voice in the background as if pointing at something.

"We're seeing maps, lady and gents," Cee clarifies.

"Ladies and gents," Jack corrects.

"Oh? Sorry if I missed someone."

"Hi, Cee, I'm Ava. I'm Morgan's best friend."

"Oh hey. I'm sorry. I didn't know you were there. Three men

and three women. What a team!" Cee quips. "Anyways, these maps show that Florida is the gate, and their main network is in Central and South America. There are spots marked with diamond icons."

"That's Tampa!" Sam exclaims. "God damn! The numbers that we thought were the IDs of the diamonds, along with their carats and values, are location codes!"

"So the riches that Callas and Diana are hunting are, in fact, the very thing that will bring them down!" I claim. How is that so satisfying? At the same time, tragic. Because at the end of the day, my parents and Hudson died because of this.

"What an irony," Jack mumbles.

"Well, there are three diamonds in Tampa. One of them is that apartment you went into, Ty," informs Cora-Lee.

"Son of a bitch!" Ty gripes.

"So these are the locations where the children have been hidden," Jack says.

"Morgan," Sam says circumspectly. "Your parents have uncovered a huge operation. What they were after is what we're after. Rescuing those kids."

Only, they were too late to report them. But at least I can rest easy. Their deaths aren't in vain.

"Why didn't they send this to the FBI?" Ava asks.

"I think your parents suspected a mole," Tyler says. "That Callas had somehow infiltrated the investigation."

I huff out my anger. "And they never thought it was their own family."

"It looks like you guys might need to go places soon. Let me know when you want me to book the plane again," Cora-Lee suggests.

"Good idea, Cee," Ty says. "With the permission of the bill-payer?" He glances at me.

"Of course," I approve.

Lou enters the room. In her motherly voice, she says, "Guys, it's four a.m. Jack and Ava, don't you have to rest? I can show you your rooms, unless you want to do it, Ty?"

Tyler slides to my side, being the pillar of strength that he is. He decides, "You show them their rooms, Mom. I need to talk to Morgan."

As we say goodnight to each other, it dawns on me. I'm no longer alone, and it's not just Ty and me. Everyone in this room —and at Red Mark—is behind me. That's one hell of a support system, and nothing can replace it.

35

MORGAN

The comforter keeps me warm, but the furnace below me that is Tyler Hunt gives me a solid, sumptuous kind of comfort. He said he wanted to talk to me, but we ended up going straight to bed.

My eyes are heavy, and waves of drowsiness caress me from the inside.

But Tyler moves, his breath coarse as if letting out a mighty burden. Or letting me know that something is burdening him.

"Ty?"

Finally, after trying to stay still and let me fall asleep again, the man calls it. "Morgan, I need to talk to you."

"Of course." I scoot myself off him. "Fire away."

"Jack is going to get his Florida connection to track Callas. We're close."

"Yeah. So as soon as we know, we fly."

"Yeah. We fly." He almost echoes my voice. "And I want you to stay with Ava here."

I bend my legs, pushing myself up and facing him. I couldn't have heard him correctly. "What? No! I'm coming with you!"

"Morgan, let me and Jack handle this."

"Hey, where is this coming from?"

"It's how we roll for this one last assault."

"Wait a minute!" I grimace, recalling my short conversation with Jack on the porch earlier. "You'd discussed this with Jack, without me?"

"I had to!"

"Huh... he was talking about how much you love me and that whatever you do, it's because you want to keep me safe."

"Is that wrong?" he deadpans.

"Ty! You don't think I can handle my own aunt? Are you not going to grant me the pleasure of looking her in the eye when she's defeated?"

"You can handle anything, but I can't risk getting you injured. Or worse."

"So what!"

"You stay here with Ava. I hate to tell you this, but you don't have a say in it. It's final." It may be his tiredness talking, but I know Ty means it—he just didn't have the energy to be diplomatic with me.

"What happens to us protecting each other?" I complain.

"You stay, you protect me."

"I'm not afraid to die, Ty."

"That's exactly why I can't take you, Wolf Girl."

I shirk the comforter off me. "That's it, isn't it? That's why you call me that! You always think I'm a girl!" It turns out my tank is as empty as his. I can't be bothered to stay civil. "And you and Jack are the grown-ups. The men who can handle anything! Well, you two can die too, you know?"

"Morgan, I've always called you that since the first time we met. It doesn't mean I think less of you. We're highly tr—"

"Yeah, yeah. You're highly trained. And I'm not!" I gripe. "But Lilly is my sister! She only trusts me!"

"She may not remember you. Then what?"

I push the covers over to him, almost throwing it at him. My feet land on the floor with a thump, and with even angrier force, I run outside.

How dare he!

Lilly will never forget me.

I sit on the porch, waiting for the lightning show, anticipating the thunder. But there's no light, there's no noise, only the roar inside my chest.

Tyler walks up to me, his step light as if I was going to turn around and pounce at him. "I'm sorry." He has come with a blanket.

I stay still.

He spreads the blanket over my shoulders with a tender touch. "It's been a long day, but there's no excuse. I shouldn't have said that about Lilly." He sits on the same bench but keeps a small gap. "Forgive me?"

I glare at him for a few seconds. But I can't be mad at him for long. I acknowledge his apology, then whisper, "What if you're right?"

"No. No. The bond between sisters will never be broken. I'm sure of that."

I lean my head on his shoulder. "You mean it?"

"Yes. But I stand by my decision."

I bite a lip. "They want me, Ty. My sister won't be safe unless they see me. I can't just sit here doing nothing."

"Point taken. But Jack and I will make sure that we prevail even without them having to see you. They will have no choice but to let Lilly go."

"You make it sound easy."

"It won't be easy. It won't be straightforward. It will be dangerous, that's for sure. But I'm with Red Mark for a reason. I know you don't want to hear me blabbering about this, but I've trained by the best, with the best, and I've proven myself. That was why you came to me, wasn't it?"

I sigh, then nod. He's in his boxers and a thin T-shirt that he seems to have put on haphazardly. "Come, let's go inside," I motion.

I lead him to the study, where my old cellphone has been charging.

"I'll make her look at this." I turn on the phone. I'm shaking, and for the first time, I feel revengeful. "Fuck, I will! I'm going to force her to look at this!" I load up a photo. "These are the Blackwells, and she isn't part of us. I'll look her in the eye and ask why, and she'll explain while she's staring at my dad, my mom, and Hudson."

In the background, my phone keeps buzzing, spitting out one missed call notification after another.

And to my horror, it rings in my hands.

I drop the phone with a squeal as if it's burning me.

"Don't answer!" Ty yells, picking it up only to switch it off.

"Shit..."

"Where did you get this phone?"

"It was already in the house at North Cascades. I presume my mom left it for me."

"When was the last time you turned it on?"

"Um... it was in Spokane before I started the wilderness hike. The battery had been dead since then, and I left it on the charger just this morning."

"You haven't turned it on since then? Well, apart from just now?"

"No, I haven't. I used another phone since, a sat phone."

"Good. Someone might just want to track our location."

My chest is pressed under an invisible stone. "I'm sure I haven't."

"It's okay, sweetheart. I'm going to call Cee now. Cellphone tracking isn't new. We know how to counter it. Whatever you do, do not turn that on."

"Okay."

Tyler makes a call, and as usual, he puts it on speaker.

"Ty." It's Sam Kelleher's voice—it's so low I wonder if the man is talking in his sleep.

"Sir? Sorry, I thought I was going through to Cora-Lee."

"Ah, yeah. I asked her to get some z's and told her I'd wake her up if something came up."

"You two are still in the office?"

"Ty, we told ya. We'd stay overnight. Hang on, I'll get Cee."

My heart melts. Red Mark isn't just about danger and adrenaline. Ty wasn't wrong to be boasting about his training— the mental toughness, the empathy. It's their values that set them apart. 'Alone' is not in their vocabulary, and they will go as far as we do. It's brotherhood at its best.

"Ty, Morgan." This time, Cee's voice comes through.

"Cee, thanks for staying up for us. Could you please place a redirect on this number? It's Morgan's old number. I'm texting it to you now." He handles his phone with one hand while the other reaches out for his laptop.

"You bet."

Ty explains, "She has been receiving calls. Old and new. As recent as ten minutes ago. We may need to talk to our caller. So, in case the call goes on long enough, I don't want them to track us."

"No big deal, Ty. Now, you should be able to receive calls to that number on your console."

Tyler observes the window on his laptop, something that resembles an old-school interface with a black background and grey buttons. "Good."

"Do you want me to attach a location to it?" Cee asks.

He thinks for a moment. "Yeah. Let's give them a realistic

one so they don't ask questions. Make it appear that Morgan's phone is somewhere near downtown Helena. They knew we were there, so make them think that we're back."

"Got it."

"Thanks, Cee. Please go home. We can take it from here," Ty says.

"You too, Mr. Kelleher," I add. I know the boss is still there.

Sam clears his throat. "Okay. But if there's anything, you call me. We'll be back here in three- or four-hours' time. We've got you, guys."

SOMETHING VIBRATES the desk we've been resting our heads on. Tyler and I make noises as we stretch, no doubt feeling the aches from sleeping in our seats.

The vibration turns out to be a ring on Tyler's laptop.

He gestures for me to wait, then he clicks the 'answer call' button on the interface and nods at me.

"Hello..." I mutter.

"Morgan." A distorted voice.

"Who is this?"

"I must admit, I underestimated you. I didn't think you'd last this long. But then again, it would've probably been easier if you had simply given yourself up two years ago. Your brother would've been alive."

It takes all my strength, and Tyler's, to rein in my emotions and not to let it all out.

I take a deep breath. *No.* She can't know yet that we've uncovered who she is.

"You son of a bitch! Let's end this. Tell me where Lilly is."

"I know you're scared of me, Morgan. I'm ruthless. And I'll tell you one more thing about me. I'm not good at dealing with desperation. So I will absolutely do anything to get what I want."

I tremble in anger. "Tell me what it is then."

"Oh come on, don't disappoint me now. You know what I want. Your parents must've thought highly of you, perhaps excessively, that they entrusted you with such dangerous information."

Tyler writes on a piece of paper: *Tell her about the diamonds.*

I snarl, "I thought you were going to start a revolution or something. Maybe you were trying to get some big names off my parents. But no. It's so basic. Just some rocks."

"Get all of the information ready. You will show it to me here, in front of me—well, us. I mean, Lilly will be here too, with a gun pointed under her chin."

"Prove that Lilly is with you!"

"That's so trivial. But fair enough. I'm sending you a picture now."

Ty and I hold our breaths. The picture stutters as it comes in, and I guess it has to go through a redirect process. When it has loaded fully, I know it's her. My long-lost sister.

I glance at Tyler, who's encouraging me to go on.

I put on an overconfident tone, letting her think I'm trying to mask my fear. "Tell me where, and I'll give it to you."

"I'll send you the details shortly. Everything will be transferred over a secure line here, Morgan. So you must have it ready."

"Alright. I'll do whatever you want. Just don't hurt Lilly."

"If you learn anything from the death of your family, you must know that getting the police involved will make this exchange null and void. If two veteran FBI informants could die like flies, you know what would happen to rookies like you."

"I have stayed away from the authorities all this time. You know I won't contact the police."

"That's the easy part," she spouts. "And no Red Mark. So that means it includes your boyfriend, whom I know is listening. Don't let today be the last loving conversation you have with him."

The call ends.

I feel hollow. Maybe I shouldn't risk it and do as she says. I can't lose Lilly.

"Ty, let me go with you."

Tyler shakes his head. "Morgan, please don't fight me."

"No, I'm not fighting you. I'm just seeing no other choice. They will hurt Lilly if they see you or Jack."

"We won't give them a chance to hurt her, Morgan."

"I want to fight *with* you," I implore.

"You can't come with us. Not because you're weak. You're the toughest human being I've known. Tougher than my colleagues."

"Then why am I the one left behind?"

"I'm not leaving you behind. You're with me. You'll be with me, although not physically."

"Callas and Diana need me. They'll keep me alive. But they don't need you."

He takes my hands so gently. "Many men readily say they would die for love. But I'm not going out there to die, Morgan. I want to live for you. I know you love me as much as I love you. I will live for you so you don't have to grieve for me. I want to be there for the rest of your life and a day. You'll never be without me, Morgan. Don't forget that."

"Ty..."

"I'll be back in your arms. And at that time, Lilly will be with me. I promise."

Tongue tight, heart squeezed as if wrung by ropes, there's nothing I can do but hug him. Everything becomes clear now. I trust him—and that means letting him go.

I nuzzle my way to his chest.

"I love it when you do that," he quips. "And I can't wait till the day you do it because you're happy, no baggage, everything has been solved."

I can feel my face lift, imagining the happiness Tyler has just painted.

"Stay here with Ava, okay?" he says.

"I will. And thank you for bringing her to me."

"What did I say? You'd see her again."

"And Gravy."

"For sure. It turned out I wasn't the only one who couldn't let you go." He touches the tip of my nose. "Now, I'll bring Lilly home."

I close my eyes and lean on him completely. "I won't fight you. You and Jack get that bitch, and that son of a bitch."

"Amen," he says. "You know, when I did something right, Tobias would've said, 'That's the way, sailor.'"

His voice breaks a little, and his gorgeous blue eyes shine with tears. I never knew Tobias, but I swear I can hear him say that to his best friend right now in this room.

Suddenly, Ty's head jerks.

"Ty?"

He gulps, blinking his tears away. "I'm sorry. I know I'm supposed to give you my undivided attention, but something just came to me." He rubs his forehead. "The photo of Lilly."

"What about it?"

He loads the image on his screen. "Her head is lying on a cushion." His finger keeps pressing the 'plus' button, zooming in.

"A logo?"

"Yeah. Look at this padded seat. It could be an outdoor sofa on someone's porch, but look at the curves and the surface. It looks way too shiny for it to be home furniture. And, I may be wrong, but judging by the shadow cast here." He points at the bottom of the picture. "This may be under-seat lighting. I think she's on a ship!"

Now I'm even more tongue-tied—in a good way. 'Something came to me,' he said. It could be his training, it could be his experience. But I think it's because he was born with tracking instincts that clues just appear like beacons.

"What does the logo say?" I squint at the blue and white pixels spread across the screen. "Star?"

"I think so. It could be the name of the ship," he suggests.

"Let's get Cora-Lee!"

Tyler dials in, and it only takes one ring before Cee answers. "Talk to me, Tyler."

"Good to know you're still alive."

"Cora-Lee only needs two-hour naps. Anyway, what can I do for you?"

"Check if Callas owns any ship. Possibly with a name that contains 'star.'"

"On it."

I can imagine the tech whizz typing, eyes vigilantly looking at the monitor to find the answer. Then we hear a sigh.

"Is that a no?" Ty guesses.

"No, well, I mean, yes, he does own a ship. I was just wondering how you arrived at that thought. Anyway, Sapphire Star. Last docked in Baja, and it's scheduled to sail to San Diego today."

We hear a knock on the door. The study has been open all this time, and we see Jack and Ava looking, well, fresh and fortified despite the lack of sleep. I think they caught Cee's last message.

Tyler turns to Jack. "Fancy getting your feet wet?"

The Marine narrows his gaze. "I heard the water is fine in California."

36

TYLER

We fly from Bozeman to San Diego using the same private jet that took us to Florida. We've become friends with the crew, and we're spoiled like celebrities. Air travel will never be the same after this.

Once in San Diego, we charter a fifty-foot Sea Ray out into the Pacific.

"Welcome home!" Jack quips as we sail past Coronado.

"Ah, the NAB." Naval Amphibious Base Coronado was my home back then. But now, home is where my Wolf Girl is.

Jack keeps combing his hair with his fingers as the wind messes up his fringe. That is a serious head of hair. The Marine will need the razor soon.

"You miss being a SEAL?" he asks.

"It was one hell of a ride. But I knew it was time, and I never looked back."

We stay on the starboard side deck, leaning against the railing, gazing at the blue spreading ahead of us. It's late summer. This side of the ocean is peppered with vacationers. No one would guess there's a Marine and a SEAL on board, ready for battle.

"When are you back on duty, Jack?"

"Next week."

"Camp Lejeune?"

"Yeah. But they're talking about relocating me to Kaneohe Bay."

"Hawaii. Not a bad office."

"Not bad at all," he scoffs, full of thoughts.

"Have you considered joining Red Mark?"

"I love the Corps. I think I still have another decade in me if not two. I've been a Force Recon Marine for a couple of years now. That was my goal when I earned my EGA." EGA—Eagle, Globe, and Anchor, the insignia of the U.S. Marine Corps. "Now, I kind of wonder, what's next? Especially after experiencing this."

He points in the general direction of the yacht. "There's something about rescuing someone in non-military context." He tilts his head up, letting the sun hit his face. "Lilly. I'd say it feels more real, but that's wrong, too. Hell, our battles out there were real. But you know, it's like you're needed, one-on-one. It's closer to you—that's what it is. Closer."

"You'll know when to leave. You will. Trust me."

Jack taps on the railing. "I hope so. I'd hate to make a wrong decision."

"I know how you feel."

"I don't know if I believe in redemption. Not the kind of redemption we were seeking all night last night. Wolf 302," he chuckles. "I mean, once the moment's gone, it's gone. You may feel you've gotten it back, but it'll never be the same. Just like my childhood."

"What would you do if you found the man who took you?"

"I keep asking the same question myself. I don't know, Ty. At some point, I may stop looking. But I haven't found a reason to. Yet."

Jack was taken when he was seven, and he didn't reconnect with his brother Sam until he was thirty. That's a huge hole in one's life. He's right. He can never feel the love of his parents and brother as a seven-year-old again. The time has passed. It's gone forever.

Our boat captain alerts us that their radar has picked up the presence of Sapphire Star.

Perhaps there will be no redemption for us if we fail this. Or *I* fail this.

We change into our diving gear, and I slot something into my front pocket.

"Don't tell me you're superstitious. Good luck charm? Really, Chief?" teases Jack.

"I don't do good luck charms, buddy. I just need something of Morgan."

"I thought you were made of steel and had no room for that kind of shit."

"A woman changes you, Jack. Believe it."

He gives me a dismissive glance as if telling me it doesn't apply to him. Then, a call comes through to the captain, and he immediately calls me to the bridge.

I take over the headset.

"Ty, it's me," Morgan says. Her tone is serious but calm. "Scarf-face just called."

Finally! The woman was certainly taking her time, perhaps trying to show who's in control. "What's her instruction?"

"She said someone will pick me up at Pier 2."

"Well, that person can wait forever, but we'll be at the party well before he realizes he's been stood up." I take my binocs. The Sapphire Star is still a dot in the ocean, but she's coming alright. "So you don't think she's suspecting anything?"

"Don't think so. She doesn't know what's coming for her!"

Hell no!

I glance at Jack. There will be no redemption needed today. When a Marine and a SEAL join forces, failure is never on the agenda.

"Ty, since someone is 'going to pick me up,' I've got a feeling the ship is going to anchor offshore," Morgan guesses.

"Good call." That woman never ceases to amaze me. She's always aware, always thinking. "You okay?"

"Yeah. I'm good," she answers emphatically. "Be careful, Ty."

"I will, sweetheart. I promise you'll see Lilly tonight, not Scarf-face."

37

MORGAN

I stand at the porch, my gaze following the bends and straights of the main trail.

I told Ty I was okay, but I'm fidgeting like a hand grenade is bouncing inside my gut. In the meantime, my bestie is sitting calmly, pencil and paper keeping her occupied.

Pepper, the young border collie, is curling at Ava's feet, while the alpha dog Salt is circling me, perhaps thinking I'm going to ride out with Zeus.

"God, Ave. Kill me now." I stride to my bestie, taking a seat on the same bench.

"He'll be fine." She carries on sketching. Now that she has defined the lines around the face, I know who has been lucky enough to be her muse today.

"Are you gonna show it to him?"

She shrugs, filling in the left iris of her subject, bringing his eye to life. "Hey, isn't it great that Gravy has been given a clean bill of health?"

"Yeah."

"You'll see him tomorrow!" she sings.

"I know," I deadpan. I appreciate her effort to distract me, and I can't wait to pat Gravy, but right now, whom I want home is Tyler.

I get up again, leaving the porch. Salt stares at me as if about to herd me. Or maybe he just wants to protect me in the absence of his master.

"Morgie, what is it?" Ava calls out.

I stride back to her. "Maybe I should charter another flight and go along with Diana's plan." I can't stomach the idea that Callas and my aunt could be planning something that may take Ty away from me—forever.

Ava releases a big sigh. She puts away her sketch, scolding me. "No! I won't let you do that, Morgie! You've got to trust your man!"

"It's not about trust. It's about risk. It's about a possibility. It's about—"

Protecting him.

"I'm going to chain you up if I must!"

A long growl launches out of my mouth. I'm angry with myself. "You're right," I concede, plonking my ass back on the bench.

Ava puts her arm around me, shaking my shoulder as if I was having a bad dream. "Everything will be fine, Morgie. Now, let me distract you."

"Please."

"Did he pop your cherry?" she asks me innocently.

"Ava!"

She giggles. Her curls bounce lightly against her shoulders. "Come on! Tell me!"

I roll my eyes. "What do you think!"

Her hands clap. "Hallelujah! I won't have to worry about my bestie staying a maiden forever. Which would've been a waste, by the way. Because you're lovely, and you deserve a loving partner." I tilt my face, perhaps blushing a little that she asks, "How was it?"

I hold my breath, feeling giddy, remembering the moment Tyler was inside me for the first time. "Amazing."

Her lips twist left and right. "You're not just saying it because he was a SEAL?"

"I know what's real and what's imagined. My swooning-over-a-book-boyfriend days are over. Really, Ave. He was amazing that night."

"Huh! So, the virgin vapidity phenomenon isn't always true?"

"I'm proof."

"You lucky so and so! You remember what mine was like?"

"Come on, we've passed our twenties now."

Ava wraps her arm around my neck, pulling me to her. "Okay. Okay. But see! Have I distracted you or what?"

"Thanks, Ave." I swipe a few unruly curls from covering her face.

"More distraction?"

"Why not."

She puts the sketch on the table in front of us. Only half of the face has details, but there's no doubt, it's Jack. Oval face, with tight jaws, low brows, and deep-set eyes that hold back a lot.

"What are you gonna do, Ave? I know how you look at him and how he looks at you."

"He's super cute. Kind."

"And single."

"But I'm not."

"What do you mean? You haven't told me anything about your boyfriend, and we've been cooped up in this house for almost twenty-four hours?"

"Here's the thing, Morgie. I'm pregnant."

"Ava!" Now I give my best friend a big hug. "I'm so happy for you, Ave." She hugs me back, but I sense sadness. "What's wrong?"

"It's Willem's."

Willem. The loser.

No. Willem, the abuser.

"I thought you broke up with him years ago!"

"I did. But things got messy with my family. Now Willem and I are getting engaged, then we're gonna get married, then have this baby."

"Ave, is he the one you want to be with for the rest of your life? Or is it what your parents want?" I know her parents are very controlling, and Willem is a man with a deep pocket.

"I should've been like you, Morgie. Strong, opinionated." She exhales heavily. "Me?"

"You're even stronger." I hold her hand, giving it a reassuring shake. "You've left him once, and I know you can do it again."

"My parents have done a lot for me."

"Did they know what Willem did to you? Ave, you had to spend two days in hospital! He broke your arm!"

"I know, I know. You don't have to remind me. But no one else knew, okay? Only you."

A pang of guilt zaps me. I should've told my parents about it. Ava didn't tell me right away. She said she broke her arm because she fell. I only found out the truth when she had recovered and left Willem.

"So, does he still hit you?"

"No. Well... not as bad." She pauses. "But I'm keeping the baby. I know you think it's stupid. But I've sworn to myself and the baby." She caresses her belly. "That I will love him or her no matter what."

I pull her into an embrace, feeling her belly against mine.

"Ava, you're doing the right thing, keeping your baby. You've always wanted to be a mom."

"Yeah."

"But you have to leave him."

"Morgie, I wish... oh God, I wish on everything I have that my baby daddy was someone else." She pulls up the collar of her jacket, smelling it—well, Jack's jacket, to be precise.

"Leave Willem. I know it's easier said than done. but—"

Ty's laptop, which we put at the other end of the table, spits out persistent rings.

"Shh!" I press the 'answer call' button.

The distorted voice of Aunt Diana blares. "It's too quiet, Morgan." This is the first time I sense frustration in her.

"You've failed to track me!"

"I don't appreciate tardiness."

"I don't either. Trust me, I'm coming."

"Good. Or Lilly will be dead."

"I've got what you want. But if I find just a scratch on my sister, I'll hunt you down, and you will wish that you'd died with my parents that night."

She scoffs. With the distortion, it sounds like a chimp snorting. "What are you going to do exactly, Morgan?"

I let silence answer. But here is what I would do—I'd tie her to a chair, forcing her to stare at the photo of my parents and Hudson. Perhaps I'd show her some video clips of them so she could hear their voices. If she refused, I'd cut her fingers. One by one. I'd stretch the moment so I could get one for every shot Hudson sustained.

The bitch is lucky she's not going to face me. Tyler would be a lot more merciful.

She scoffs again. "You're a smart girl. I know you love Lilly —she's the only one you have. So you won't give me any funny tricks, will you?"

"You'll see."

"Just be quiet about your entrance."

"Trust me, you won't want me to make too much noise. And I will be nice to your chauffeur. He's waiting for me at Pier 2, didn't you say? He'd better be ready."

"I won't hurt Lilly, but I can't guarantee my partner won't. Take that as a warning, Morgan."

The hand grenade that has been bouncing in my gut may have just exploded. She's right. While Diana may have an emotional attachment to Lilly, Callas doesn't.

My hand clenches as I get up. "I'm on my way."

The call ends, and Ava stares at me.

38

———

TYLER

The Sapphire Star sails past us like any other yacht. It's a lot bigger than ours. It's a seventy-footer capable of carrying around eighty people.

Jack and I observe with our binocs.

"Can't see anyone inside," Jack says. "The blinds are all down."

"Hmm. I guess they value their privacy. At least no one's outside, so that's a good thing."

We keep our distance as the ship slows down. Morgan was spot on. It's going to anchor soon. Lucky for us, we're not the only ones enjoying the California water this afternoon, so we can keep our disguise.

"They're releasing a tender," Jack notices.

I follow the movement of two men breaking away from the main yacht, sailing on a smaller craft. "They must be heading to Pier 2 to pick up Morgan."

"What are you gonna do, Chief?"

I approach our boat captain. "Skip, let's position ourselves next to that fishing boat—The Fair Lady. Give us about forty yards to swim to the Star."

"Got it."

The captain drives on, almost circling the Sapphire Star, keeping a wide berth. Then he slowly maneuvers the boat closer.

We're in position.

Standing at the stern, I turn to Jack. "You sure about this?"

"Fuck yeah!"

We've decided to stay light—ready for action as soon as we climb on board. So we're going to swim underwater without oxygen tanks.

As a SEAL, I'm in my element. As for my Marine partner, Marines are ultimately riflemen, but some are combatant divers. Lucky for me, Jack Kelleher is as close to a frog as a Marine can be.

We dive in, navigating the gap between our boat and the Star by swimming breaststroke in stealth.

The last time I swam underwater for fifty meters with a single breath was during my BUD/S. There's no fancy trick, and there's no superhuman feat. You simply have to stay calm and have a good technique. Once you'd done it, it stays in you.

The only differences between a pool and the open ocean are the wave and current. But they're not deterring us.

I check in with Jack as we reach the halfway point. He gives me an 'okay.'

About a minute later, we reach the Sapphire Star's port side. We slither up the fiberglass surface like a couple of reptiles hitching a ride.

We reach the deck unchallenged.

I give Jack a nod—confirming we're sticking to our plan. We've got to cover a large area, so we split up. Jack heads below deck while I scour the top.

Apart from the captain on the bridge, the ship is quiet.

I check every room I pass. There's leftover food and half-filled glasses. There's a cigarette smell all over, too. There are people here.

Just next to the kitchen, I see a roll of rope, its end frayed. It's been recently used. More disturbingly, there's a syringe and an empty bottle of Midazolam. My neck warms. I bet that tranquilizer was for Lilly.

"Jack," I whisper into my mouthpiece. This is the first time we're taking our underwater comms technology to the test. It'd better hold up after just a short, shallow swim.

"Ty. I've found Lilly's room, but she's not here."

"Keep looking. I think she's been sedated."

I pad to the upper deck.

Shit!

I duck, keeping myself out of view. Someone is coming out of a room in the corner of the deck. Heavy steps.

I crawl forward to get a clear view of who it is, still keeping myself hidden behind a sofa.

Eduardo Callas—carrying an unconscious Lilly.

"They're here," I whisper to Jack. But there's no answer, only static. I think it's a transmission issue rather than him getting into trouble.

Out of nowhere, a man jumps in front of me. He would've got me with a shot had he not landed too close. With a kick, I disarm him. I then hurl him to the floor and shoot his leg.

Spooked, Callas runs all the way up to the top deck, carrying Lilly like she was a bag.

I pursue him.

"Jack! They're here!" I speak into the radio. But I'm still getting nothing from my partner.

Cornered, Callas sets Lilly down, but he's still holding her with one arm, forcing her to stay upstanding despite her being unconscious. She's dangling over his arm. Her wrists are bound in front of her. There is no sign of apparent injuries, but the state of her concerns me. How much did they put the tranquilizer in her?

Callas' other hand is now gripping a gun, pointed at Lilly's head.

"Hand the girl to me, Callas. It's over!" I point the gun at him.

Callas steps backward. "Either she'll die with a bullet lodged in her brain or with water in her lungs."

Nine out of ten, I know when a man is bluffing. And he's not.

"Unless you give me Morgan!" he adds.

Before I can answer, something hits my back.

Jesus!

Then, the back of my knees. It's not just something. It's a fucking steel bar, and it hurts like a motherfucker!

I fall to my knees. Now, two guns are pointed at my head.

"Diana Blackwell," I grit out. She has come with her guard —the one who hit me and who quickly kicks my gun away from my reach.

I could retaliate and take on both of them, but that will mean provoking Callas to gamble with Lilly. I will avoid that at any cost, especially since they're positioned too close to the edge of the deck.

"Where's Morgan?" Diana asks. She's unmasked, and although she looks a little surprised to see me, cockiness is all over her face.

I raise my eyes to her emphatically. "She says, 'Fuck you!'"

Her feet fidget, and her lips press together for half a second. But she stays composed while entertaining my provocation. "Isolation can make a person angry, I know. Now that cunt knows what it's like to be on her own."

"So, all this because you want to get rich?" I snarl.

"Don't think I have a shred of love for her! I had no

qualms about her parents' deaths either. I was just their nanny, their afterthought." Hatred bubbles out of her mouth. "You know, Mr. Hunt? It wasn't just them. Even my parents were under their spell. God! My brother, Morgan's dad, received a wholesome two million. 'They have a family, Diana,' my parents told me." Her mouth twists bitterly. "And I don't, so they gave me a meager three hundred thousand. What a joke!"

"The joke's on you, Diana. Morgan ain't coming."

The woman thrusts the barrel of her gun against my forehead. "Don't fuck with me, Mr. Hunt. I'm a woman, but I won't hesitate to blow your head off."

"Oh, I believe you. Morgan has taught me a lot about women."

"She can't hide forever. If you hand her over to me, we can still have a peaceful talk."

"Well, she doesn't have to hide anymore. And she certainly doesn't need to see your sorry face again."

A call comes through to her guard. What I can hear off the line is unintelligible, but I bet it's one of the men on the tender informing them Morgan never showed up.

Her attitude changes as if she realizes the tables are turned. Her gun cocks, I can feel the click against my head. Then she says to Callas, "He's not gonna give her up. He has to die!"

"Di, just remember, we want the diamonds. Morgan is just one little bitch, and he's just her lap dog."

I don't think these two realize that Jack is on board, and I'm acting like it—no looking around, no anticipating. However, I am wondering where he is.

Callas adds, "If you shoot him, that little bitch is going to run, just like how she always has."

"You'll never find her," I snap. "She's safe with her family."

Hell yeah, my Wolf Girl is no longer running scared alone.

She has her best friend, my family, and the Red Mark family all behind her.

Callas ignores me, keeping his focus on Diana. "If you can't handle him, I will."

"I *am* handling him!" Diana yells.

"Di! You kill him, we'll lose twenty million."

Diana breathes fast, as if she were in front of a time bomb and deliberating whether to cut the red or the blue wire. She then grumbles to herself, withdrawing. "Fine." She gives a sign to her guard to restrain me.

The big man swivels to face me head-on, only to thump his knee against my gut. Damn! Somehow, it hurts more than the steel hits. Direct contact always hurts more! The guard then hooks his arm behind me, locking my hands.

Meanwhile, Diana strides over to Callas. "I won't kill him. But *you* deal with him. Give me Lilly."

The statement seems to stir Callas, who has appeared in control all this time. He steps forward, meeting Diana, but Lilly is still in his grip. "You're still in this, aren't you, darling?"

"Yes. Of course. Do what you want with that ex-SEAL. Give me Lilly."

The air shifts. Callas moves backward, creating a gap between himself and her, returning to where he was—close to the edge. "I'm doing all this for us, Di. Don't you forget it."

"I know, Ed. I'm with you all the way. Just give me Lilly."

He narrows his gaze so sharply that she stops approaching him. But her hand moves.

Callas' eyes widen like a stag overcome by rabies. Whether it's panic or anger, he fires at her.

I shove the guard who has been keeping me in place like a length of truck chains. I twist his arm, pointing the gun at himself. Too late to stop his finger on the trigger, the man ends up shooting his own stomach.

Meanwhile, seeing his lover bloodied and lifeless, Callas goes mad. He wails at her body, gun still in her hand. "Look what you've made me do!"

I couldn't care less about the tragedy unfolding in front of me. My attention stays on Lilly—Callas is shoving her overboard!

I ignore the pain from the blows to my body. Not even Callas' bullets can stop me. I propel myself to catch her before she free-falls on her own. I manage to do so, but it's too late to stop the both of us from tumbling.

We travel vertically into the ocean. I swathe her, protecting her head and her spine. If we hit the surface the right way, we'll be okay. And I'll make sure it's me who brunt most of the impact. This is what a SEAL is built for. This is what I'm built for.

First, the slap, then the splash. Then, the blue water bubbles around us as we dive like a torpedo. I let myself flow, morphing into an underwater beast who's protecting his young.

We keep traveling down. Finally, the momentum eases. With Lilly still firmly in my embrace, I swim up.

I gasp as we emerge from the surface.

The impact and the cold water seem to have woken Lilly up. She shakes in my arms, humming inanely.

"Lilly, stay calm. Stay with me." I hold on to her but let her float on her own, checking if she's okay. "My name is Tyler. Your sister sent me."

She keeps shaking.

"You okay?"

Her trembling voice barely utters, "Yeah."

"Morgan sent me." I wipe water off her face so she can see me clearly. But instead, it's me who's in awe seeing her face. She reminds me so much of Morgan—those big brown eyes.

Her trembling eases and I cut the rope that binds her hands. Then a boat approaches us. The Coast Guard.

"Let the girl go!" an officer orders. The others beside him seem ready to draw their guns.

"Lilly, they're on our side," I try to keep her calm. "You have to get on board now."

She doesn't seem to resist when I hand her over to the guards.

"Her name is Lilly Blackwell," I inform them.

The officer in charge stops me from jumping on. "Identify yourself!"

"My name is Tyler Hunt. I'm from Red Mark Rescue & Protect. I have been tasked with saving this girl."

The officer nods, giving me a hand to climb aboard.

I haul myself out of the water. *Fuck me*, the wracking pain! It's like my body is about to split at the waist.

The guards are tending to Lilly, administering an IV solution. I immediately go to her side, but she tries to roll away.

"Mr. Hunt," warns one of the guards.

"Lilly, hey, I'm Tyler. I told you your sister sent me."

She shakes her head feebly.

I persist. She's got to remember her sister! "She's um... she has a huge wolf tattoo. Here." I point at my left biceps. I wish I had Morgan's photo with me.

Lilly looks at me blankly.

But I do have something of Morgan. I take out the Yellowstone coin from my wet suit's front pocket. "This is hers. Remember?"

She gasps, her eyes wide, taking the coin into her hand as if she has just found a lost treasure.

"She misses you so much, Lilly."

Finally, a smile. She places the coin on her chest, then

covers it with her trembling palm. At her side, her other hand moves. I feel tiny fingers nudging my palm, then a squeeze.

"You can keep it," I murmur. "When you see her, show it to her. Tell her I gave it to you."

I gaze at the top deck of the Sapphire Star. Jack is giving me a thumbs-up—whatever took him so long! I think more of Callas' men had held him up below deck. Right now, I don't see any other movement apart from the Coast Guard personnel. Jack has secured the ship, and I think he has shot Callas.

So, in the end, Diana turned against her lover. I'm sure she was going to run away with Lilly—perhaps love had driven her to do so. On the other hand, Callas showed that evil was capable of love, too.

But I wonder. Was it love? Or was it simply obsession?

39

MORGAN

"Shit, Morgie! I really thought you were serious," Ava complains.

Lying to Scarf-face turned out to be easy. Especially since I know Cee had been placing my so-called cell locations to mimic a trip from Helena to San Diego.

"I've promised my man that I'd stay, Ave. And I'm keeping it." I draw my chin up like a proud girlfriend.

"Now we wait," she sighs. Then she reaches for her finished sketch. "Give this to Jack, will you?"

The Marine's face stares right back at me. All this time, I've seen Jack as this tough, handsome military man, unstoppable when he's determined to finish something. But only Ava saw it in him. Pain. It's in her drawing. That black-and-white version of the man is holding a lot of pain.

"Why don't you give it to him yourself?"

She bows her head. "Nah. Please. You'd do it for me?"

"Okay. But it means you're going to sort things out with Willem."

"I can't promise anything. Besides, I hardly know Jack. It may be just a silly infatuation."

"He's a good man."

"Yeah. The question is, am I good for him? I have too much baggage, Morgie."

"Maybe. But give him the benefit of the doubt. If, in the end, he breaks your heart, think about this. Would you rather be heartbroken by that woman-beater? Or by an honorable man?"

"Geez... I never thought about it that way."

"Just think about it, Ave."

Hours have passed. The sun has set.

"Where are they?" I murmur, pacing the length of the porch. Ty and Jack should've concluded the mission because I should've arrived in San Diego hours ago.

Suddenly, Salt and Pepper go berserk, followed by the familiar whir that has been coming and going above this farm.

I don't even wait. I sprint to the paddock as soon as the helicopter comes into view. Ava isn't far behind me.

Tyler jumps out of the chopper.

"Ty!"

That victorious smile, announcing to me that he's delivered on his promise and he's home. He's wearing a tight fatigue top. A pair of cargo pants hangs flirtatiously off his tapered hips.

Bless my heart. That handsome wall of muscle stands assured—and he's sizzling hot!

And he's mine.

I hug him as tightly as I can.

"Ugh..." He groans.

"Ty? You're hurt!" I pat him carefully. "Did you get shot?"

"I'm fine, Morgan. Just a few aches."

I round my arms over him loosely.

"That's good, that's good," Tyler murmurs, resting his face on my crown.

"Lilly?" My whole body tingles, anticipating his answer.

"She's safe."

I feel my legs fold under me, and I land on Tyler's massive chest—the place that never fails me whether I'm searching for safety or sharing joy.

"Did she remember me?"

His knuckles run soothing strokes along my cheekbone. "She did."

Tears prick the inside of my lids. I close my eyes, letting them fall.

Gradually, I bat my lids open. "Diana?"

Tyler shakes his head. "She and Callas are dead."

Relief sweeps through me. This is really over.

Ava approaches us nervously. "Jack?"

"He stayed back with Lilly. Those two seem to have a bond. I must say, she warmed up to him more quickly than she did me."

My best friend chuckles sweetly. "Perhaps Jack was unknowingly watching over her when he was surveying Callas in Tampa?"

"Wow. Now, that's a thought!" Ty praises. "Come on. We've got to go."

"Can I come?" Ava asks.

"Of course," Ty replies. "This time, Ava West, you're gonna get there in style. It's going to be a fine evening."

We lift off. On the ground, Salt and Pepper bark with their tail wagging furiously, circling around as if cheering us on. In the distance, Peter and Lou Hunt stand arm in arm, giving us a happy wave.

I'VE BEEN WAITING for this moment for two goddamn years, imagining what it would be like, what I would say. Now that I'm only a hallway turn from her, I'm a bundle of nerves.

Jack and Ava give me a signal to move on while they stay in the waiting room.

"God, Ty. Are you sure she remembers me?"

"She does. But my advice? Take it easy to start with. Her memory of you might be different from what she sees when you come into her room."

"Yeah. Yeah. You're right," I stutter, staring at the door to Lilly's room.

"Go on. I'll wait here."

A nurse pushes the door slowly open.

I step in. The room is dim, but the girl lying in the bed has been moving around, so I know she's awake.

"Lilly..."

My sister stares at me, her eyes trying to focus in the dim light. Perhaps realizing I'm not a nurse, she drawls, "Who are you?" Soft, curious.

"I'm Morgan. I'm your sister."

Lilly sits up, her hand clutching the hem of the blanket. I stand by her side.

"Morgie..." she whispers.

The most beautiful sound I've heard in years.

I open my arms, letting her come to me. I feel her—my little sister. As if the tie that bundles my nerves has been yanked away, without shame, I cry on her shoulder. "Lilly. I miss you so much."

"Morgie..."

"Are you okay?"

Lilly nods, then lets me go. "You look different."

"I guess so. A lot has happened, Lil."

She reaches out her hand to me, touching my black rose pendant.

"I lost mine in Florida."

"Did you know?" I narrow my gaze, taking out the chain and pendant from my pocket.

"No way!"

"Tyler found it. May I?" I present it to her, and she nods.

The pendant looks so beautiful on her. But most of all, it belongs there.

"And Tyler gave this to me." Lilly shows my Yellowstone coin. "Lucky he did, otherwise I... it's stupid, but I wouldn't have remembered you."

"You helped me choose, remember, in that crowded souvenir shop?"

She chuckles. "Out of anything, that was what I remembered first on that boat—I think it was the Coast Guard's."

"Memory is a funny thing."

"And you still have your wolf tattoo?"

I roll up my sleeve.

"Hmm." Lilly inspects my inked arm. "I'm still not sure about the design, but it's grown on me."

"We saw those wolves and their pups the day after I got this tattoo. Remember?"

Her eyes sparkle. "Yes! They howled every night."

"And so did we." I put my hands in front of my chest, bending my fingers, posing like a wolf showing off their paws. "Awooo! Awooo!" I mimic what we did those nights in our cottage.

And soon Lilly joins in. "Awooo!"

I cry and laugh at the same time, hugging my little sister. She was in my life, then taken away. In my darkest time, she only existed in a sketch. Now she's safe in my arms again.

"I didn't mean to forget you, Morgie," she sighs.

"I know, Lil."

"Aunt Diana told me you were dead. And it felt like I'd been sleeping a lot. Waking up in different places."

I caress her hand. "It's over now. You're with me."

Suddenly, she straightens, feeling a presence. "Tyler!" she calls.

I spin my head back. Yes, it's him. That's the man responsible for this reunion. As if interrupting, Tyler stands at the door.

"Is it okay if he comes in?" I ask Lilly.

"Yes, of course. He saved me." She then gestures at me to get closer, whispering right in my ear, "And he's so handsome!"

I smile at her, perhaps blushing a bit. "Come on in, Ty," I call.

Tyler ambles into the room. With me sitting down, and Lilly lying on the bed, and the dimness of the room, his figure seems to loom larger than usual. But his voice is sweet. "Hey, Lilly. How are you feeling?"

Lilly slides down. "I'm alright, but starting to get sleepy again."

"Go and sleep then," I murmur.

"You're not gonna leave me?" Her eyes droop, coated by tears from a yawn.

"No. I promise."

"Okay."

"Can Tyler stay?" I ask her.

"Of course. You need him." She smirks as if telling me she knows because she's my sister. She's back. I know Lilly is back.

Tyler and I stay quietly beside her bed, holding hands. As I watch Lilly drifting off, I smile to myself. This is the beginning of my new life.

I feel a squeeze on my hand as he invites me to stand up. He then pulls me into a corner behind the privacy curtain, securing an arm around my waist. His other arm snakes behind my neck, pressing my nape. A heavy breath lands on the side of my jaw. Then, the breath turns into a whisper. "Your sister said you needed me. The fact is, I need you. I need this, feeling you."

"You've brought Lilly back. As you promised," I murmur, nuzzling into his chest.

"Didn't I say I like it when you do that?" A few gentle kisses land on my crown.

I tilt my head up and look at him. *Damn*, even in the shadows, I know those blue eyes have gotten brighter. "You did. And I'm doing it because I'm happy."

"We did it, Wolf Girl."

"We did, Mr. Steadfast." I play-thump his side with my fist.

"Oomph..." he gasps.

"Oh shit, sorry, sorry." I caress the spot I just hit.

"I'm not sure about steadfast. I'm pretty cooked, to be honest," he concedes. "But I wouldn't swap this for anything."

The ocean found us, and he asked me why. I think I've found the answer. Because nature always gets it right.

40

TYLER

A week after our mission aboard the Sapphire Star, Morgan and Lilly moved into my house in Helena. It was like going from zero to a hundred in a blink of an eye, but I wouldn't have it any other way.

Hudson's body was found about fifty miles from the spot where he was killed. He's now resting next to his mother and father. The inscription on his tombstone says: *The strength of his spirit will never be conquered.*

The tragedy hit Lilly hard. But that's what a big sister is for—Morgan has been nothing but steadfast. Lilly has a long recovery ahead of her, but I'm sure the teenager will take strength from the woman who has proven that there's no adversity they can't beat.

The information inside the diamond folder has helped the FBI carry on the legacy of two of their best informants. So far, twelve boys and girls have been rescued from being trafficked as a result. And there will be more to come.

It's winter now. Morgan and I are renting a lodge in Yellowstone while Lilly is staying with Mark.

It's the two of us here, with a surprise addition—Gravy. Just when I thought he would be the ultimate city dog, he proved me wrong. The mutt seems to be at home in the wilderness—somehow reminding me of Morgan. But today, he'll stay behind at the lodge as we're going to do some serious wolf tracking.

Morgan is on the phone with her sister. "So, everything's okay?"

Lilly answers, "Yeah. Noah and I have just helped Mrs. Connor bathe the twins."

My boss and his wife Ivy welcomed their bundles of cuteness two months ago. Noah, Ivy Connor's son from her previous marriage, seems to be taking his role as big brother very seriously.

"That's great, Lil," says Morgan. "Hey, we'll be off-grid for most of today. But I'll call you later tonight, okay?"

"'Kay," responds Lilly. In the background, Noah is calling for her. Apparently, there's been an unexpected need for a change of diapers.

"You go and help Noah. I love you."

"I love you too, Morgie."

She puts the phone away, smiling.

I nudge myself closer to her. "Are you always this well-put-together when you're out in the field?"

Wolf Girl is in her hiking gear, but she would fit right in if she was going to a party. Her hair is tied back in an impeccable bun, and her shiny fringe falls to her cheeks. She's applied some mascara to her already long lashes.

And those shimmery lips. I don't have to imagine anymore. That pout has been all over me.

She kisses me, leaving a red mark on my neck—literally. "Only when I'm with you. And I've just marked my territory."

"Hm... just don't tempt those wolves."

She puts on a face. "Well, before we go, I have something for you."

She hands me a T-shirt. Obviously, it's not thick enough for winter, but it makes me wish it was already nighttime.

Lefties are better lovers.

I laugh at her silliness. "What are you trying to do, Morgan Blackwell?"

"Just to commemorate our victory." She spreads the T-shirt over my chest. "It suits you."

"Have I won you over, then?" I push myself against her, driving her to the wall.

"Total victory."

She escapes from my hold, zipping her jacket up.

I lazily move away from her and sit down to put on my socks. And suddenly, Gravy jumps up, putting his snout on my lap.

"What is it, buddy? You don't want to be left behind?"

"Oh, Gravy... not again."

"Look at him..." I pat the top of his head. "How can you say no to that face?"

"No. He can't come with us," she insists. "Gravy, bed!"

"Gee, you're one tough mama!"

"Leadership, Ty. Leadership."

Gravy throws another attempt to get me on his side. Oh, those begging eyes! But after a whistle from Morgan, the mutt leaves my lap and then curls up in his fluffy, donut-like bed.

She pats Gravy lovingly. "Good boy. Good boy. You stay and relax."

That's what she would call 'tough love.'

Morgan then pulls down her beanie, covering her whole head and almost half her face. Now, I'm almost certain that the makeup and hair were simply to tease me—perhaps testing my self-control and the restraint of my left arm.

"Come on then!" She gestures at the door.

We hit the park on snowshoes, hiking a trail along a pine forest.

"So, Ava and Jack—do you think it's on?" I ask. "I saw the sketch you gave him. That was pretty impressive. I think the man looked more handsome in that drawing than he really is."

"That's how Ava sees him, I'm sure. I kinda feel that they're like unfinished business. How's Jack anyway?"

"It's confirmed. He'll move to Hawaii next month."

"Damn. I really hope he comes back soon. I mean, to us, to this part of the world."

"Me too. Much as the military has a pull over him, I'm telling you, he belongs with Red Mark. Do you think there's a way you can make it work?"

"Well, I don't have any influence over Red Mark."

"Yeah, but you do over Ava."

"Yes. Yes. And I'm working on it, Ty. A woman's pull is stronger than any duty call, whether you agree or not," she challenges. "Most of all, Ava's fiancé is an ass. I *will* make it work."

"Let me know how I can help."

"I will, Ty." She then motions me to stop, pointing at the paw prints in the snow. "They were here!"

We keep trudging, avoiding the prints as much as we can. Passing a snow-covered rock, she suddenly becomes excited. "Oh look, wolf pee!"

"You're a good hunter," I praise her. "But I can't believe you squeal like that over a squirt of urine!"

"My name may be Blackwell, but I've always been a *hunter*," she raves.

Is that a hint?

"Should I make it official?"

She blushes. "Are you proposing to me?"

"Oh, come on! I'm not kneeling next to a patch of wolf pee. Please! I've got class."

Morgan twists her lips, but she's got to know I intend to make her a Hunt, have a family, and all that. But most of all, I want her to be herself.

I continue, "With me, you're free to do whatever your heart wishes. I won't hold you back. You know that, right?"

"I'm too wild to be held back." She pinches my cheek, and we carry on our hike.

The path leads to a clearing, giving us an unprecedented view of the valley below.

I've been to places, and Montana is my home. But nothing compares when you're in the heart of the wilderness. The air of solitude grounds you. The feeling of insignificance when you're just a speck in the giant white landscape—it humbles you.

"Let's hide here," Morgan points and kneels behind a sage bush. I follow suit. Then she freezes. "Shh... listen..."

A few twigs snap in the wind. Then, a wolf howls from the opposite side of the valley.

Morgan smiles wide as the echo carries the call far and wide.

Soon, another howl follows, as if responding.

Morgan nudges me. She puts on her binocs, scanning the valley below us. I take out mine, too, following her direction.

"The Junction Butte Pack," she whispers.

One by one, the magnificent creatures come out of the forest. The feeling of solitude is taken over by awe. It's bitterly cold, but this is when feelings rise above anything else. It gives you a different perspective, a different lens on what life is about, far away from the city limits. Yet, I can't help thinking we're not that different. Family, survival, and connection— that's what a pack lives for.

"Jesus. There are lots of them!" I comment.

"The last tally says there're twenty-two in the pack. That's the alpha female, 907."

"Wow... she's huge! But where are the pups?"

"Well, her pups from last year have grown a bit. I see one of them there."

I see a smaller wolf chasing the tail of another. "The childish one."

"Winter is mating season. You'll have to wait till spring to see the small pups."

I don't know why the thought excites me as if I'm anticipating my own pack. Her enthusiasm is contagious, it seems. "Are you planning to come back then?"

"Hell yeah!"

"I don't know where I'll be then, Wolf Girl, but I'll try my best to be part of your expedition."

She kisses me. "We'll make it work, Ty. I know what's demanded of you as a Red Mark, and I won't be the one who interferes with you saving those children. I'll never be without you, and you'll never be without me."

"I like that."

"Not that I'll be following you like a lost puppy, but you know what I mean?"

Didn't I think that I couldn't have it all?

I did. But I hadn't met a wolf biologist called Morgan Blackwell then.

I drop my binocs and push hers away from her grip, inviting her to my side. "Come here and hug your Malamute."

I nudge her face toward me and welcome her laughter. I don't wait till she settles. I ravage her lips, smearing lipstick all over my mouth. I'll never get sick of the taste of her.

Steadfastness means nothing when you're on your own. Steadfastness needs a partner. And God bless this wilderness, I've found mine.

THANK you for reading *Her Steadfast Protector*. I hope you enjoyed Tyler and Morgan's story.

Remember to grab the next book, **Her Faithful Protector**, and immerse yourself in the captivating tale of Ava and Jack as their profound bond is put to the test. Plus, will Jack finally uncover the identity of the person responsible for his kidnapping?

Join my newsletter for release updates, free books, special deals, and more ➜ alessakelly.com.

If you haven't already, buy the first book in the series, **Her Unbreakable Protector**, and read the story of Sam and Cass.

ALSO BY ALESSA KELLY

Download the FREE prequel to the series, STAYING FOR YOU.

Burning for You: From Enemies to Fearless Lovers

He's a simple farm boy at heart. She's a big-city girl. Thrown together by revenge, will their explosive chemistry endure a hostile takeover?

Fighting for You: From Strangers to Fearless Lovers

She's ready for a soulmate. He's sealed away his heart. When attempted murder brings them together, can they survive long enough to find love?

Longing for You: From Secret to Fearless Lovers

He's a notorious mercenary boss, she's a no-nonsense oil tycoon. When legal entanglements take them on a collision course, will they rise to beat unsurmountable odds?

The Hartley Brothers Series

Hold Me Forever

She's a traumatized survivor. He's a closed-off veteran. Can two lost souls find safe harbor together?

Cherish Me Forever

Two wounded hearts. When unexpected love comes within their grasp, can they learn to trust before it's ripped away?

Standalone

Protecting Her

He's a disgraced ex-cop. She's on a mad quest for justice. When they're trapped in a deadly game, can they escape into each other's arms?

Join my newsletter for release updates, free books, and more ➜ alessakelly.com.

Her Steadfast Protector: A Rescue & Protect Romance Suspense Novel (Red Mark Rescue & Protect Book 3)

www.alessakelly.com

© 2023 Alessa Kelly

ISBN

ePub: 978-1-922363-31-2

Paperback: 978-1-922363-32-9